MEGA 4
BEHEMOTH ISLAND
JAKE BIBLE

Chapter One- Prey

The young man was fit and very clean cut. Very clean cut. Blindingly clean cut.

Dressed in a white button-down shirt, black slacks, and shiny black shoes, the young man could have been any MBA from a Fortune 500 company. His grey eyes told the world he was all business; his fit form told the world he could back up that business physically, if needed.

All Popeye's eyes and form said was that he couldn't give a shit about this very clean cut asshole that sat before him.

Not young, not clean cut, and considering he was strapped to a hospital bed, not very fit, Trevor "Popeye" DeBruhl glared at the young man, one of his eyes squinted almost closed, giving him the look of that famous cartoon sailor.

Forearms wiry and muscled from years as a boatswain, Popeye strained against the restraints that held him in the bed. He would have kicked out, but he was missing his right leg from the thigh down, and it seemed lame for him to just kick with the one leg.

"Mr. DeBruhl, please calm yourself," Jowarski said, his business eyes beaming from that clean-cut, good-looks face. "I only need to ask a couple questions and then you can rest."

"Where's the lady?" Popeye growled. "That woman that said she was Ballantine's wife? Where's she at? She know you're in here? She didn't like it the last time you questioned me."

"Yes, we discussed that, she and I," Jowarski replied. "All squared away now. She has more important things to deal with. I am the specialist when it comes to interrogation, so it makes more sense for me to be here while she is out there."

"Out where? Where the hell is this place?" Popeye asked. He yanked at his restraints again and again then relaxed. "Why the hell am I all trussed up like this? You guys government? This some CIA black ops facility? What the hell do you think I know? I ain't saying anything to a little piece of piss like you. I shit turds older than you, golden boy."

"Golden boy?" Jowarski laughed. "My sister used to call me that. I hated it. She'd say it over and over, yelling it at me as I chased her through the apple orchard in our backyard. Boy could she run."

Leaning forward in the generic padded chair that complimented the generic decor of the room, Jowarski set aside a clipboard and steepled his fingers.

"Don't call me golden boy, Mr. DeBruhl," Jowarski said. His voice was smooth and easy, but held an edge that could not be missed. "You are welcome to refer to me as Mr. Jowarski or as sir. But not golden boy." Popeye started to respond, but Jowarski held up a finger. "Also, no more questions. I'm here to do that. Your job is to answer the questions I ask. Are we understood?"

Popeye lay there for a minute then grinned, his weathered face split in two as he laid his head back and laughed. Jowarski picked up the clipboard and settled back into the generic chair, his grey eyes watching, waiting, until Popeye was finished.

"Feel better?" Jowarski asked.

"Nope," Popeye said. "Not by a long shot."

"Ready to answer some of my questions?" Jowarski asked.

"Go ahead and ask," Popeye said, shrugging. "But I can tell you right now I have no idea where Ballantine is. I was shot and fell overboard the B3. Last I saw that ship, and everyone on it, it was steaming deep into the South Pacific. That boat could be anywhere by now."

"No, no, not anywhere, Mr. DeBruhl," Jowarski replied. "It has arrived at a very specific place. I believe you when you say you don't know where that place is."

"Then why the hell ask me a bunch of questions?" Popeye asked. "Oops, sorry, that was a question. You gonna spank me now? Uh-oh, that's another question."

Jowarski frowned and took a deep breath. He seemed to be considering what Popeye said then shook his head.

Popeye rolled his eyes and continued speaking. "Seems like a waste of time. And from what I heard the other day, you ain't got time to waste."

"No, I suppose we don't have time to waste," Jowarski replied. "That is why I will need you to be completely honest. I will ask questions that don't seem relevant, but they are. Just answer to the best of your knowledge and we'll be fine."

"What if I don't feel like answering your questions?" Popeye asked. He watched Jowarski very carefully. He knew the man was dangerous. He could almost smell the predator in him.

"Not answering would be a very bad idea," Jowarski said. "Just like when my sister finally couldn't outrun me in the apple orchard and stopped between the drooping trees. That was not a good idea for her."

"What the hell are you talking about?" Popeye asked. "What'd you do to your sister?"

"I caught her, Mr. DeBruhl," Jowarski said. "And I tend to not be nice to things I catch."

*****

The man's chest heaved as he ran, his legs, fueled by fear and terror, drove him through the dense underbrush of the rainforest. He snapped twigs and small branches, pushing through the foliage, mad to get free of what chased him. The man could hear it coming, not the snapping of twigs and branches, but the crashing and falling of full grown trees. The destruction of trunks like shotgun blasts, the impacts of the fallen trees like concussion grenades.

The man slapped at his belt, hoping he still had the pistol there. His right hand found the familiar solidity of the grip and he felt a tiny bit of relief wash over him. He was pretty sure he had a full magazine which would give him nine .357 rounds to put more than a couple of holes in the thing if it caught up to him.

But he hoped, prayed, wished that it never came down to that. Even with the huge semi-automatic holstered to his hip, the man knew he didn't have much chance against the behemoth behind him. His only real chance was to get out of the thing's territory and make it back to the cave and get as deep inside as he could; tuck himself back into the darkness where the beast couldn't reach him.

A large bird flew up in front of him, the bright red wings blinding him for a moment as it bolted from the massive fern to his left. The man stumbled and nearly fell, his bladder loosing at the surprise, and he let out a horrified squeak. On a normal day (Ha!) he would have been scared shitless about coming in such close contact to the prehistoric bird, but the owner of the massive wingspan with the serrated beak and sharp talons that flew by, lifting up to the canopy of trees overhead, was the least of his problems.

A roar that shook the man's molars pushed through the rainforest and he swore he saw ferns ahead of him bend at the force of the noise. A second roar nearly lifted him off his feet and he knew that he only had one chance at living.

Instead of heading east as he should have, the man bolted west, a new destination in mind. It wasn't the plan, wasn't Logan's protocol if you were caught out in the open, but fuck plans and protocols. Plans and protocols could kiss his shit-soiled ass.

He shoved aside a sapling, ancestor of the modern magnolia, that was already ten feet tall and getting thick around the trunk, and found a trace of the path he wasn't supposed to take. West was never a good idea on the island. There was lots of fresh water that way which meant there were lots of creatures that wanted that fresh water. Good idea or not, it was the only idea the man had that he thought would even come close to keeping him alive.

Another roar and the man was more than sure his bladder had filled itself just to empty all over again.

**

"Comfortable?" Jowarski asked. "Need anything?"

"My left foot up your ass?" Popeye replied.

Jowarski wagged a finger and then looked down at the clipboard.

"You have duel citizenship, correct? The US and South Africa?" Jowarski flipped a page and read it for a second. "No immediate family to speak of. Maybe a cousin or two here and there, but no ties to anything other than a couple of documents that say you can rightfully sing two different national anthems."

Jowarski frowned and rubbed at his clean-shaven chin.

"What is the national anthem of South Africa?"

"Hard to explain," Popeye said. "It was one thing when I was young, now it's two things. A mash-up, like the kids say."

"Right, right, because of apartheid," Jowarski said and nodded. "Where did you stand on that?"

"On what?" Popeye asked.

"Apartheid," Jowarski explained. "Were you for or against? Be honest. It helps me to gauge your answers better if I know a couple things that aren't in this." He tapped the papers on the clipboard. "And your views on race aren't in this. Which is lazy reporting, if you ask me. Whoever compiled this did not do a thorough job. I'll fix that as much as I can."

He waited as Popeye stared at him. The room was silent for several minutes.

"Mr. DeBruhl?" Jowarski asked. "Your views on apartheid?"

"It was shite," Popeye said. "My parents didn't like it, I didn't like it, no one I knew liked it. It was for rich snobs that wanted to keep their land and gold. For the rest of us, it was just another thing to get drunk and fight about. Total shite."

"Total shite," Jowarski mumbled as he wrote on the clipboard. "Good to hear, good to hear. Now, what is it that got you interested in being a sailor? In making your life and living off the sea?"

"What does that have to do with Ballantine?" Popeye asked.

"Nothing," Jowarski said. "But it has everything to do with you. And that's what I want to know right now. All about Popeye DeBruhl. The more I know about you, the more I know what to ask that might, just might, trigger something deep inside you that could help us find Ballantine."

"Why are you so scared of Ballantine?" Popeye asked. "You double cross him? Boy, I wouldn't want to double cross that creepy son of a bitch. You think those giant sharks we were chasing were the scariest things in the sea? No way. Ballantine is."

"Quite," Jowarski nodded. "How about you answer my question, Mr. DeBruhl? Why did you decide to become a sailor?"

"I'm good at it," Popeye replied.

"Yes, I'm sure you are, but how did you find that out? A person doesn't just hop on a ship one day out of the blue," Jowarski said. "What motivated you to choose that career path?"

"I hopped on a ship one day out of the blue," Popeye replied. His squint became even more pronounced and he flexed his arms, pulling at the restraints again. "Hey, you want answers? Then let me out of these things. Until then, you can write whatever you want on your clipboard, but you'll have to make it all up because I'm done talking to you."

"Is that so?" Jowarski asked.

His tone made Popeye shiver.

"If you are done talking to me, Mr. DeBruhl, then you are of no use to me," Jowarski continued. "People that are of no use to me are a drain on resources. We have limited resources at the moment and I cannot justify keeping you around."

"So let me go," Popeye smirked. "I wouldn't want to be a drain."

"Yes...let you go," Jowarski sighed. "If only it were that easy."

***

Vines clung to the man's arms, wrapping themselves about his wrists as he pushed through the dense foliage. He ripped free, shouldering past the massive leaves that swooped down to consume him.

To consume him.

He almost laughed at the thought. To think only a few months previously he and his colleagues had been shaking their heads at why they weren't making the right progress with the biospheres.

Not a problem for any of them anymore.

His scientist brain quickly ran through the many vectors needed to create the anomaly, but he came up empty like always. Like they all had. Something sparked the release of energy. The uncontrollable proliferation of life that swept the island almost overnight.

Logan had said that it was a total accident, but...

But the man did not trust Logan further than he could throw him. And he was pretty sure Logan wasn't even really *Logan* anymore. Not in the way the man wasn't Dr. Moses Chen. They'd all gone through serious changes. But Logan just seemed *off*. Dr. Chen couldn't put his finger on it.

The roar behind him snapped Dr. Chen from his thoughts. He screamed then clamped his hands over his mouth as he continued his struggle with the local flora. The leaves stopped their attack and the vines withdrew as Dr. Chen burst from the edge of the jungle and into an open meadow filled with eight-foot wildflowers and thick, swaying grasses.

He stopped and tried not to cry. The grasses hadn't been there last week. Or if they had, Logan hadn't put them in his report. Which means they hadn't been there. Logan put everything in his reports. He was beyond OCD when it came to the details. Years of field research and a near miss with a Nobel made him that way.

Dr. Chen stared at the meadow. His eyes tried to find a path, find a way through without suffering too much damage. He couldn't find that path.

He checked himself, so pissed he hadn't thought to bring a machete with him. Who needs a machete when the plan is to only go a few yards from the cave? The guy chased from watching a simple sunrise, that's who.

Dr. Chen made a choice. He stripped off the long-sleeve shirt that was tattered and torn and wrapped it around his head and face, leaving space for him to breathe and see, but for nothing else. He checked the pockets of his cargo pants and nearly cried with relief when he found he had brought his sunglasses. He yanked them free and ignored the fact they were bent and twisted from his jungle flight. He wasn't going for style, just protection.

He slipped the sunglasses on and made sure the shirt was tight around his head then took a deep breath and started running once more.

He was three feet into the tall grass when the first blades swung out at him. They swooped down, going for his face immediately. He flinched and cringed with each impact of grass on sunglass plastic. He felt more blades swiping at his head, but both the sunglasses and the shirt stayed in place, keeping him from being sliced and diced right there in the meadow.

Unfortunately, his arms and torso didn't have the same protection. The sweat-stained tank top he wore became rags before he was a full twenty yards into the meadow, hanging off him by strings and grime. He hadn't showered in days since they couldn't spare the fresh water, so his body oils and sweat kept quite a bit of the tank top plastered to him. In seconds, blood was the main cement holding the material in place.

Dr. Chen's arms were crisscrossed with a hundred cuts, both superficial and potentially problematic. The adrenaline in his system kept him from worrying too much, not to mention the distraction of dozens and dozens of blades of grass coming at his face over and over again. He pushed on, leaving a bloody trail of himself behind. He knew the scent would drive the creature mad once the thing reached the meadow.

If he didn't get to the other side before that point then he didn't expect to make it out of the meadow at all. The grass was dangerous, but not to something as huge as the creature. The blades would be stopped quickly by the thing's thick hide. They'd cut and shave bits off here and there, but never deep enough to do any real damage.

Loud poofing noises reached his covered ears, but Dr. Chen couldn't worry about those. He glanced up quickly, seeing the plumes of pollen burst into the air. Blue, purple, green. Not the orange or yellow, or even red, that one would expect from wildflowers. But these wildflowers, in all their eight-foot glory, were not what anyone would expect.

Dr. Chen took a deep breath and held it as spiky particles began to fall through the grass and cling to his clothes, his skin, trapped in his blood that never stopped flowing.

Never stopped flowing. Shit.

Dr. Chen realized that the grass must have developed some type of anti-coagulating properties. Even with the immense amount of perspiration seeping from his pores, some of the blood should have started to thicken. But it didn't. His mind did the calculations and he knew he had perhaps five minutes, maybe ten, before grass or flowers or even the giant thing behind him were the least of his problems. He'd bleed to death well before any of that took him down.

Then he saw it, darkness at the end of the meadow. He shoved through the last row of grass and slid to a stop, his eyes trying to pierce the darkness of the jungle ahead of him. He couldn't tell if anything lay in wait, ready to make a snack of him before his eyes could adjust to the gloom.

He counted to three then took off into the jungle. But he stopped only a few feet in as the creature's roar grabbed his attention. It sounded different. Sounded like it was high up and not on the other side of the meadow. Dr. Chen spun about and watched in horror as a massive shadow darkened the middle of the meadow. The shadow raced towards him and he couldn't figure out what it was. Then he looked up and saw the monster soaring over the grasses and wildflowers. It was in mid-leap, clearing any danger the meadow may have presented with one push of its powerful hind legs.

"You can't do that," Dr. Chen muttered, realizing the stupidity of his words before he even finished saying them.

Apparently it could do that.

The creature's eyes were locked on where he stood just inside the jungle's tree line and Dr. Chen felt trapped. Trapped by the gaze from those black, black eyes. Trapped by the knowledge that everything he thought he knew, everything they all thought they knew, was complete and utter bullshit. The rules did not apply anymore. Despite the fact that they had invented the rules.

A scream lodged in his throat, Dr. Chen turned and ran as fast as he could. He ignored the continual blood loss. He ignored the fatigue and cramps that started to set in. He ignored the creature that had broken all the rules. All he thought about was getting another ten yards, another twenty, thirty, fifty.

If he could get through that part of the jungle then he would have a chance. A small chance, but still a chance.

***

"I'll give you one more chance, Mr. DeBruhl," Jowarski said. "Just play along with me and answer my questions and you could get yourself out of this room alive."

"That's one damn empty promise," Popeye said. "What happens when I get out of this room alive? You kill me out there?"

"I do not want you dead, Mr. DeBruhl," Jowarski sighed. "I want you alive and cooperative. But those work hand in hand. Cooperate and stay alive."

Popeye studied Jowarski for a few seconds then nodded. "Fine. I became a sailor because it was a way to escape without running away. I had a future, if I worked hard enough. And I'm a damned hard worker. You don't become boatswain without busting your ass over and over again."

"Do you like the sea?" Jowarski asked.

"I love it," Popeye said. "More than anything else. Besides my own hide."

"Is that so? I would think after the first encounter with the giant sharks that you would have considered a new line of work," Jowarski said. "To save that hide. Signing on permanently with Ballantine was not exactly the best move towards self-preservation."

"I didn't sign on with Ballantine," Popeye said. "I signed on with Darren, with Marty, with Cougher and the rest of the crew."

"Gunnar? Dr. Peterson? Was he part of that as well?" Jowarski asked.

"Gun was there, yeah, but he was more like the ship's mascot," Popeye said.

"Really?" Jowarski laughed. "I had you pegged for that role." He glanced down at Popeye's stump. "No pun intended."

"The mascot helps with morale," Popeye said, ignoring the slight. "I'm boatswain. Morale is important, but not my priority. My priority is making sure the ship runs to its highest efficiency. Sometimes you have to take a shit on morale for that to happen. Gun always knew how to break the tension and keep the crew from getting too pissy."

"Why do you think that is?" Jowarski asked.

"He grew up around the Thornes and Darren," Popeye replied. "If you are part of that crowd then you learn how to diffuse tension in a hurry or you'll get chewed up and spit out."

"Have the Thornes always been such a violent family?" Jowarski asked. "Were they aggressive even back then?"

"Military families sometimes are," Popeye shrugged. "But I don't know enough about them to say what their history is. I do know that Kinsey is one tough-as-nails firecracker. You cross her and you'll be holding your junk in your hands before you can blink. Her dad ain't much better."

"What about Mr. Chambers? Is he just as dangerous?" Jowarski asked.

"Darren? Nah. He has anger management issues, but then so does pretty much everyone I know," Popeye said. "He can keep the anger in check. Unless you mess with Gun or Kinsey. Then I'd say he's probably not the guy you want to be around."

"He's protective of them?" Jowarski asked.

"Hell yeah," Popeye said. "He loves that girl like nobody's business. He'd kill, die, come back to life, and kill again for her. Same for Gunnar. Those two are thicker than brothers."

"Speaking of brothers," Jowarski smiled. "Tell me about the Reynolds boys. How do they fit into the family dynamic?"

"The Reynolds? Shit, those two are misfits of the worst kind," Popeye replied. "They never shut up and never stop cracking wise. Drives Thorne nuts. Drives most of us nuts. But you gotta love 'em."

"Why is that?" Jowarski asked.

"Because they know their jobs and they are great at them," Popeye replied. "Drive you nuts or not, them boys can shoot, can fight, can find a way to survive. Shit, look at them. All burned and torn up. One's missing half his face and the other is missing an eye. See 'em with their shirts off and it's nothing but a fucking Rand McNally map of scars on display."

Popeye started to say something else, but stopped and shook his head.

"What? What is it?" Jowarski asked.

"Nothing," Popeye said. "Just thought about how Max looked at that Darby woman. Makes me think of how Darren looks at Kinsey. Funny how shit happens on a boat."

"Darby?" Jowarski asked, leaning forward quickly. "What does Darby have to do with Max Reynolds?"

"Ha!" Popeye laughed. "Ain't that the question of the century! What could a stone-cold chick like that see in a clown like him? Don't make a lick of sense. Personally, I'd be scared to death to be alone with that woman."

"You are not the only one, Mr. DeBruhl," Jowarski said. "That's a wild animal being domesticated. It never ends well."

***

The sound of rushing water drove Dr. Chen on. Not that the sound of the trees behind him being broken and mangled wasn't enough to keep his ass moving. It was plenty. But those were sounds that almost made him want to fall in a heap and just lie on the ground in the fetal position. The rushing water meant he was close to escape. Close to maybe surviving the nightmare that his day had become.

He stumbled and nearly ran headlong into the trunk of what he guessed was in the metasequoia family. The massive redwood-like tree had to be nearly forty feet wide and stretched up into the air almost farther than the man could see. He shoved himself away from the giant conifer and stumbled around the massive trunk.

His breath caught as he saw what was before him. The edge of the jungle was backed up against a sheer cliff. Dr. Chen hurried to the edge, careful of the crumbling earth beneath his feet. He looked left and saw a way to get down, but he knew he didn't have time for that path. The monster behind him was only a few paces, a few collapsed and crushed trees, from snatching him up in its oversized jaws.

To the right, close to a hundred yards away, was a majestic waterfall that would give sightseers and photographers heart attacks from its beauty alone. It roared over the edge of the cliff, falling at least a hundred feet before turning into a rainbow mist against the hidden rocks and boulders of the river below. Dr. Chen could reach the waterfall, but he doubted he could survive the fall.

Unless he changed, which he had been loathe to do despite the others' assurances it was the most amazing thing ever.

It was a hard choice, one made even harder by the constant pounding of giant feet coming for him.

Die from beast or die from waterfall? Stay himself or become something else entirely?

He made his choice and sprinted to the right just as the trees behind him were turned into nothing but splinters and toothpicks. Woody shrapnel exploded around him and he screamed as he felt new wounds added to his already marred body. There were a million ways he could die in the next few minutes, but only one chance at survival.

The ubiquitous roar shoved at him like a strong wind. He ignored it, blocked it out, focused only on the waterfall ahead of him. One hundred yards became eighty, became fifty, became twenty, became nothing.

Hesitancy was death and the man didn't want to die so he did not hesitate. He reached the edge and kept going, leaping out as far as his fatigued legs would carry him. His arms pinwheeled and the scream of fear he bellowed changed pitch and tone until it became a wail of survival, a plea to anything that would listen to save him from being an impossible monster's meal.

Or snack. Yeah, he was only snack-sized for the creature that charged at him.

He turned in the air, his body already changing, and caught sight of the creature that had been pursuing him—a tower of a beast with a huge body, short arms, a head nearly as big as its torso, and powerful legs that looked like nothing but quivering muscle. Which they were.

He could feel his own quivering muscles as he turned into whatever he would turn into.

That was the thought in his head as he hit the water and was spun about by the force of the river that fell from above.

Dr. Chen was swept down, down, down, away from the edge of the cliff, away from the beast, that nightmare made of muscle and violence, away from the world above and into the world below. He took a deep breath and then lost it instantly as his back impacted with a heavy boulder. He roared and choked on water, his heavy body pulled downriver by the immense power of nature.

Whether that nature was actually natural or not, was up for debate.

***

"What locations or destinations did Ballantine ever talk about?" Jowarski asked. "Any special places he was fond of? Possible vacations he'd taken in the past? Maybe even a bucket list of travel spots he wanted to see?"

Popeye blinked a few times then scrunched up his face and leaned as far forward as the restraints would allow. "Do you even know Ballantine?"

"I've met the man, yes," Jowarski replied. "I understand those seem like strange questions for someone like Ballantine, but I have to be thorough."

"Yeah, thorough," Popeye chuckled. "You must be desperate to ask questions like that. I'd think Ballantine's wifey would know those things. Why the hell ask me?"

"Dr. Ballantine has not had the privilege of her husband's company in some time," Jowarski replied. "But we'll keep that between you and me." He waited with his pen poised above his clipboard.

Popeye shook his head and leaned back. "Ballantine didn't share."

"Is that so?" Jowarski asked. "Nothing while you and the rest of the crew travelled with him over the open oceans? Nothing before, during, or after one of your many monster missions? He didn't say anything off handedly? A quick joke or sarcastic remark?"

"The guy was always saying quick jokes and sarcastic remarks," Popeye said. "That was all he said. You couldn't get a straight answer out of him if you jammed ten feet of reinforced steel up his ass."

"Colorful," Jowarski said. "So, no off-hand comments about places he wanted to visit or had visited?"

"You sure don't listen for a guy asking a bunch of questions," Popeye said. "There were no off-hand comments with Ballantine. The guy was as controlled as they get. If he said something then he meant to say it whether he pretended to or not. Nothing to chance with that one."

"Yes, we are aware of that," Jowarski said.

"What did you do to him?" Popeye asked. "Why are you so afraid of Ballantine?"

Jowarski shook his head and gave Popeye a wan smile.

"Commander Thorne," Jowarski said. "Where does he stand with Ballantine? Are the two co-leaders?"

"I don't think they know," Popeye said. "Ballantine always says Thorne is in charge of Team Grendel, but Ballantine is an A-plus control freak, so I don't think he lets anyone be in charge of anything."

"Do they fight? Quarrel? Bicker?" Jowarski asked.

"All those words mean the same thing," Popeye said. "And yeah, they do. Or did. Don't know what they do now. They could be dead for all I know."

"I doubt they are," Jowarski said.

"Really? Why you think that?" Popeye asked.

The wan smile returned to Jowarski's face.

***

Dr. Chen's face felt a thousand pounds too heavy. The skin and muscle swelled, puffing up from the collision with the many boulders that he'd encountered as he was shoved down under the water, pummeled by the waterfall and the river itself. At least the water was cold enough to numb the pain slightly. But only slightly.

He grasped at the edge of the riverbank, his fingers impossibly long and grey. He gripped sturdy roots that dripped down into the river, thirsty for relief from the tropical sun that beat relentlessly on the island. Dr. Chen tugged at the roots, wrapped his hands about them, pulled, but he made no headway. He just didn't have the strength to get himself out of the water. He'd spent every last bit of energy staying alive. Any energy he did have deep down in reserve would have to be used to keep from drowning at the edge of the river.

And to change back. If he could figure out how. The others hadn't said how they did it.

Far above, half a mile away, stood the monster, its jaws open, its throat rippling as it bellowed. It raged, stomping back and forth, crushing anything and everything in its path at the top of the waterfall. It kicked boulders, sending them rocketing out and down.

Dr. Chen flinched and cried out as one of the boulders came within twenty feet of him. It was as big as a Volkswagen Beetle and probably weighed twice as much. He knew he couldn't stay where he was. The creature kept looking for a way down off the cliff, hunting for a path that would hold it and allow it to come down and finish the job it started. The man didn't understand why. The thing should have given up a long time ago.

But then nothing on the island acted like it should. Every one of their grand plans fell apart in a swirling rush of exploding metal and roaring flames. Catalysts catalyzed what they shouldn't have and the growth that resulted was exponential. What should have taken years, and on a much smaller scale, happened in less than a week.

And still happened.

Dr. Chen's muscles felt like they were detached from his bones, floating inside his skin sack, ready to dissolve and melt if they were exposed to the air. But somehow he managed to move from his spot, reaching up and grabbing roots hand over hand, using them to propel himself down the river and well out of sight of the pacing, stomping, bellowing creature.

He was grateful for one thing and that was the giant creature seemed to have scared off any other animals that may have been lurking close to the water. Hard to miss the sound of a seventy-five foot beast ripping through the jungle. The other fauna of the island had plenty of warning that it was a good time to make themselves scarce.

Of course, they didn't just disappear. They went somewhere. And after nearly a half hour of slow, careful, hand-over-hand movement, Dr. Chen found out where they went.

He came around a bend in the river and stopped. There, wading in a large pool that had formed on the opposite side, stood six creatures that shouldn't exist. In fact, they never would have if he hadn't personally entered the sequence into the matrix facilitator. That felt like a hundred years ago.

Modeled closely on the spinosaurus, the creatures snapped and hissed at each other, jostling for position to catch the many Mawsonia-like fish that flopped in the shallow pool. The fish must have also been scared downstream, retreating from their deep pool haven at the bottom of the waterfall.

Dr. Chen watched, terrified yet also fascinated as the spinosauruses seemed to compete with each other, but also work in harmony to keep as many of the Mawsonia from fleeing further downstream. It was not a hunting behavior he would have even guessed the spinosauruses were capable of.

But then part of the reason the island existed was to see what all the creatures were capable of. Just not on the scale that occurred. No, the scale they had wanted was maybe ten percent of what had occurred. A controlled, and controllable, group of miniatures, all studied and observed from the perfect safety of a contained facility.

Dr. Chen shook his head at their hubris. How they thought they could create living prehistoric dioramas without anything going wrong was ludicrous. He looked at his hands, his incredibly misshapen hands, and shook his head, feeling the weight of his enlarged cranium strain his neck.

He was about to cry when his hands started to return to normal, to shift and shrink before his eyes. Dr. Chen marveled at the transformation, not even kidding himself that he knew how the entire process was even possible. An island of impossibilities. He had to wonder if he was lucky or cursed to be a part of it all.

Those were the last thoughts that ran through his head as the creature above him, rising out of the dirt and mud of the riverbank, opened its jaws wide and lunged.

***

Captain Marty Lake and Chief Engineer Morgan "Cougher" Colfer stopped what they were doing and looked from the deck of the Beowulf III and out at the bay they had just sailed into.

"D? You hear that?" Lake called.

"Yeah," Darren Chambers replied over the com.

Lake turned to the bridge and Darren stuck his head out, looking at the white sand beach that surrounded the crystal blue bay.

"That sounded like a person," Darren said over the com.

"That was for sure human," Max Reynolds added, joining the com conversation.

"Totally human," his brother Shane agreed. There was the sound of something being sucked and then a cough and a slow exhale. "Man, I am so glad that Lucy totally snagged some of our stash and hid it from us."

"Not the time, Shane," Darren said.

"Are there people on that island?" Cougher asked.

"Ballantine said he didn't see any signs of his science staff surviving what he said was a pretty fucking big explosion," Lake replied. "But it stands to reason someone made it out in one piece."

"Not anymore, man," Max said, immediately making his own sucking, coughing, exhaling sound. "Dude. This shit is harsh. We need to teach the Luce how to take better care of her weed."

"Take a look at that island," Shane said. "We could grow our own. Gunnar has seeds. I know he does. Somewhere down in his lab. He's a sneaky bastard."

"Guys!" Darren shouted. "Shut up about the weed! Nobody cares about your weed!"

There were several loud grumbles of disagreement over the com.

"Jesus, how many people are in on this conversation?" Darren asked.

"Pretty much all essential personnel," Lake said. "I called on an open channel."

"Did I hear correctly that a person may have screamed from the island?" Ballantine asked as he stepped from a hatch and onto the main deck.

Mid-forties, dressed in his usual khakis and polo shirt, Ballantine looked like a golf pro with a psychotic twinkle in his eye. Fit, tan, muscular, he moved with a confidence and ease that made most that came in contact with him less than confident and very uneasy. He held a pair of high-powered binoculars and turned to face the island.

"Which way?" Ballantine asked as he came up next to Lake.

"I don't know," Lake replied. "It echoed out from the bay. That's all I know."

Ballantine glanced at Cougher, but the man only shrugged.

"Not much help," Ballantine said, putting the binoculars to his eyes. He scanned the bay then tilted the binoculars up, focusing on the jungle and low mountains beyond. "Hmmm."

"What do you see?" Lake asked. "Another monster?"

"Please, Captain Lake, let's not call the creatures monsters," Ballantine said. "I have explained to all of you the type of work that the facility here was conducting. They are live specimens. Perhaps a little too alive, but far from being monsters. These creatures are pure miracles of science."

"And they will eat us in a fucking second, right?" Lake smirked.

"Well, yes, there is that," Ballantine said. "Oh, look!"

He handed the binoculars over to Lake and took the man by the shoulders.

"What the hell?" Lake said, but didn't fight it as Ballantine directed him to look in a specific area. Lake put the binoculars to his eyes. "What am I looking for?"

"Halfway up the second mountain," Ballantine said. "Trust me. You'll know it when you see it."

Lake studied the island for a while then gasped and pulled the binoculars away.

"Are you shitting me?" he asked.

"What?" the Reynolds brothers asked over the com at the same time.

"There are flying ones!" Lake said. "Big, red, flying ones!"

"Flying ones are bad," Max said.

"Very bad," Shane agreed. "We do not approve of flying monsters."

"I really wish you would stop calling them monsters," Ballantine said. "It's so disrespectful to the scientists that gave their lives creating these creatures."

"What is going on up here?" Commander Vincent Thorne asked as he came out of the same hatch that Ballantine had exited only minutes before. "Did you see any of the monsters or not?"

Ballantine sighed and shook his head. "Why do I even try?"

Chapter Two- Can't Stay On This Boat Forever

Team Grendel stood on the deck of the Beowulf III, all waiting for Ballantine to begin his briefing. Usually they met in the large, ornate briefing room above the main deck, but the huge nuclear EMP that killed the engines also killed most of the tech in that room, making it basically useless. Except on poker nights.

A triple hulled "research vessel" at over 90 meters, the B3 was styled along the lines of the Google research vessel R/V Falkor, but with a much different purpose. That purpose was obvious as Team Grendel waited, fully armed and geared for their mission on the island that framed the background behind them.

Former commander of the Navy SEALs BUD/S training program, Vincent Thorne was leader of Team Grendel, the band of ex-SEALs and other SpecOps misfits that Ballantine had brought together to handle less than ordinary situations. In his sixties, but still fit enough to take down men half his age, Thorne was not a man that minced words or wasted his time with pointless pleasantries.

"Let's get on with this, Ballantine," Thorne growled.

"We will, we will," Ballantine said as he tapped his loafered toe. With his arms crossed, he pointed his sunglasses-covered eyes towards the island. "Just waiting on the elves, as usual."

"Do they have any toys worth playing with?" Max Reynolds asked. "The EMP didn't fry them all?"

"They could have at least tried to save a PlayStation or something," Shane Reynolds said. "You can only do so much target practice each day before you go cuckoo nuts."

"Did you just say that?" Max scoffed. "My own brother has betrayed the sniper code by saying he gets bored with target practice. It's like I don't even know you."

"Hey, bro, I can't help it if I'm a perfect shot and there's just nowhere to improve," Shane replied. "I wouldn't recommend you stop practicing, though. You pull to the left on your second shot. Don't feel bad. It happens."

The Reynolds brothers were nine months apart and looked almost identical, both with yellow-blond hair, green eyes, freckles across the nose, deep tans, and that Southern California surfer boy attitude. But there was more than one way to tell the difference between them- Max was missing his left ear and had scar tissue running from his scalp, down his neck, and onto his shoulder while Shane was missing his right eye completely and had a black eye patch covering the socket, a Rasta-colored pot leaf stitched into the material.

Both had very thick joints tucked into the corners of their mouths.

"Boys, knock it the fuck off," Thorne said, stepping from the group to face the brothers.

"Sorry, Uncle Vinny," Max replied.

"Our bad, Uncle Vinny," Shane added.

They didn't budge.

"The joints!" Thorne barked. "I'm talking about the joints!"

"Oh, I thought you just wanted us to shut up like always," Max said, taking the joint from his mouth and carefully putting it out with the wet tips of his thumb and forefinger. He tucked it into a pocket on his gear vest and patted it gently. "You stay safe, mighty spliff."

"I want you to shut up too," Thorne replied. "That's a fucking given."

Next to the Reynolds stood their cousin, Kinsey Thorne, a muscular woman of average height with short-cropped blonde hair and wrap-around sunglasses that reflected her father's face back at him as he surveyed the rest of the Team.

"You know you can't ever win the shut the fuck up battle, right Daddy?" Kinsey smirked. "I don't think they even understand the concept."

22

"Max no understand shutting up," Max said. "Max stupid."

"Beside the point," Darren Chambers chuckled.

Dirty blond hair that blew in the ocean breeze, bright blue eyes, a tight black t-shirt hugging his muscled torso, Darren looked like a bulked up GQ model, not an ex-SEAL. He lifted his sunglasses and gave Kinsey a wink.

"Good thing their stupid doesn't run in the family," Darren said.

"Shut up, Ditcher," Shane said. "Stop sucking up to Sis. She divorced your ass for a reason."

"Ancient history and water under bridges and all that," Darren said. "And what the fuck did I do? I was just playing."

"You were winking at my cuz, bro," Max said.

"I'm your bro, not him," Shane responded.

"That was a derogatory bro, bro," Max said. "I save the love bros for you, bro."

"You're the best, bro," Shane said. "Come here, bro. Give me a bro hug."

"Do you have any control over this?" Thorne asked, looking at Darby.

Barely five feet tall, Darby had shoulder-length black hair tied back in a pony tail, a tan tank top, and cut off cargo pants that had strings hanging down from the unhemmed edges. She was maybe a hundred pounds wet, but everything about her projected a sense that when you were in the company of Darby, you were in the company of a true apex predator.

She blinked her dark eyes and sighed. "Because I'm sleeping with your nephew, you think I have control over him?"

"Yes," Thorne said. "Max is pliable that way."

"Hey," Max protested, but without any real vigor. "I'm far from pliable. In fact, I can get downright—"

"Nope," Kinsey interrupted. "I do not want to hear the next words out of your mouth."

"Can you keep him in line for just a few minutes?" Thorne asked Darby. Darby shrugged. "Thank you."

"Stay in line," Darby said to Max.

"Or what?" he replied, a lascivious smirk on his face.

"Or we play bullfighter again," Darby replied, turning away as if that settled the conversation.

Apparently it did. Max grimaced then made a lock the lips and throw away the key pantomime.

"What the fuck is bullfighter?" Darren asked.

"We don't want to know," Kinsey said before Darby could respond, not that she looked like she would. "TMFI."

The last member of Team Grendel, Lucy Durning, stood off to the side of everyone, her attention focused through the large binoculars she held to her eyes.

"There's shit in the water," she said. Everyone turned to look at her, but she didn't remove the binoculars. "Yeah. There is definitely shit in the water. The island isn't the only place with critters. Great. Prehistoric birds in the air and what-the-fuck-evers in the water."

Nearly six feet tall, wide at the shoulder, with a head of shockingly red hair, Lucy could have been intimidating, but instead she was an easy-going woman that didn't buy into macho bullshit and had nothing to prove like Kinsey or Darby seemed to. Unless it was proving she was the best at target practice against the Reynolds boys. Shooters gotta shoot, snipers gotta snipe.

"Yes, I was afraid the facility may have been working on aquatics," Ballantine said. "They weren't scheduled to for some time, but you know how science always progresses. It may have been necessary in order to recreate the biosphere of a specific species. These things domino quickly."

Team Grendel stared at him. Ballantine smiled and stared back until Thorne growled and said, "Do I need to go down there and carry the assholes up myself?"

"That's not very nice," Ingrid said as she and Carlos came up from below decks. "I have been nothing but pleasant to you, Commander Thorne. No need to call me names."

"Except for the traitor thing," Darby said. "That wasn't exactly pleasant."

The Team frowned at the mention of Ingrid's duplicity.

Having gotten herself into a tight situation, Ingrid, one of the three weapons smiths and techs that worked below in what was known as the Toyshop, had been forced to plant and activate a tracking device so that the B3's enemies could find them quickly.

Unbeknownst to her, Ballantine had anticipated the betrayal and used it to his advantage. As he tended to do with most situations.

"Now, now, Ingrid has been put through enough," Ballantine said. "She made a mistake, something every single one of you here can consider yourselves experts in, but she turned it around and is back to being a valuable member of this crew."

"Where's Mike?" Kinsey asked. "Did you guys certify his legs?"

Carlos, having been sullen and silent since stepping onto the deck, rolled his eyes.

"Certify," Carlos scoffed. "The legs aren't a used Mac. You can't just run diagnostics on them and a bell dings."

"So that's a no?" Darren asked.

"Michael will remain on the B3," Ballantine said. "Until we know for certain his prosthetics were not damaged by the EMP."

"Been a few weeks. Wouldn't you know by now?" Max asked.

"Yeah, his legs seem fine when he's walking around," Shane said. "They guy can even dance. Got some moves."

"No," Thorne said, pointing a finger at Shane without looking at him. The dance Shane was about to do stopped instantly. "Mike will join us on the Team as soon as I am sure those legs won't shit the bed. We do not want to be on an op and have him suddenly immobile. Could kill him, could kill us."

"An op?" Max laughed, looking out at the island. "This isn't an op. This is Jurassic Park 3, man. The second island. The one that time forgot."

"You couldn't be further from the truth, Maxwell," Ballantine said. "Time did not forget this island. In fact, it sounds like time found it and grabbed it by the nuts, twisting and twisting until both balls popped and exploded everywhere."

There were more than a few squirms.

"Lovely," Darby sighed. She looked at Ingrid and Carlos who both seemed about to puke. "What do you have? I'd like to get this freak show on the road."

Thorne looked like he was about to object to Darby hijacking his Team then he shook his head and aimed a thumb at her.

"What the lady said," Thorne barked. "We have work to do."

"He called your girl a lady," Shane whispered loudly to Max. "Ha. Darby's a lady."

"I know," Max said, whispering back just as inconspicuously. "I've seen her lady parts. Been all up in that."

Thorne growled so low and deep that the deck nearly rumbled.

"Damn," Shane said. "I think you just went elephant on us, Uncle Vinny."

"Yeah, totally," Max agreed. "And what my brother means by that is elephants can communicate long distances on low frequencies that we—"

"SHUT UP!" the rest of the Team shouted, even Darby.

"Oh my," Shane gasped in a faux British accent.

"How rude," Max gasped as well, mimicking the accent.

"Never a dull moment," Ballantine said.

"Are there creatures out in the water?" Ingrid asked. "I better get your compression suits."

She hurried off as half the Team began to complain.

"The compression suits in this heat? Are you fucking nuts?" Max asked.

"Don't bring up nuts," Shane said. "Ballantine will get distracted."

"Yeah, what was up with that twisting and twisting thing, man?" Max asked Ballantine. "Not cool."

"What do you have for us?" Thorne asked Carlos, ignoring his nephews as much as he could. "I've seen the thing we're up against." He patted the butt of his heavily modified M4 carbine. "This will only piss it off."

"If the information Ballantine has given us is correct," Carlos said. He rolled his eyes at the look Ballantine gave him. "If it is correct then the creature will have skin thicker than an elephant's hide."

"Uncle Vinny can talk it down," Max said.

"Yeah, he speaks elephant," Shane added.

"As I was saying, the creature's hide will be extremely thick," Carlos continued. "The normal rounds in your M4s will not penetrate."

Max and Shane patted their sniper rifles.

"Speak for yourself, nerd," Max said. "Some of us aren't using M4s. My .300 Win Mag will stop almost anything."

"My .338 Mac will do even better," Shane said.

"Want to bet?" Max asked.

"Sure. How much?" Shane replied.

"We should make it interesting," Max said. "Maybe— Oh, fuck! OW!"

He looked down at Darby's hand that had him by the crotch. She flexed once and he squeaked.

"Build me something that can do that on command," Thorne said as he looked at Carlos and pointed at Max. "For both the boys."

"Hostile work environment much?" Shane muttered.

"Even your high-powered rifles won't do much against that thing," Carlos said.

Ballantine made a clucking noise at the word "thing." Carlos ignored it as he set down a crate he had been holding.

"Line up," Carlos said. "I have new ammo for you. Armor piercing with explosive rounds. Even if they don't get all the way through the creature's hide, they'll do some extreme damage when they blow."

"He said blow," Shane chuckled and looked at his brother. Max only shook his head, his crotch still under Darby's control. "Oh, right, you're muzzled. No fun all on my own."

"That's the point," Darby said.

"A good point too, sweet ass cheeks from heaven and beyond," Max said. "You always make the best points."

Team Grendel ejected the magazines they already had in place in their various weapons of choice, handed them to Carlos, and accepted the new magazines eagerly. Magazines in their kits were swapped out as well and they were all busy getting their gear stowed again when Ingrid returned.

"Here they are," Ingrid said. "Compression suits for everybody."

There were some quiet complaints, but having all had their lives saved at some point by the functionality of the suits, no one objected too harshly. The team stripped down to their underwear, modesty not something that any of the military veterans subscribed to, donned their suits then went about double checking each other to make sure seals were in place.

As one they activated their suits and the mesh material cinched up instantly, fitting each person's form like a second skin. The suits were designed to maintain a specific pressure when diving into and surfacing from deep water, helping the wearers avoid the normal health issues that came from descending or ascending too quickly. What they all found out during their many battles with human and not-so-human foes was that the suits also helped maintain pressure on and seal around wounds.

Not to mention they were nearly impervious and could harden like armor if the wearers found themselves in the jaws of an impossible creature. Which seemed to be the unfortunate fate of Team Grendel all too often. A roar from the island quickly reminded them of that fact.

"This better not be it," Thorne snapped. "Better bullets and compression suits will not be enough."

"The compression suits aren't better," Ingrid said. "They're just— Oh, right, you only meant the bullets." She smiled sheepishly and pulled out several black boxes from the bottom of the case Carlos had brought up. "These should help."

"Containment nets," Carlos said. "We have tested each of them and they were not affected by the EMP."

He set one of the boxes on the deck and pressed on it with his foot three times. A bright blue grid of light erupted from the box, hovering in the air in front of Team Grendel. About ten feet by ten feet square, the grid was a crisscrossed pattern of electric lines that sparked and shimmered in the tropical sunlight.

"Yeah, that'll stop an angry dachshund, but that's about it," Max said.

"You plan on us waving that blue hanky around and hope to distract the monster?" Shane laughed. "Did no one give you the specs on the thing? It's fucking huge?"

"I feel like we're in Spinal Tap," Max said.

"Yeah, that is totally Stonehenge right there," Shane agreed.

"I know they won't stop the creature, or any creatures," Carlos said, exasperated as usual by the brothers. "They were not designed to handle creatures so large. But they will keep you from being devoured at night when you sleep."

"Oh. Cool," Max said. "I'm a big fan of not getting eaten when I sleep."

"Whoa. Sleep?" Shane asked. "How long are we going to be on the island? I thought this was a day op. Just a recon mission to see what we can see then back here in time for drinks and apps."

"That reminds me," Max said. "I have a two for one coupon I need to use before it expires."

"Only counts on apps, not drinks," Shane replied.

"Really? What kind of cheap-ass, chicken-shit outfit is this?" Max laughed.

"No, seriously," Shane said before Thorne could light into them. "We're staying overnight?"

"Best to be prepared," Ballantine said. "The island has already proven that even the best laid plans are no match for its will."

"You talk like this island is alive, Ballantine," Kinsey said. "Anything else you need to tell us?"

"Nope," Ballantine answered without the slightest hesitation.

"You are so lying," Darren said.

"He's always lying," Darby responded. "Keep up, Operator."

Ballantine clapped his hands together. "Well, Team Grendel, I hate to see you leave, but you can't stay on this boat forever, now can you?"

Thorne sighed. "Grendel. Load up. We need to get through this bay and on that beach in ten minutes."

Team Grendel hustled to the sides of the B3 and the waiting Zodiac rafts with their shielded and modified motors. A couple of deckhands waited for them, ready with the winches when the Team was all loaded up. Ballantine waved as they were dropped into the water then turned to Carlos and Ingrid.

"Where are the doctors?" he asked.

"Meeting in Gunnar's lab," Ingrid said. "Going over all the data you gave them on the facility."

"Good," Ballantine said. He looked over his shoulder as the Zodiacs sped across the bay, dodging the sudden appearance of fins and flippers that should not exist. "Hopefully the brains onboard can figure out how to reverse this. I don't believe brawn is going to win this fight."

"It never does," Carlos snorted as he turned and left, mumbling complaints the whole way to the hatch.

"Care to join me?" Ballantine asked Ingrid once Carlos was gone.

"I have a ton of work," Ingrid said.

"I am aware of that, but Moshi has it covered," Ballantine said. "You should come. I think being around the doctors will be good for you. The operators are all aggression and loyalty. It's going to take them longer to forgive you. The doctors will forgive you the second you contribute an intelligent idea to our dilemma."

Ingrid squirmed, looking very uncomfortable.

"Come on," Ballantine laughed, taking her gently by the elbow. "It'll be fun."

"I don't think you understand what fun is," Ingrid said, almost whispering.

Ballantine laughed again, but didn't stop as he steered her towards the hatch.

***

Of Scandinavian descent, Dr. Gunnar Peterson had a strong build, but nothing like the military physiques of Team Grendel. Red/blonde hair mussed completely, and the scruff of a similarly colored beard on his face, Gunnar leaned heavily on the lab table that was covered in papers, maps, schematics, and other detritus from the constant hunt to figure out what went wrong on the island with the limited information they had been given.

He frowned deeply as Ballantine and Ingrid walked into the lab.

"I am guessing a progress report is too much to ask for," Ballantine stated.

"You guess right," Gunnar said, pulling up a stool and sitting on it. He waved his hand at the mess. "Without seeing the island and destroyed facility, it will be hard for us to piece together what exactly happened."

The "us" were also seated around the lab table, their heads heavy, eyes looking weary and exhausted.

To Gunnar's right was Dr. Lisa Morganton, late forties, with short, bobbed blonde hair and hazel eyes. She was not her usual calm and collected self. Her hair was as mussed as Gunnar's and she had deep circles under her normally alert eyes. She barely gave Ballantine's sudden appearance any acknowledgement, her focus strictly on the task at hand.

Next to her was Dr. Boris Kelnichov, whose face was etched and lined by deep crags and furrows, putting his age at over sixty despite the fact he wore youthful looking Bermuda shorts and a bright yellow t-shirt that looked like it hadn't been washed in some time. His hair was a stand up mess of salt and pepper, sticking out at all angles in wild, unkempt tufts.

Ballantine frowned at everyone's appearance except for Ronald's.

"I see you took the time for personal hygiene, Ronald," Ballantine said, addressing the wildest looking of the bunch.

Ronald was a gigantopithecus. It was that simple. He stood about ten feet tall with extremely long arms hanging at his sides. His legs were nearly as long as his arms, but were much more muscular. Ronald's entire body was covered in thick, brown fur.

Basically, he was a Bigfoot.

But everyone had stopped referring to him as such when he dangled both of the Reynolds brothers over the side of the B3 one night and made them promise to stop calling him such a derogatory and simple name. He was not, as he insisted, a Discovery Channel special.

"Hi, Ronald," Ingrid said as she stepped out from behind Ballantine.

"Oh, Ingrid, hello," Ronald said, his voice deep and rumbling, but with a careful and precise diction. "It is good of you to join us. I am afraid even with Dr. Morganton's expertise in biomechanics, we are all just simple biologists here. There seems to have been an exorbitant amount of unidentified technology utilized by the staff of this facility. Your technological abilities could prove helpful."

"See," Ballantine said as he grinned and pushed Ingrid forward. "Forgiveness is just around the corner."

"Speak for yourself, Ballantine," a voice said from the corner of the room.

"Hello, Michael," Ballantine said, turning towards the voice. "I didn't see you there."

"That's the point," Mike said as he set aside a worn and tattered paperback. He was sitting on a stool, his metal legs propped up on a counter. His eyes moved from Ballantine to Ingrid. "If I can't go on the op with the rest of the Team then I figured playing security detail for the brain trust here would be the best gig. That is until you sign off on my battle gams."

"That is Commander Thorne's call, I'm afraid," Ballantine replied.

"It's my call," Dr. Morganton said. "As well as Carlos's. Once we know for sure the tech in your legs is one hundred percent reliable, then you will be cleared for duty."

"Great," Mike said, picking the paperback up again. "Until then I get to babysit you all and make sure Ingrid doesn't decide to go all double agent again."

"Mike, stop," Gunnar said. "Leave the girl alone. She fucked up. She knows she fucked up. And she's in the same shitty situation as the rest of us. We need her help with these schematics, so knock off the macho harassment bullshit or you're sleeping alone tonight."

Mike shrugged then looked down at his book and did a horrible job of pretending to start reading again.

"Please, Ingrid, join us," Ronald said, patting an open stool by him. Then he grimaced and picked up the stool, moving it to his other side. "This spot might be more inviting. I'm afraid Boris has not washed that t-shirt in some time and his aroma is quite pungent. And being of a species that is known for its glandular strength, that is saying a lot."

He chuckled with enthusiasm and several of the items on the table shook and shuddered from the rumbling.

"Okay," Ingrid said as she smiled at everyone then took her seat. "What am I looking at?"

"We don't know," Gunnar sighed. "That's the problem. It is obviously some type of generator."

"Oh, I wouldn't say obviously," Boris argued. "I have dealt with many generators on my island and none of them looked like this."

"Maybe it was meant to generate energy," Dr. Morganton said. "Maybe it was meant to generate something else."

"We've already been through this," Gunnar replied. "What else could it generate other than energy? Why even call it a generator at all then?"

"I didn't," Dr. Morganton snapped. "You did. You have been the one insisting it is a generator. None of us have agreed with that."

"Well, we're calling it a generator until we can call it something else," Gunnar snapped.

"What about an incubator?" Ingrid asked as she picked up the schematics and turned them this way and that way. "Could it be an incubator?"

"That would be a massive incubator," Boris said. "I had several in use on my island, as you can imagine considering the work I was doing with the extinct species there, but none were even close to this size."

"I believe I will leave you to your work," Ballantine said. "Ladies, gentlemen, a pleasure as always."

Gunnar dismissed him with a wave and concentrated on what Ingrid had said.

"Okay, let's say it is an incubator," Gunnar conceded. "What does it incubate? Ballantine said that the facility here was working on miniature models of different biospheres and biomes. None of the animals, plants, or organisms created would need an apparatus this large."

"Not unless they were incubating the entire biosphere," Ingrid replied. "What if instead of making one component at a time, they were making it all at once? Feeding in the data to the system and letting the creatures and their environment grow and develop together?"

"My lord," Ronald said. "The complexity of that undertaking would be immense. Yes, it would save hundreds upon hundreds of hours in labor and growth, but the risks would be enormous."

"No shit," Mike said. "You realize the island is all kinds of fucked, right? I'd say the risk didn't pay off."

"Alright, an incubator," Gunnar said. He stared at the schematics for a few seconds then closed his eyes and shook his head. "Unfortunately, with our systems wiped out, we can't even create a virtual model of this to prove that theory."

"That's not completely true," Ingrid said.

"You have a supercomputer that can build this in a virtual environment so we can see what it does?" Gunnar asked.

"Not exactly," Ingrid said. "But I know something that will be close. And it won't be virtual. It'll actually build this. Just on a teeny, tiny scale."

"Great," Mike laughed. "That way when it blows up, like it did on the island, the explosion will be teeny and tiny."

"We do not know that this is what blew up," Gunnar said. "And just keep reading your book, smart ass. Let the adults handle the big stuff."

Mike shrugged.

"Human relationships are so complicated," Ronald said. "Love and hate seem almost intertwined."

"Tell me about it," Gunnar replied. He tapped a finger on the schematics and focused all of his attention on Ingrid. "It's your show now. Time to pull back the curtain."

"Show? Curtain? Ugh, can you be more gay?" Mike sighed.

"That's it, you are staying here, asshole," Gunnar said, pointing a finger at Mike. "And you are sleeping in your own bunk tonight."

"I was just kidding," Mike responded. "Chill out, Gun."

"Ingrid? Where are we going?" Gunnar asked.

"The Toyshop," Ingrid said. "Where else would I take you?"

***

The Zodiacs hit the white sand beach and slid up onto land as Darren killed the motor in one and Darby killed the motor in the other. Most of Team Grendel immediately hopped out of the rafts and started tossing gear and supplies to each other, while Lucy and Max covered them with their sniper rifles. Once they were certain nothing was going to come for them right away, they eased up and helped grab gear as well.

Yet, no one relaxed. Their weapons were slung so that they could be grabbed up without a moment's hesitation.

"We sure those things won't be coming out to say hello?" Max asked, looking back at the bay and the occasional appearance of a large fin or flipper.

"They didn't fuck with us while we were in the water," Shane said. "They probably won't fuck with us up here on land."

"High tide line is there," Thorne said, pointing to a small line of shells and darker sand a meter away. "We set up between that line and the jungle. Max and Darby will stay here at the FOB while we recon the area."

"Whoa, what?" Max exclaimed. "Why am I staying here?" He hooked a thumb over at Darby. "More importantly, why is she staying here?"

"Legs," Darby said. "Our legs are still healing."

"It's been weeks," Max whined. "Come on, Uncle Vinny, you've seen us both workout and know our legs are in tip top shape."

"True," Thorne replied. "But someone has to stay here and watch the equipment and make sure the Zodiacs are ready to bug out at the first sign of trouble. Makes more sense to have you and Darby stay since both of you had severe leg wounds recently. Not to mention that if we come busting ass out of that jungle, I'd prefer to have a shooter covering. That means it's either you or your brother or Lucy. You want to tell me how I narrow that down?"

"If you say one word about me being only Coast Guard and not a SEAL, I'll whoop your ass right here on this beach," Lucy said, pointing her finger at Max. "And Darby will let me."

"I will," Darby said, busy unpacking gear and getting it set up in the levelest spot on the beach. "She'll kick your ass."

"All the women on this beach can kick your ass," Kinsey said, grinning from ear to ear. "It's just a fact of life, cuz. Stay here and help your lady get set up. Then make her a sandwich and rub her feet when you're done."

Max sputtered for a moment, threw his arms up in the air and stomped off to the largest pile of gear.

"That was fun," Kinsey said.

"Wasn't it?" Lucy laughed.

"He's easy to get upset," Darby said. "Little bitch."

The women kept laughing as they picked up gear and moved it further up the beach, well out of the way of the tide when it comes in.

"I'm not so comfortable with how they have bonded," Darren said to Shane. "I feel grossly outnumbered."

"It's a brand new world, Ditcher," Shane said. "I fear we must get used to it."

"Dude, don't call me Ditcher," Darren sighed.

"Ditchers ditch, man," Shane said and shrugged. "You ditched Kinsey, so you are Ditcher."

"I really thought we were past all that," Darren replied. "It's just not funny anymore."

"Isn't supposed to be," Shane said. "Until Kinsey says you aren't Ditcher anymore then you are Ditcher."

"Hey, 'Sey!" Darren shouted at Kinsey.

"Yes, 'Ren?" Kinsey replied, a sly smirk on her face.

"Will you tell your cousin to stop calling me Ditcher, please?" Darren asked.

"Is he doing that again?" Kinsey asked.

"Yes, yes I am," Shane responded.

"What do you think?" Kinsey asked, turning to Darby and Lucy. "Should I end the poor boy's misery?"

"Why?" Lucy asked. "I once hid my ex's Mustang in a garage three towns over until she apologized for cheating on me. Then I kept it another three months until I knew for sure she wasn't still seeing the little bitch she cheated on me with."

"I sliced off an ex-lover's genitals and fed them to his dog," Darby said. "He didn't ever get them back. Unless he kept the dog shit. I didn't wait around to find out."

Lucy held up a hand and Darby casually high-fived it.

"Did you hear that, 'Ren?" Kinsey called over to Darren. "I think you're getting a pretty good deal."

"I'd quit while you're behind, man," Shane said.

"Fucking A," Darren sighed as he took off his pack and started double checking his kit. "Will I ever win with her?"

"Not if you think it's a competition," Max said, walking by with his arms filled with jugs of water. "Just let go, D. Just let go."

"I like how you called him D," Shane said. "It could stand for Darren or it could be Ditcher. Nice."

"It's the subtle ribbing that sets me apart from the others," Max said. "I have a certain finesse about me that—"

"Boys!" Thorne snapped. "I'm done."

"Uncle Vinny is done," Max said.

"Apparently," Shane replied. "Love you, Uncle Vinny!"

"He flipped us off," Max said.

"With love," Shane replied.

"Always with love," Max said.

The two brothers blew their uncle a kiss.

"Oh, for fuck's sake," Thorne growled as he took a sip of water and surveyed the jungle's tree line.

He watched the trees, looking for signs of life, but other than the breeze that stirred the many ferns and palms that lined the beach, nothing moved. It took him a second to realize that aside from the same ferns and palms, nothing made a sound either. No movement with no sound was not good.

"Grendel, weapons up and hot," he said quietly.

Even though his voice was barely above a conversational whisper, the entire Team stopped what they were doing and lifted rifles and carbines to their shoulders, eyes locked on the jungle. Thorne lifted his left hand and waved it to the left. Lucy and Kinsey spread out that way, crouching down and walking sideways until they were about twenty meters away. Thorne motioned right and Shane and Darren mirrored Kinsey and Lucy's movements.

Darby and Max came up on each side of Thorne, each taking a knee. Once they flanked Thorne, he took a few steps towards the jungle, his finger resting on the trigger guard of his M4. He closed half the distance then dropped to his own knee.

The Team watched closely, senses on high alert, all noticing the distinct lack of sound coming from what should have been a jungle teeming with life. What kind of life? None could say, but there had been plenty of noise coming off the jungle when they entered the bay. Now there was nothing but ominous silence.

"What's the call, Vinny?" Darren asked quietly. "We staying put or going in?"

"Staying put for the moment," Thorne responded, just as quietly. "Ten minutes then we move in."

They waited there, the sun beating down on them, reflecting up and glaring from the white sand. When the ten minutes was up, they all stood as one and closed ranks.

"Continue setting up," Thorne said to Darby. "But I want one of you watching this tree line at all times. If something needs two of you to put together then forget about it."

"There goes the sex swing," Max said. He winced as Darby slugged him hard in the arm. "Hey. I use this arm, you know."

"Coms on Team channel only," Thorne said. "I'm sure Ballantine will be listening, but he has strict instructions not to interrupt or interact with any of us unless in an emergency situation."

Thorne stuck a finger under Shane's nose then under Max's.

"Being smart asses is not an emergency situation, so do not fuck around," Thorne ordered. "Am I understood?"

"Understood," the Reynolds said together. Their tone made it obvious they were ready for business and the jokes were going to wait.

"Good," Thorne said. "This is how we're going to go. Darren is on point with Kinsey, myself, Lucy, and Shane behind. Darren has the call on this. I trust his eyes in there better than mine."

Thorne looked at his nephews, but neither made an old man joke. He nodded his approval.

"We do not split up," Thorne said. "If we get separated for any reason then you are to bug back here and wait. Do not start wandering through this island looking for everyone. Back here and wait. Got it?"

"Hooyah," they all said.

"Hooyah," Thorne replied. "In we go."

They lined up in the order that Thorne had given then slowly made their way into the jungle. Darby and Max waited on the beach, their eyes, and weapons, locked onto the insertion point. After about ten minutes, they eased back and looked at each other.

"You think we can bang one out while one of us still keeps an eye on the jungle?" Max asked.

"No," Darby said. "And don't say shit like that. I'm horny enough as it is."

"Field action gets you hot, doesn't it?" Max chuckled.

"Shut up," Darby scolded then pointed to the equipment. "You're on grunt duty. I'll take first watch."

"You're sexy when you're bossy," Max said, not arguing. He secured his rifle to his back and began unpacking boxes, getting equipment sorted and ready for set up.

"I'm sexy all the time," Darby said, giving him a sly smile before turning her full attention on the jungle.

"True dat, hot stuff," Max said. "True dat."

It was nearly thirty minutes of constant work before Max had everything ready to put together. All of their gear—food, water, ammunition, communications array, tents, folding tables and chairs, plus much more—was organized and laid out by category and difficulty of set up.

Max started on the main tent, working hard at getting it set up by himself, moving from one corner to the next and back again until he had poles jammed into the sand and had stretched the canopy across it. He'd just gotten the synthetic material in place when a huge gust of wind tore it all away from him, sending the tent tumbling down the beach, parallel with the tree line.

"Son of a bitch!" Max snarled as he took off after the tent. "You have got to be kidding me!"

He was about fifty yards away from Darby and the pile of gear when he came to a sudden halt and nearly pissed himself. Several large tendrils of green shot out from the jungle and wrapped themselves around the escaping tent. They yanked it into the jungle and it was lost from Max's sight.

"Darby?" he called over his shoulder, slowly backing up. "Hey, Darby, my love?"

"I saw it," Darby called over to him. Then her voice was in the com. "Just a heads up that the plant life is active. I repeat. The plant life is active."

The tent came flying out of the jungle. It tumbled through the air and hit the surf, its poles snapped in half and canopy torn to shreds. The small waves lapped at it, carrying it from the beach and out into the bay.

"Guys?" Max called over the com. "Give me a click if you heard what Darby said. The plant life is active, hungry, and picky about what it eats. Tents are not on the menu. Operators may be."

There were five clicks in his ear as he hustled back to Darby, telling them both that the rest of the Team heard them and were warned about the new threats the jungle presented.

"Big, giant monster sharks and shit are one thing," Max said. "But grabby plants that chew up tents and spit them out? Fuck that. Just fuck that."

Darby nodded, but didn't say a word, her carbine trained on the jungle, her arms and hands rock solid and steady.

Chapter Three- Can't Stay On This Island At All

Thorne and the rest of Team Grendel moved slowly, cautiously through the dense undergrowth of the jungle. It took all of Thorne's willpower not to jump whenever a low branch snagged against him or a short bush brushed his leg. He'd look over or glance down and take a deep breath, relieved that the encounter was a passive occurrence, not an active attack like Max had warned them about.

By his count, they were at about one klick into the jungle and had yet to see an end to it. Ballantine had said the island itself was at least one hundred square miles, but from what Thorne had seen as they sailed their way from the cliffs they had originally arrived at and around to the bay, the island was considerably larger than one hundred square miles. Unless, for some strange reason, the side he hadn't observed yet was missing a large chunk.

They continued on, their eyes watching everything at once, their weapons up, an extension of those eyes, and their feet carefully finding step after step in the never ending verdant landscape. It didn't take them long to discover an unofficial trail. Although, it was probably only unofficial to them. To the creatures of the island, small by the looks of the trail, it could have been a major superhighway.

The trail curved to the right and took them along a row of what looked to be banana trees, although the bunches of fruit that hung from the thin branches did not look like any bananas Thorne had ever encountered. In his former life in the Navy, he had traveled extensively across the globe and knew that plant species varied from region to region. Yet what he saw was not a variant, but a different thing all together.

Kinsey reached out and snapped off one of the fruits, grasping it in her palm like it was about to try to squirm and squiggle away in some desperate attempt to escape its sad fate. Without slowing her stride or losing a single pace behind Darren, Kinsey tore into the fruit with her teeth and ripped back the peel to expose the fruity flesh inside.

She immediately tossed the fruit away and began to gag.

The smell of the fruit reached Thorne and he had to fight his own gorge. The fruit smelled like a corpse. Literally like a body that had been rotting in the sun for a couple of days. The stench coated the back of Thorne's throat and he swallowed and spit again and again to try to dislodge it.

Kinsey looked over her shoulder quickly and gave them all an apologetic grimace. Thorne didn't blame her; he would have done the same thing. They needed to learn about their surroundings as fast as possible, and despite the obvious dangers, only trial and error was going to cut it. They didn't have the luxury of one of the scientists with them to sort it all out. Nor did they have the tech to stream video back to the B3 and let the eggheads whisper answers in their ear.

He wasn't exactly sad about the latter.

Darren raised a fist and they stopped, crouching instantly. Thorne glanced behind him and saw Shane and Lucy each turn a different direction, watching for possible attacks as they waited for Darren to sign them forward or explain what he saw.

After a couple of seconds, Darren crouch walked back to Thorne, letting Kinsey take point, and huddled close.

"There is definitely something ahead of us," Darren said. "Pretty sure it has been shadowing us on our right for a good half klick, but now it's moved forward and is either leading us or getting set to cut us off."

"Size?" Thorne asked.

"Pony-sized, maybe," Darren replied. "Hard to tell with the way the light is. All the shadows from the trees and leaves are fucking with my depth perception."

"Try having only one eye," Shane said. "That'll really fuck with depth perception."

"Not a pissing match," Thorne stated. "Do you want to move forward or skirt the thing?"

"I'd prefer to split up and surround it," Darren said.

"But that's not happening. No splitting up," Thorne responded. "Forward or to the side?"

"Forward," Darren said. "My gut says it isn't dangerous, just something to watch out for."

"Everything on this island is something to watch out for," Thorne said. "But we'll go with your gut. Lead on."

Darren retook his place as point. Kinsey glanced over her shoulder at Thorne and he nodded to her, showing he was in agreement with Darren. She gave an imperceptible shrug as the Team stood and continued moving again.

A high-pitched squawk rang out above them and the entire Team glanced up, watching as a huge red bird flew from one treetop to another. The thing's legs seemed impossibly long and were tipped by three claws, each with talons nearly a foot long. The bird squawked once more as it jammed its sharp, serrated beak into a hole in the trunk of one of the trees, yanking free a wriggling worm-like animal that it chomped in half and swallowed in one bite.

The bird's head turned and its golden eyes surveyed them. It blinked a few times, the lids coming in from the sides like a reptile's, then squawked one last time and thrust itself up out of the canopy and into the bright sky beyond.

The bird proved to be a dangerous distraction.

When they turned their attention back to the path, they found their way blocked by a herd of pony-sized creatures. But they were most certainly not ponies. Not by any stretch of the imagination.

Looking very bird-like themselves, the creatures were each a little over two meters tall with elongated heads that ended in a strange mix between a beak and a lizard jaw. Feathers covered their heads and most of their body. Their arms had feathers as well, quite a few, but the appendages didn't look like they had the strength to swat a fly let alone help the things actually fly. Their spines were long and angled, with tails that trailed out behind them, swishing back and forth in an agitated, feline way.

But it was the feet that got Team Grendel's attention. Three-toed, two of the toes ending in long, sharp claws while the third had a thick, raised claw that stuck far into the air. The third claw was at least a foot long and the tip glinted in the dappled sunlight, telling everyone and everything that it was sharp as shit and meant for one thing only.

The creatures packed together in a group of six, their black eyes focused directly on Grendel.

"Thorne?" Darren whispered. "What's the call?"

"The call is stand as still as fucking possible," Thorne said. "See if maybe they'll lose interest and move on."

"I don't think that's their plan," Shane said. "We've got two hostiles on our nine."

"Two more on our three and one on our six," Lucy added. "We're surrounded, folks."

"Daddy?" Kinsey asked. "Permission to light these weird chickens up, please?"

"Weird chickens," Shane chuckled.

"Permission denied," Thorne said. "We do not want to engage if we do not know what we are engaging. We wait. If they make a move then cut them the fuck down. If they go away then we've avoided a fight and also avoided alerting the whole island to our presence."

"Your plan is boring and safe," Kinsey joked. There was a slight waver in her voice and she took a quick look back at Thorne, giving him a frightened smile.

"Hang tight, operators," Thorne said. "Be cool."

They were.

The five of them stood there, eyes and weapons locked onto their new friends. Black avian/reptilian eyes watched the Team and the Team watched back.

Thorne could tell the creatures were studying the Team. He watched as what he guessed was the alpha in the pack kept glancing from the barrel of his carbine then back to directly in his eyes. The other creatures looked him up and down, assessing his strengths, his weaknesses, his will. The standoff lasted for close to thirty minutes.

Then as one, the creatures moved in.

They did not attack like wolves or lions or any other predator pack Thorne was familiar with. The closest he could approximate would be hyenas. That chaotic rush and then the everyone-for-themselves attitude of violence. Get your piece and go.

After the silence of the standoff, the barking of the rifles and carbines was near deafening. Only Team Grendel's experience and discipline kept any of them from jumping as the first triggers were pulled.

The six in front moved so fast that Darren dove to the side as he fired, avoiding a couple quick slashes by the thick, sharp third claws. He hit the ground on his shoulder and grunted, but didn't let up as he squeezed the trigger again and again.

Kinsey dropped to a knee and opened fire, aiming for the creatures' legs, not their chests or heads. Three went down from her carefully placed shots, their bent knees exploding in a spray of blood and bone. She emptied her magazine by the time the other three reached her. Kinsey didn't have time to reload. The creatures were on her and those jaw-beaks, those third claws, came at her face and belly.

The air above her erupted as Thorne moved forward, standing over her, his M4 barking. He nudged her with his knee in the back and she quickly tossed her carbine aside, choosing to pull her .45s from her hips. She was a good shot with her M4, but she was an expert with her pistols.

Thorne moved to her side, laying down a protective fire, giving Kinsey time to roll away and come up shooting. The two Thornes pressed their attack, driving the three creatures back into the dense foliage of the jungle, the explosive rounds blowing chunks out of everything they touched.

But that was all they could do, drive them back. The things were incredibly fast so the explosive rounds rarely touched the targets. They jumped and ducked, moving and weaving back and forth like supersonic boxers, avoiding the gunfire as if they had stepped out of the Matrix. Ferns were obliterated, small trees were cut down, the stench of the death bananas filled the air, joining the sharp stink of gunpowder and fear.

"Fuck me!" Shane yelled from behind the Thornes. "Fucking die, you fucks!"

Thorne didn't dare turn to look at the rest of the Team. He had to make sure he kept the bullets flying in front of him, giving Kinsey time to slap two fresh magazines into her pistols. As soon as she was reloaded and firing again, he ejected and replaced his almost spent magazine.

Instead of holding his position, Thorne started moving forward, pressing the attack, driving the creatures not just to a standoff, but further into the jungle. He heard Kinsey call his name, he even thought he heard Max and Darby calling over the com, but he ignored it all. By his best estimate, they had maybe another ten minutes in them before they ran out of ammo. Standing ground was no longer an option.

The creatures, three of them, split up and Thorne found himself in the middle of a dinosaur—since that was what he had to admit to himself that they were—triangle. The sounds of gunshots lessened and Thorne realized he had effectively hobbled Kinsey and Darren because if they tried to shoot at the creatures then they would be shooting at him. It was a rookie mistake and Thorne cursed himself for it.

The first creature to attack leapt into the air, its third claws leading the way. Thorne timed it, counting off in his head, then dropped and rolled to the side, letting the creature hit empty ground where he had just been standing. Instead of firing at the attacker, Thorne came up and fired into the belly of the creature he nearly rolled right into. The thing's midsection blew wide open, but it didn't drop at first. It wobbled for a second then fell forward.

That proved to be a problem. The creature landed on top of Thorne, pinning the man to the ground, more importantly, pining his carbine against his chest. His left hand was free, but he couldn't get his right, and his M4, loose. It was not an ideal scenario.

The plus side was he was out of the way of friendly fire and Kinsey and Darren started shooting again immediately. The first creature, the leapy one, came at Thorne's head, beak-jaw wide open, shiny edged and sharp, stunted teeth on display. The beak-jaw turned into chitinous mist as Kinsey moved forward and emptied one pistol point blank into the thing's head.

Thorne smiled up at her as she nodded then turned to take on the third creature. But Darren had that covered. The thing swayed on its feet as round after deadly round tore into its side. Blood and flesh splattered the jungle, the specialized rounds exploding as designed, shredding the creature from the inside out.

Kinsey helped get the dead creature off Thorne. He rolled over and slowly pushed up onto his hands and knees. His compression suit had done a good job of keeping his ribs from being crushed by the weight of the thing, which was considerably heavier than he would have guessed. Most things were when they lay on top of you dead.

"Clear!" Shane called out.

Thorne looked up from all fours and watched as his daughter holstered her pistols and grabbed up Thorne's M4, putting it to her shoulder and scanning the immediate area.

"Clear!" she called out as well.

Darren and Lucy followed, announcing that the brief battle was over and the jungle was safe once again.

Thorne got gingerly to his feet, mentally assessing any hidden injuries that hadn't revealed themselves. Other than a bump over his left eye, he was in good condition.

"Report," Thorne grunted.

"Good," Shane said.

"Good," Darren said.

"Good," Lucy said.

"Good," Kinsey said. "Daddy?"

"Good," Thorne replied. "Anyone want to guess what those were?"

"Velociraptors?" Shane asked.

"Same family, but not quite," Darren said. "I think. I don't know much about prehistoric reptiles, just enough to play Jeopardy. I'm more the ocean mammals guy."

"We all have our kinks," Shane said.

"Hey!" Max barked into the com. "You guys good?"

"Yes," Thorne reported. "How is the beach?"

"Secure," Max said. "Maybe you'd like to head back this way? I think the sun is going to set soon. You've been out there for a couple hours now. It'll take you about an hour to get back. Darby is making s'mores."

"I am not," Darby responded over the com. "We are out of marshmallows."

"My bad," Shane said. "It was a moment of weakness. A six bag, no stopping until gorged, moment of weakness."

"It's why stoners make shitty survivalists," Darren said. "They'd eat all the provisions the first night."

"I resemble that remark," Shane said.

"Daddy? The call?" Kinsey asked.

She handed him his M4 then walked over and retrieved her own. She slapped in a fresh magazine and looked over, expectantly. The whole Team did.

"Back to base," Thorne said. "We regroup and try again at dawn. We know more than we did when we first came in here."

Team Grendel nodded then moved into formation, the same as before yet pointed in the opposite direction. They made it about twenty yards before the world exploded into a chaotic blur of giant, leathery flesh and mangled foliage.

***

Standing on the beach, their weapons aimed at the jungle, Max and Darby could do nothing about the sounds they heard in their coms. The yelling, the shooting, the roars. The panic.

"Darby," Max hissed.

"We hold the beach," Darby said. "We stay at base and wait."

The shots stopped. So did the roars.

"*Darby*," Max hissed louder. "We can't leave them in there."

"We are not leaving them," Darby said. "We are following orders and maintaining our position."

Max started to take a step and Darby slammed a fist into his shoulder.

"Fuck!" he shouted, his arm going numb. His rifle dipped and he glared over at her. "What the hell?"

"You have to wait at least twenty minutes before you have full use of that arm," Darby said. "You go in that jungle and you are dead."

"So, I wait twenty minutes and go in then," Max snapped.

"I'll only punch you again," Darby said. "And if that doesn't stop you then I'll dislocate your shoulder."

"What good will that do?" Max shouted. "I'll be useless and defenseless."

"I'll defend us both," Darby said. "Here. At the base. On the beach."

"Darby!" Max yelled.

"NO!" Darby roared. "You stay with me, goddammit! You will not die in that jungle! I won't let it happen!"

Max took a couple of steps back and looked at her. She refused to turn his way, keeping her M4 pointed at the jungle. But he saw the tear that welled in her eye. He saw how her jaw quivered.

"Hey, hey, it's cool," Max said softly. "I'm staying right here."

"Yes, you fucking are," Darby snapped, her voice choked with emotion. "You are staying right here."

"Right here," Max said, nodding. "We'll wait for them."

"Right here," Darby said.

Max rolled his shoulder a couple times until it didn't hurt too much then took his stance again, rifle up and aimed at the jungle.

The two of them held their position for nearly an hour, occasionally calling over the com for the others, but the steady hiss of static told them that they weren't getting any answers soon. The sun began to dip over the jungle and the glare made it nearly impossible to keep up their guard.

"We should eat," Max said finally. "We'll keep watch, but we need to eat. And drink water. We've been standing here forever."

"You eat," Darby said. "I'm good."

"Fuck that," Max said. "You're eating with me. We'll face the jungle while we munch on some lovely dehydrated shit, followed by a dessert of dehydrated crap. I prefer the crap and would leave the shit untouched, but you can't have your pudding unless you eat your meat."

He slung his rifle and jogged back to the camp they had set up. After rummaging for a minute, he jogged back with two pouches and two forks in hand. He smacked the pouches hard and watched as they swelled up, puffing into Mylar balloons. Max ripped open one, stuffed a fork into the steaming contents, and handed it to Darby.

She took it after hesitating a few seconds, sniffing at the food without attempting to hide her disgust.

"Smells like shit," she said and jammed a forkful into her mouth. "Tastes like shit."

"Yep," Max said. "Never gets better."

Before he tore his own pouch open, he dragged over two folding stools and set them into the soft sand. He took a seat, slapped the second stool for Darby to take a load off, then opened his meal. He swallowed hard, said a prayer under his breath, and ate as fast as he could.

Darby watched him with disgust as he finished his pouch in seconds, belched loudly, then tossed the empty container onto the sand.

"I'm going to pick it up," Max said before Darby could get on him. "Ready for dessert? It's total crap. Yummy."

Darby shook her head as she choked down her main course. Unlike Max, she carefully chewed and swallowed each bite.

"You're only making it worse," Max said.

"I'm maximizing nutritional intake by chewing properly," she said. "I'll get more energy from the meal and need to eat less. Which means taste less in the future."

"Oh," Max said, looking at his empty container in the sand. "I should have chewed more."

"Yes, you should have," Darby agreed.

She finished her food and stood up, retrieving Max's pouch for him without saying a word. He watched her dispose of the pouches then fetch them both two bottles of water. Seated once again, she handed him his water and then continued staring at the jungle.

Max stared with her then looked back at the beached Zodiacs.

"Should one of us go back and get Mike?" Max said. "We could use the numbers."

"Ballantine will send him, if he feels it's necessary," Darby said. "I am sure he heard the whole thing."

"Yet he hasn't said a word," Max said.

"Thorne specifically told him to stay out of operations," Darby said, shrugging. "I think he listened for once."

"They had to have heard the gunshots and roars," Max said.

"They expected to hear gunshots and roars," Darby said. "We didn't come here to pick flowers."

"So, we wait?" Max asked.

"We wait," Darby said. "And we watch."

Max sighed then settled in, his rifle resting in the crook of his arm, ready to snap to attention at the first sign of trouble.

***

The sky darkened and the sun set, creating a multitude of pinks, purples, reds, and oranges above the island. When the last of the light finally faded, Max stood, stretched and walked back to the main tent. He grabbed what he needed from a folding table and rejoined Darby.

"Here," he said, handing over a set of NVGs. "Just in case."

"I'm keeping my eyes natural," Darby responded, but took the NVGs anyway. She clipped them to her belt, started to speak then shook her head and stayed quiet.

"What?" Max asked. "What do you want to say?"

He hadn't donned his night vision goggles either, but he kept them resting on his leg, ready for action if he needed them.

"Sorry," Darby said quietly.

"What the fuck for?" Max asked.

"For breaking earlier," Darby said. "It was unprofessional."

"Okay, okay, first, have you met me and my brother? We're as far from professional as it gets," Max replied. "Second, you call that breaking? Sugar tits, I have seen breaking and that was not it."

Darby nodded, her head a silhouette in the brightening moonlight that reflected off the bay behind them. Max waited, but she didn't continue.

"Care to tell me what got you so emotional, my little beast of deliciousness?" Max asked.

Darby laughed softly and reached out, patting his leg.

"Not right now," she said. "But thank you."

Max took her hand and kissed it. He started kissing her wrist then working up her arm until she gently pulled back.

"Don't start," she said, not unkindly. "We can't get distracted."

"Baby, I'm always distracted when you're around," Max replied. "But don't tell Uncle Vinny that. He'd never let us go on an op together again."

"I should tell him anyway," Darby said. "A distracted shooter is a useless shooter."

"Woman, I got skills enough to handle distraction and still get the job done," Max laughed.

"Don't call me woman," Darby said. "Sugar tits is okay, though."

Max laughed again. "I wish the rest of the Team could see you like this. They have no idea the Darby I know. Does Ballantine?"

Darby turned and looked directly at Max, but he couldn't see the look on her face in the shadowed moonlight.

"Ballantine has seen me a lot of ways, but not like this," Darby said. "This is for you. This is for me."

"Got it," Max said.

A spot in his chest warmed at her words. He knew he was really, really into Darby, but he hadn't dared admit the "L word" to himself. That moment changed a few things. He was about to say as much when Darby started talking again.

"I watched them drag the girls into the jungle and there was nothing I could do," Darby said. "They were fifteen, maybe, at the oldest. I wasn't pinned down, but I had to hold my position and provide cover for the rest of the Team. The bastards kept coming at us and there was no stopping."

Her whole body shuddered.

"By the time it was over, every one of them was dead," Darby said.

Max waited. It took a minute, but Darby continued.

"The objective was to protect the mine," Darby said. "It was small, not a huge producer, but worth enough that the company I worked for, not the "company" company, but a different outfit all together, had been hired as security until the latest load could be safely extracted and shipped out."

"Where do the girls figure into it?" Max asked.

"They don't," Darby said. "Or they shouldn't have. We were set up in a close village. Half of our Team was on site while the other half was in the village. We rotated out so there was twenty-four hour coverage. Nothing left to chance. Except we all know that's bullshit, right?"

"No shit," Max said.

"They came at us, some local gang," Darby said. "They came at us in the village. I honestly don't know if they were there to take us on or there for the girls. Doesn't matter now. The firefight was brutal and we lost two of ours before we wiped them out. A few escaped, abandoning their junker trucks and SUVs in order to get lost in the jungle. I followed."

She swallowed hard, picked up her water bottle, drained it, belched, then sat there, her head held straight, her hands worrying the grip of her carbine.

"Six of them," Darby said. "They'd nabbed six of them. Dragged them into the jungle and destroyed them. Completely destroyed them. Even during a firefight like that the animals found time to whip out their dicks and have their fun. Then they went to work with machetes."

"Fuck me," Max whispered. He'd seen some nasty shit in Afghanistan, but not that nasty. "Where was this? Africa?"

"No," Darby said. "Indonesia. A small island. Like this."

"Oh," Max said. It all clicked. Too many similarities jammed together. It could overwhelm anyone.

"One was left alive," Darby said. "I had to make a choice. Let her live, with no hands or feet, her body so broken that it was doubtful there was a doctor within a thousand square miles that could put her back together. Or end her suffering right there in the jungle."

Max let the silence settle. He didn't ask her what choice she made. He was pretty sure he knew. The seconds, minutes ticked off in his head before he decided he should reach out to her. His hand was almost to her when he heard the rustling.

"Darby?" he whispered.

"I heard it," she whispered back.

Max put on his NVGs and turned them on. The night vision goggles turned his vision into a monochromatic scene of green and black shadows. He scanned the area, but saw nothing. The rustling had stopped. Darby stood and put her carbine up to her shoulder, her face naked, no NVGs in place. Max didn't worry. He knew she was part cat and could almost see perfectly in the dark.

There was a quick flash and then a sizzle and the NVGs on Max's face began to spark and smoke.

"Fuck," he exclaimed as he yanked them from his head and tossed them onto the beach, burying them in sand with his foot to stop the sparking and smoking. "These are no good."

"I was afraid of that. The EMP was stronger than the elves will admit," Darby whispered. "You blind?"

"Pretty much," Max whispered back. There were motes of light and swirls of color that danced in his eyes, fucking up his sight. "You good?"

"I closed my eyes when I heard the first spark," Darby said. "Stay put. I'm going to check out the tree line over here."

"Like fuck you are," Max said. "No splitting up, remember?"

"Stay put," Darby said again and walked off, taking slow, careful steps.

Max tried to follow her progress, but the moonlight wasn't strong enough to counteract the still dancing motes and swirls. He closed his eyes, hoping it would let him adjust, and counted to thirty.

When he opened his eyes again, he saw a dark shape closing on Darby quickly.

"Dar—!" he cried out just before his head rocked back and stars were added to the motes and swirls. The pain was excruciating and he heard a soft flapping noise before more pain erupted in his skull.

He found himself face down in the sand, a heavy weight on his back. A person's weight. Max let himself go wild. He bucked and shoved up with his arms. He got his legs under him and pushed as hard as he could into the soft sand. There was a brief shout then the weight was gone.

Despite the pain, the stars, the swirls, the motes, Max got to his feet. Animal instinct said that if he didn't, he was as good as dead. And as the spiked club whipped past his face by half an inch, he knew animal instinct was completely fucking right.

No time to find a weapon, Max lifted his fists, settled his feet into the sand, and watched the person-shaped shadow come for him again. The club swung out and Max easily dodged it. It was a wild, desperate swing. No training or real thought put into it. A strange sense of relief flooded Max. The attacker was not a pro. How nice. He was sick of fighting pros all the damn time.

Another swing of the club and Max reached out lightning fast, snagging the weapon from his attacker's grip without much effort. The attacker grunted and cried out, protesting at the sudden turn of events. Then he/she/it rushed Max, tackling him about the waist.

Max was not expecting the move and he fell onto the beach, landing hard in the sand. The wind was knocked from him, but he ignored the suffocating feeling and boxed the attacker's ears once, twice, a third time. The attacker cried out again and tried to scramble off Max, but he had had enough.

Grabbing the attacker by the head, Max twisted as hard as he could. The snapping sound was like pure, sweet music. He shoved the corpse off him and scrambled back up to his feet. Then he was down on his knees.

He didn't remember there being time or space between the standing and the falling. The world sort of swam and wavered. Max forced himself to focus, refusing to give into what he knew was probably a slight concussion.

He reached up and touched his scalp, nearly screaming at the pain. His hand came away dark black with his blood. Gently, gingerly, he put his hand to his head again, probing with cautious fingertips.

Half his scalp was hanging loose.

"Well, fuck me," he muttered. "Super fuck me."

The shape came at him so fast he didn't have time to get his arms up to ward it off. But he didn't have to. It was Darby. She was in his face and she looked terrified. There were streaks of black blood across her face and neck, darkening her suit, but Max had the distinct impression that the blood wasn't hers.

"Skull is fine," Max said before Darby could ask. "It's all just skin damage. A little dizziness, but I didn't lose consciousness."

"We need to stitch you up now," Darby barked, helping him to his feet and over to the main tent.

"You get the others?" Max asked. "Were there others?"

"There were," Darby said. "Not anymore."

"How many?" Max asked.

"Four," Darby said. "They were fast, but couldn't fight worth a fuck."

"Yeah, I know," Max said. "If I hadn't gotten sucker clocked, I would have handled mine a lot easier."

"They had these," Darby said, holding up a small dart. "Blowguns over there."

"You get hit?" Max asked.

"No," Darby said. "Almost. I got in close before they could get a bead on me."

"Poison?" Max asked.

"No way to know," Darby said. "The tip doesn't smell like anything I recognize. May have just been to knock us out."

"Fuck that," Max said.

Darby sat Max down by a small table and cracked two glow sticks. Max didn't ask why so little light, he knew she was being cautious in case more showed up. The glow sticks wouldn't ruin her night vision and still gave her enough illumination to work by.

Max sat as still as he could. It took her a long time, probably a full hour, to stitch his scalp back together. He didn't cry out once, but he would have been lying if he said he didn't piss himself a little at one point in the procedure. Scalp reconstruction by glow stick on a Land Of The Lost beach was not a gentle event.

"Done," Darby said finally.

"We need to gear up and go after the fuckers, wherever they went," Max said.

"We're as geared up as we can get," Darby said. "Take a look around."

Not occupied by having his head sewn back together, Max was able to take the time and assess the FOB's situation. It could be classified as fucked.

"Where's the gear? The weapons? Ammo?" Max cried. "Where the fuck is my rifle?"

Darby hooked a thumb over her shoulder at the surf. "They dumped everything in the bay."

She looked at him for a moment then turned her full attention back to the jungle, which she had been facing the whole time, one eye on the procedure, one eye on a possible second attack.

Max looked out where she had indicated and saw crates floating and bobbing in the small waves. He focused further out, towards the bay and the far off shape of the B3 out in the water. The moon had risen enough that the bay was a twinkly light show of wave tips and currents. The fins and flippers still roamed the waters, ever active, ever present.

Something about the scene grabbed his attention, spoke to him, said that things were more fucked up than just their equipment trashed. It took a couple minutes before he figured out what it was. Then he stood up so quickly that he almost knocked Darby over. Despite the brutally painful head rush he received, Max stayed on his feet and pointed out of the tent at the beach.

"One of the fucking rafts is gone," he exclaimed.

Darby stood and whirled about.

"Fuck," she said.

Only one of the Zodiacs was left on the beach. The other was nowhere to be seen.

"Call it in," Darby ordered as she walked slowly from the tent, turning this way and that, looking for more trouble. "Let them know that hostiles may be en route."

"It's been an hour, Darby," Max said. "If hostiles were en route then they have already showed up on the B3."

"Call it in!" Darby yelled.

Max called it in.

***

Mike stirred as the com came to life in his ear. He was sitting up on the bridge, taking a turn at watch and giving Lake some needed rest. He'd been dozing in and out, that light rest one got while watching TV or riding in the passenger seat during a long car ride. It couldn't be called sleep, but it wasn't full wakefulness either.

"B3! B3! This is Max! Come in!"

"Max, what's up?" Mike responded.

"Oh, fuck, thank God!" Max exclaimed over the com. "What's your status, Mike? What's the status of the ship?"

"Status? Boring as all fuck," Mike replied. "How the hell are you? Ballantine forced us not to call you guys when we heard the shit going down. Everyone accounted for?"

"No, but that's not the problem," Max responded. "It's only one of them. Listen, Darby and I were attacked on the beach by people, man. Crazy fucking people. We handled it, but one of the Zodiacs is missing. We think you may have hostiles either on the way or already at the ship."

Mike perked up, his SEAL training pushing away any sleepiness he may have been feeling.

"What? How many? What kind of hostiles? Armed or not?" Mike asked, the questions tumbling out as he grabbed the pistol resting on the navigation station where he sat. He was up on his feet and heading for the hatch to the stairs that would lead to the upper deck. "Give me details, Max!"

"I don't fucking have any!" Max responded. "No idea how many or if they are armed! The ones we dealt with had crude clubs and fought like amateurs. But they are sneaky as fuck, so watch out for the silent attack."

Mike stepped from the bridge and looked down at the deck below him, his eyes adjusting from light to darkness. He thought he saw a shadow that shouldn't have been there.

"Mike, you need to alert the entire ship now!" Max said.

"On it," Mike replied as he started to switch the com channel to ship wide.

He never made the switch as his world became a sudden sting to his neck and a quickly rising deck coming to meet his face.

Chapter Four- We Are Not Alone

Vines lashed out at her face, but Kinsey swatted them away, refusing to let them grab onto her, to slow her down, to stop her mad flight through the jungle.

The Team was separated. It was the exact opposite of what they wanted to happen, but there was no choice. Even after taking out the pack of whatever-the-fuck-raptors that came at them, they hadn't even been close to out of the woods. In fact, they were deeper than ever.

The noise.

It had to have been the noise that brought them.

Three massive monsters. Fifty feet tall, at least. Maybe taller.

Huge motherfuckers with heads the size of compact cars and teeth bigger than her legs, the things had ripped through the trees as if they weren't there. They had come in fast and hard, their mouths open, roaring, declaring that it was dinner time and the main course was served.

Team Grendel had opened fire, unleashing everything they had on the things, but it wasn't enough. They ran out of ammo fast, even with the specialized rounds. Only one of the monsters had gone down. The other two were wounded, but far from taken out.

Her dad had ordered them to flee, to run, to book ass as far away as possible. They were supposed to head back towards the beach. That was the plan. But all it took was a few minutes of furious running for Kinsey to be completely turned around. The jungle looked the same. East, West, North, South. It didn't matter which way she turned. All she saw were the dark shapes of huge trees, giant ferns, and plants she wouldn't have been able to identify even if it was daytime.

Then came the vines.

They pawed at her, clawed at her, grabbing her suit, stripping away gear that she hadn't strapped down tight enough. She fled again and hadn't stopped moving, stopped running, for hours. Her legs were exhausted, her lungs burned, her head swam with fatigue. But the vines were relentless. They would not let her rest. If she even dared to slow down, they went straight for her legs.

They were everywhere.

"Shane! 'Ren! Lucy!" Kinsey shouted into the com. "Daddy!"

No answer. Nothing. Even the earlier static was gone.

The com was dead.

On she ran. Her M4 was missing, taken by one of the hundreds of offending vines, and her .45s were empty, no full magazines left. Kinsey had a combat knife, but she was afraid that if she unclasped it and pulled it free it would just go the way of her carbine, lost to the deadly foliage.

So she ran. Endless flight. Constant movement.

Despite the fear, despite the insanity of the nightmare she was thrust into, Kinsey was still a Thorne, still a trained professional that lived a life far outside the norm. And the professional part of her began to realize something.

She was going in circles and those circles were intentional.

Yes, the jungle all looked the same, but trees were not just trees. Some had specific traits, such as obvious gashes that had healed after something tore into the bark. Distinct markings that caught her eye as she raced past for the sixth time.

The jungle was trying to get her to turn a specific direction and it wanted her exhausted when she did.

"Fuck you," she said as she skidded to a halt, done with the constant running. "Fuck all of you."

A vine shot out from her left and grabbed her upper left arm. She circled her arm around the vine, taking the initiative to grab it back. She wrapped the vine about her forearm and clung to it with her hand.

More vines came at her, and she avoided as many as possible, but she had made her choice. It was time to see where the vines wanted her to go. If she kept running then she'd be exhausted to the point of helplessness.

And Kinsey Thorne was far from helpless.

"You all can suck my dick," she snarled as the vines began to lead/drag her through the more benign and non-offensive foliage. "Suck it hard."

She stumbled, fell, righted herself, fell again, then let the vines pull her across the loam and moss of the jungle floor. The tropical climate kept things in a state of perpetual rot, so it wasn't like the ground was a rough surface.

Kinsey let go and decided to roll with it. It was a strategy she had used too many times back when she was a junkie and surviving on pure instinct and will. It didn't matter how trained she was, being a junkie meant her skills were compromised back then. She could fight better than most people on the planet, but the need to scratch that addiction itch threw those skills out the window at the promise of a fix.

So she had learned to roll with it. She got herself in situations that no woman, no person, should have gotten into. She pushed the boundaries of survival, all for a taste of whatever was at hand at that moment. Then, once her itch was scratched and she had gotten right, she dealt with the situation. That usually, almost exclusively, meant a lot of blood and someone ending up dead.

Her eyes focused on the vines that moved her through the jungle and she wondered if they had any clue what kind of predator she was. Or if they even had any kind of clue at all. Were they separate individuals, autonomous vines that worked in unison towards a specific goal? Or were they all part of some larger organism, just appendages sent out to troll for food and bring it back to the main body?

Kinsey was almost excited to find out. The fear of the island, and the monsters on it, fueled her mind, her body, her being, with a predatory curiosity generally reserved for cats. Something in her relaxed and she started to enjoy the ride, looking forward to the possibility of letting go. When she reached the end point, Kinsey had every intention of going blank and unleashing something she had been keeping bottled inside for the past year.

She intended to murder the fuck out of whatever she faced.

Yes, she had killed plenty of Somali pirates, cartel soldiers, members of Ballantine's original Team, and even the odd cannibal here and there during Team Grendel's brief interludes between massive crises, but since boarding the Beowulf (it was Beowulf II back then) she had yet to really let go.

It was time to unleash the Kinsey Thorne that she had created when she'd been ejected from the Navy SEAL BUD/S training for using amphetamines. It was time to get wild and be the predator, the feral cat, the killer, the hunter, the unstoppable force, that she knew deep down inside was her true self.

Darren wouldn't understand. Her father wouldn't understand. Not even her cousins, or any of Team Grendel, would understand. What she was, what she believed in every cell of her body, was too much for any of them. The longing and pull of drugs was always there, but it was a minor annoyance, a fly in the house, buzzing against the window. The true addiction she had been fighting, the one that even Gunnar couldn't help her get through, was the need to take a life with her bare hands, to wrap her fingers around a throat, to punch through a rib cage, to gouge out eyes and to snap necks.

She craved the taste of death, and more than that, she craved the satisfaction of willingly bringing that death without remorse or regret. Team Grendel wouldn't understand that. They'd be horrified by it. Except perhaps Darby, but Kinsey had a feeling that even Darby didn't have the blood lust deep down that she had.

With those thoughts finally free, her mind fully unburdened, Kinsey's journey came to an end. As did the jungle.

The vines pulled her from the tree line and flung her out into open space. Kinsey was no longer being dragged on the ground, but flying out over a deep, dark pit. She only had a second or two to realize that what she thought at first were rows of jagged rocks below were actually teeth.

Long, vibrating teeth that flexed and twitched as her body fell closer and closer.

Kinsey's bloodlust, her new honesty with herself, took a backseat when she realized that the vines were simply vehicles to transport food from Point A to Point B. She just happened to be the food and the pit she was falling into was Point B.

"Fuck me," Kinsey said as she fumbled at her belt, a sudden remembrance hitting her like a ton of bricks.

Which is exactly how she hit the side of the pit as her body slammed into the dark green flesh of the thing that had gone to great lengths to track her, catch her, and drag her to her doom. A tooth the size of her forearm nearly sliced her in half, but Kinsey twisted at the last second so it only bumped her side.

Star Wars slammed into the front of her brain and Kinsey suddenly realized what her predicament reminded her of. That sand monster that ate Boba Fett in Return of the Jedi. She had no clue what the thing's name was. Her cousins would know. The elves in the Toyshop would know. Hell, Gunnar and Darren and probably everyone on the B3 would know. Kinsey did not.

Nor did she really want to. She had better things to do than play nerd trivia.

Such as getting the small black box free from her belt. The black box that held the containment shield that she had been given by the elves. Kinsey felt guilty for thinking of them as nerds, but the guilt went away quickly as she freed the box and activated it.

Bright blue lines of energy shot from the box and began to crisscross, changing into a symmetrical ten foot by ten foot grid. The living pit shuddered at the touch of the net and Kinsey smiled. That was the effect she had hoped for. Without knowing exactly what she was doing, Kinsey reached out and grabbed the edge of the containment net and pulled it to her.

The net instantly formed itself into a protective cage around her, sealing her inside the blue lines. The living pit undulated violently, reacting to the energy net as if it was the most painful thing ever. Kinsey quickly found herself flung from the side of the pit and out in open air.

The hole below her, the dark circle that lay just below the rows of teeth, widened and Kinsey had a distinct impression that whatever creature she was in, it was holding its nose and going to swallow her in one gulp, just like a kid eating his or her least favorite food.

As Kinsey fell, she noticed that the air tasted like a fresh thunderstorm and every hair on her body stood on end. But the energy didn't burn. Again, she had to give the elves credit for a job well done. They had intended to modify the net to be a personal shield and it looked like they had succeeded.

Kinsey fell fast then was lost inside the living pit. The light from the net illuminated the new world she found herself in. Once past the multiple rows of plant teeth, the world about Kinsey constricted, becoming a vertical shaft of dark green flesh. Plant or animal, Kinsey did not know. She did not care. All she wanted to know was how to survive and how to kill the thing she was being swallowed whole by.

Then the ride ended and Kinsey found herself splashing down into a sickeningly sweet pool of thick, sappy liquid. It was like rotten honey. The smell made Kinsey gag and she struggled to keep her head above it. Her containment net was designed to protect her from solid threats, threats with arms and claws and teeth and sharp toenails. It was not designed to keep her from drowning in living pit honey.

The burning began almost immediately.

Her exposed skin started to tingle then itch. The itch turned to a stinging and the stinging turned to a full-on burning. Kinsey knew enough about botany, and about carnivorous plants, to realize she had fallen into a honey pot of some type. A really, really big honey pot. A honey pot with hundreds of teeth above it, which was not normal for honey pots, but it was still a honey pot.

The teeth above were only there to deal with the larger creatures that were either dragged or lured into the living pit's maw. The teeth were angled downward, aimed at keeping anything large enough from clawing and climbing its way out so the death honey could do its thing below. Other creatures, smaller creatures like Kinsey, were actually supposed to bypass the teeth and go straight to death honey jail, do not pass Go, do not collect any chance of living.

Kinsey was fucked.

Her exposed skin felt like she'd been stuck out in the sun for hours, naked and without sunscreen, despite the fact she was wearing her compression suit. The realization that her suit had been breached, which meant basically useless, hit her as she felt the pull of its weight try to drag her under. Just what she needed, more trouble.

She could see the floating bones, picked completely clean, of other victims that had tumbled to their sweet, sweet demise. It became harder and harder for her to tread the thick death honey, to keep her head above the surface. It wasn't like treading water, it was heavy and exhausting. Her already fatigued muscles were protesting that they had been pushed past their breaking point.

Yet...

Yet, Kinsey was the ultimate survivor. Her primal brain took a full inventory of her options. Her mind gathered and calculated data at a subconscious level so that when the solution came to her, it was as if inspiration had struck without any effort at all.

Her eyes tracked how her containment net reacted to the death honey. All around her the substance steamed and hissed as the blue lines of energy did to the death honey what the death honey was doing to Kinsey. It burned.

Ignoring the pain while still intensely aware of it, which was a junkie skill set if there ever was one, Kinsey studied the sides of the living pit. She noted the sudden angled nature and realized that the death honey couldn't be too deep. It may have been a pool of death, but it was a shallow pool of death.

Kinsey grabbed onto her net, took a deep breath, closed her eyes, and let the heaviness of her suit pull her under.

***

Shane had the tiny raptor by the throat, the gloves of his compression suit squeezing until the small dinosaur's eyes bulged then popped out of its skull. Tossing the corpse aside, Shane swung out with his left arm, a wide haymaker that was intended to clear, not club. The four raptors that had just leapt at him collided with his fist and forearm. They went flying this way and that way, their feathers no use to them as they were merely covering, not part of any winged limbs.

"Fucking little rats!" Shane shouted as he kicked a fifth raptor in the jaw, snapping its head around one hundred eighty degrees. The animal fell to the jungle floor, dead. Shane stomped on it for good measure. "Fuck these things!"

"Keep fighting!" Thorne yelled. "Do not let them get in at you!"

Two raptors hung from Thorne's left arm, their teeth hooked in the metal mesh of his compression suit. He tried to shake them off, but they refused to budge, their needle teeth stuck in a material that should not allow needle teeth to get stuck in it.

"Fucking elves," Thorne cursed as he shook his arm over and over while he swatted at the rest of the raptor pack that continued to leap and jump at his face. "Fuck them all!"

"Hey now," Lucy said as she grabbed a raptor in mid-leap and smashed its head against the trunk of a palm tree. "There was no way they could have known we'd come up against little dinosaurs. You can't plan for every contingency."

"It's their fucking job to plan for every contingency!" Thorne yelled, ducking under a leaping raptor. He kept shaking his arm, but the raptors would not be thrown loose. "Fuck!"

"Here, hold still," Darren said, appearing at Thorne's side with a thick, heavy branch in his hands. "Try not to move."

"Fuck you, Chambers," Thorne growled.

Despite his obvious annoyance, Thorne did not move as Darren went batters up on the small dinosaurs. Darren dislodged them with one swing of the makeshift bat and the raptors screeched briefly as their broken bodies tumbled through the air. Their screeches ended suddenly as Lucy caught the first one then the second one and slammed them into each other, popping both on impact.

Darren kept at the swinging, knocking back wave after wave of the tiny raptors until the creatures decided that the humans that had invaded their territory were too much of a threat and they fled, screeching and chirping as their small legs sent them running into the underbrush and out of sight.

"They'll be back," Thorne said. "I can feel it. The little fuckers will be back. Keep moving."

"Uncle Vinny, as much as I believe you, which I do, I'm not sure keep running is the best advice," Shane said, nudging a raptor corpse with the toe of his boot. The thing was only half a meter long, barely longer than Shane's foot. "What we need to do is climb a tree and get some rest. Take shifts sleeping until we are all recharged and ready to get back in the fight."

"Do you honestly think I'm going to agree with that plan?" Thorne asked.

"Not at all," Shane replied and shrugged. "But it was worth a shot." Thorne glared. "Or not."

"He has a point," Lucy said. "We're all exhausted."

"We are also trained to push through that exhaustion," Thorne said.

"No offense, Commander, but I was trained as a shooter," Lucy responded. "I didn't go through BUD/S like you tough guys. I wasn't a SEAL. I'm Coast Guard and my job was to shoot shit with a big gun from a moving helicopter. I may be in great shape—"

"Awesome shape," Shane interrupted. "And I mean that as a compliment to a colleague, not as a creepy sexy thing."

"I know," Lucy said. "As I was saying, I am in great shape, but not run all night in a fucking jungle while dinosaurs chase us and try to eat us shape. We need to find shelter and hole up for a few hours. Regroup, catch our bearings, and then move forward."

"We do not stop," Thorne growled.

"She's fine," Darren said. Moving so he was directly in front of Thorne and there was nowhere else for the commander to look. "Yes, we have no idea where she is, but Kinsey is fine. You know that. That woman can survive anything."

"I'd like to confirm that myself," Thorne said. "Which means we keep going." He looked at the rest for Team Grendel. "We have a teammate missing. We do not, under any circumstance, leave a teammate behind. That is the basic tenant of all SpecOps. A man goes down and we pick him up and carry him home. That man is my daughter which means there is no way in this jungle fuck of a hell that I will even consider the notion of quitting, of resting, of taking one motherfucking second away from searching for her. If you want to stay then stay, but I am continuing on and finding Kinsey. Understood?"

"Understood," Darren replied. "But we aren't saying we should leave her behind. We're saying we need to regroup and think this through while also getting some much needed rest. We have no idea where we are, we have no idea where she is, and we have no idea what other threats are out there that could end our search in three seconds with a couple well-placed chomps. We need a plan. Running blindly through a neo-prehistoric jungle is not a plan, it's a disaster."

"What he said," Shane responded. He winced at the look he got from Thorne. "Sorry, Uncle Vinny, but as much as I hate to admit Ditcher is right, which, trust me, I hate doing, he is right. It's that simple."

"You already know my thoughts," Lucy said. "We can't keep going if we don't know where we're going. That's just not smart soldiering."

Thorne looked like he was about to explode. His whole being shook and violent tension came off him in waves. Team Grendel simply waited until he got himself under control.

"Alright," Thorne sighed. The tension was still there, but the violence had subsided. "We rest, come up with a plan, then go get my girl back." He scanned the dark jungle and frowned. "Any ideas on where we're going to do that?"

"I suggested we find some trees and climb our asses up into them," Shane said.

"You saw how big those other things were, right?" Lucy laughed. "Climbing a tree only puts us at eye level."

"Unless you see a Motel Six around here then what else are we going to do?" Shane asked.

"Motel Six? Way to dream big," Lucy said. She turned about, her hands on her hips. "Did we come from that direction?" She pointed to their left.

"Yes," Thorne nodded. "Why?"

"I think I saw something back that way when we were running," Lucy replied. "I don't know how far away it is, but if I'm right then we may have at least a little protection while we rest."

"What did you see?" Thorne asked.

"A group of boulders," Lucy said. "Maybe there's enough space between them for us. That'll at least provide some type of barrier if more big things come at us."

"And solid surfaces for you to go smashy smashy if the little ones come back," Shane said.

"That too," Lucy grinned.

"Okay," Thorne said. "You take point. Lead us there."

Lucy nodded and took a deep breath then led them from the raptor corpse-covered clearing and back into the thick of the jungle.

***

Kinsey felt like her lungs were burning from the inside out and she almost panicked at the thought that maybe she had swallowed some of the death honey. But she shoved the thought from her head and kept going. The blue lines of her containment net lit up the whole area and she could see the undulating surface of the living pit's belly. Or stomach lining. Or whatever it was.

Kinsey couldn't give two shits what it was exactly, all she cared about was whether or not it could feel pain.

She reached the bottom and shoved the containment net at the living pit's belly bottom.

Nothing happened.

Her burning lungs told her to get her ass to the surface and breathe, but her will refused. Kinsey Thorne had never quit anything in her life. Yes, she cheated during her BUD/S training by using amphetamines. Yes, she let Darren walk away from their marriage. Yes, she had become a hard-core junkie that would shoot, snort, drink, swallow anything put in front of her.

But she never quit.

She shoved the containment net at the bottom of the living pit's belly again, this time using her legs, pressing down with her boots, pushing the electric blue lines deep into the dark green flesh.

The whole place shook.

Even in the gel-like substance that she called death honey, Kinsey could feel the living pit shudder as she pushed the lines deeper and deeper into the plant's (maybe?) flesh. A ray of hope opened up in her. So did her need to breathe. Hope and desire, a desire for air, filled her body as she pushed harder and harder down on the containment net lines.

Black motes swam before her eyes and Kinsey knew she was only seconds from losing consciousness. If she didn't get back to the surface and fill her lungs with fresh air then she'd end up opening her mouth and swallowing the death honey. That was something she knew she wouldn't survive. That shit would dissolve her innards in seconds. It would have dissolved her skin if she didn't have the compression suit on.

Kinsey's fight became a war of wills against herself. She almost laughed at the thought. Her father always said she was her own worst enemy. She was about to prove it to herself.

Yet she didn't get the chance.

With one last shove of her boots, the containment net lines sliced into the living pit's belly, sending black clouds of plant blood oozing into the death honey. The shuddering grew so violent that Kinsey was tossed to the side, the containment net and her body slamming into the pit wall.

Then she was up and moving.

It wasn't her choice. The lack of oxygen had pretty much sapped her of all conscious decision-making ability. What made the decision for her were a dozen thick vines that grabbed her about the arms, the chest, the waist, yanking her free of the death honey and up out of the living pit's massive mouth.

Kinsey was thrown from the living pit, tossed like a wet rag out into the darkness of the jungle. She flew from the clearing that the living pit called home. She flew through stands of giant palms and huge conifers. She spun end over end, her feet up, her head up, her feet up, until she slammed down through a thick patch of thorny brambles that nearly impaled her and came to a sudden, violent stop.

Her body ached and Kinsey knew that when she took off her compression suit, despite its protective nature, she would be black and blue and basically a walking, talking bruise. She started to laugh. It hurt like a bitch, but she kept doing it. It made her feel alive and that's all she cared about. Even if she did end up as a walking, talking bruise, she would at least be walking and talking. And laughing.

"Fuck you," Kinsey whispered as she raised both hands and flipped off the entire jungle. "Suck my dick."

"That would not be anatomically possible," a voice said from a few feet away.

Kinsey rolled over, careful of the huge thorns that were inches from stabbing her to death, pushed up to her feet and stood ready to fight. The jungle swayed and rocked, but she stayed upright. She hadn't quit when she was submerged in death honey and she sure as fuck didn't intend to quit when some mystery voice decided to sneak up on her.

"I am not in the fucking mood," Kinsey snapped. "Show yourself, state your purpose, and get ready to have the split fuck beat out of you if I don't like either."

"Relax," the voice said. "We've been watching you. How you survived the *Brocchinia gargantua*, I have no idea. It was quite a surprise to see you come flying out of there."

"Bronchitis what?" Kinsey asked.

Her world swam and she staggered a couple steps to the side before she regained her balance.

"Doesn't matter," the voice said. It was a man's voice. Confident, sure. A voice of authority, used to giving orders and having those orders followed. "I can see you're wearing some sort of suit. That must be what kept you from being digested quickly."

"I'm guessing so," Kinsey said. "No fun falling into a honey pot."

"Pitcher plant," the voice said. "Calling it a honey pot wouldn't quite be accurate. Although, strictly speaking, calling it *Brocchinia gargantua* isn't accurate either, since bromeliads don't have prehensile vines that hunt for and carry prey back to the digestive region. We're still figuring it all out."

"I don't give a shit about what it's called," Kinsey said. "I got out. That's all that fucking matters." Another stagger and Kinsey almost fell. "Who are you?"

"Sorry," the voice said and a shape detached from the foliage. "Dr. Will Logan. I used to be in charge of this island."

"Used to be?" Kinsey asked. Her chest constricted and she felt a painful shiver rip through her body. "Oh…"

"Your suit didn't protect you completely," Dr. Logan said. "The alkaloid in the nectar must have gotten into your bloodstream. Sit down and let me have a look at you."

Kinsey laughed. "Sitting isn't happening." She staggered as her legs began to vibrate uncontrollably then she toppled over, her head slamming into the thick earth of the jungle floor. "Maybe falling is. Shit."

Kinsey looked up and the shadow of Dr. Logan loomed over her. He seemed a thousand feet tall even when he crouched down close to her. His hand went to her forehead and she shivered at his touch, her nerves on fire.

"Dammit," Dr. Logan said from a million miles away. "Harley! Come help me! She's going into tachycardia! Oh, shit! Now's she seizing!"

Kinsey tried to speak, but her jaw felt like heavy iron and she couldn't get it to move.

"Just try to relax," Dr. Logan said. "We'll get you stabilized and somewhere safe. Just hold on. Don't you quit on me."

"I...don't...quit," Kinsey growled through gritted teeth, forcing the words with all of her will.

"That's good," Dr. Logan sighed. "Because our facilities are far from ideal. You refusing to quit may be all that saves your life."

***

The boulders were nothing but vague shapes in the night's darkness. The moon had set and the jungle hung over the huge stones like a shroud. Team Grendel pulled up and studied the boulders for several seconds, keeping a safe distance, before they cautiously moved in closer.

Thorne gestured for Shane and Lucy to each take a side and circle the boulders as he and Darren waited, their eyes scanning the shadows and darkness that surrounded them all.

Night noises were everywhere, sounds that Thorne couldn't identify, and with every squawk and screech, his muscles tensed even further. If he didn't get a chance to put his back up against something solid and relax, he was afraid he'd snap a tendon just standing there.

Lucy came around from one side then Shane came from the other side. They both shook their heads and looked up at the boulders. Thorne assessed the best route to climb up by and he snapped his fingers to get their attention. He shook his head and the two operators walked back to him.

Shane gave him a quizzical look, but Thorne just shook his head. He turned about then found a fist-sized stone on the ground a few feet away. He picked it up and bounced it in his hand a few times before he drew his arm back and chucked the stone up into the boulders. It clacked and conked, stone on stone, then fell silent.

There was a thunk and a loud grunt. Then another thunk.

Shane's shoulders dropped and Lucy balled her fists while Darren only stood there, his eyes locked onto the boulders, his head cocked and listening. Thorne grumbled and took a deep breath, his anger rising as he realized their chance at finding a hide was shot to shit. Something was already in there.

The snapping of a twig drew his attention away from the growing disappointment and he spun about, the rest of Team Grendel following suit. Bodies tense and ready for a fight, the four operators waited, senses on high alert.

Another twig snapped, but it was a few yards to the right of the first noise. Then a third snapped, several yards in the opposite direction. A rustle was heard from behind them, but it sounded like something had been thrown, not like something was actually there. Thorne sighed.

"They're fucking with us," Darren whispered.

"I know," Thorne whispered back.

"What kind of animals fuck around like that?" Shane asked.

"Human animals," Thorne said. He cleared his throat. "Might as well show yourselves. You obviously want us to know you're there."

Nothing. No twigs snapped, nobody stepped out from behind a palm or pushed aside a fern. Thorne didn't expect them to. It was obviously a game. He'd been soldiering for long enough to know when a combatant wanted to mess with you. He just didn't have the patience to deal with it anymore.

"Listen, we aren't here to hurt you," Thorne said. "We haven't invaded the island to take it over or anything. We're stranded like you are. All we want to do is figure out what happened and how we can help."

"And how we can get the fuck away from here," Shane added, his voice low and directed at Darren.

"No shit," Darren agreed.

"Two over there," Lucy whispered, nodding her head to the left. "By those whatever they are plants. One short, one tall."

"I see them," Thorne said. "Darren? Shane?"

"I don't see any others," Darren replied.

"Me neither," Shane said.

"You two," Thorne said loudly, turning to address the figures standing by a set of thorny bushes that looked like cacti crossed with orchids. "I'm Commander Vincent Thorne of the Beowulf III. We came here with a man called Ballantine. He sent us—"

Before he could finish the figures ducked back into the deep darkness, lost from everyone's sight. Team Grendel waited, but they didn't reappear anywhere.

"Maybe dropping Ballantine's name wasn't such a good idea," Lucy said. "The man doesn't exactly make many friends."

"These are supposed to be his people," Thorne said. "If they survived the blast then they should be happy we have showed up. We're here to rescue them."

"Since when?" Shane asked then winced as Thorne slugged him hard in the shoulder. "Ow."

"That is our mission," Thorne growled. His voice was raised loud enough for anyone in close proximity to hear. "We came to the island with Ballantine to check on the facility. Once we saw the destruction, we switched the operation to a rescue mission."

"Right," Shane said. "I got confused. Forgot the mission had changed when we saw the facility thingy all explodey and shit."

"Jesus," Thorne said quietly. "Can you sound like more of an idiot?"

"I can try," Shane said. "Give me a second."

"We don't have one," Darren said, his voice serious. "More on our three."

The Team turned to face their right and saw six figures framed against the dark foliage. They all held something long in their hands.

"Ballantine?" a voice asked. It was a woman's voice, but there was something wrong with it. It sounded thick, choked, like she hadn't spoken in a while. "Ballantine?"

"Yes. Ballantine," Thorne answered. "We came with him."

"Where?" the woman asked.

"He's not here now," Thorne said. "He's back on the ship."

"The ship?"

"Yes."

"Ballantine on ship?" the woman asked, her thick voice taking on a hint of excitement.

"Right," Thorne said, interpreting the excitement as the woman's happiness at the possibility of being rescued. "We have rafts on the beach we can use to get all of you off this island."

"Raft," the woman stated.

Thorne frowned in confusion. "I'm sorry?"

"Raft," the woman said. "No rafts. Raft."

"No, we have two rafts on the beach," Thorne said. "The only problem is we got turned around in this damned jungle. If you lead us back to the beach then we can get you to the ship."

"And Ballantine," the woman responded.

"Yes…and Ballantine," Thorne replied. The hair on his neck stood on end.

"Vincent?" Darren said.

"I know," Thorne said. "Doesn't feel right, does it?"

"Not even close," Darren said.

Team Grendel waited. The figures waited.

"Uh, we can take you to Ballantine," Thorne pushed when the woman didn't speak for a full minute. "We just need to get—"

"Ballantine come here," the woman said.

The figures lifted their arms as one and there were the sounds of several small coughs.

Thorne slapped at a sudden, sharp pain in his neck. He found something sticking from his skin.

"Motherfucker," Shane said next to him.

Thorne pulled the thing from his neck and looked down at it, barely able to make out what it was because of the darkness.

A dart.

Thorne was about to agree with his nephew, but he quickly found his lips and tongue going numb. Then the rest of him went numb and he collapsed onto the ground, landing in a pile with Team Grendel. He expected unconsciousness to follow, but it didn't, just a full body numbness that spread and spread until he didn't even know if he was breathing or not.

A face leaned down and got right in his. Thorne wasn't sure if it was a side effect of whatever the dart had on it or not, but the face looked very strange. Thick, thick brow, heavy cheekbones, a protruding jaw. It took as a second for Thorne to realize he was looking at a woman, despite the tufts of hair that sprouted from random places on the face's cheeks and chin.

"Ballantine come here," the woman said and grinned.

Her teeth were razor sharp and they filled her mouth with violent menace.

Chapter Five- Someone's Lost Their Shit

Ballantine sighed.

It was a heavy, bored sigh. One that started at the top of his head and spread down to his toes. It was a sigh he was quite practiced in making.

He held a suppressed .45 in each hand, their grips cold against his palms despite the heat that permeated the below decks sections of the Beowulf III. Not having a working engine meant not having a working generator which meant not having air conditioning.

Ballantine was sick of not having air conditioning.

Yet, despite the lack of cold air, Ballantine maintained his normal cool and calm composure. He walked the length of the corridor, his ears sharp, his eyes narrowed, and the pistols ready. He knew there were intruders on board. He always knew when there were intruders on board. Ballantine made a point of knowing every single movement, every last detail, every bit of information pertaining to the goings on of the Beowulf III.

Not knowing would just be stupid. Ballantine was not stupid.

There was a loud creak down at the end of the corridor and Ballantine stopped walking. He pressed himself against the grey metal wall and waited, his eyes penetrating the red gloom that the emergency lights provided. Again, without a generator, there could be no full illumination. The crew had to settle for small, red bulbs powered by a meager bank of solar cells and batteries that the elves had rigged up, even though they had full power in the Toyshop.

Ballantine didn't begrudge them that. The Toyshop was essential to survival. Without the many gadgets and gizmos Carlos, Ingrid, and Moshi produced, the B3 and its crew, including Team Grendel, would be sitting ducks in a world that wanted them very dead. During the day, they diverted some of their esoteric power (he had no idea what apparatus they used to generate it with) to the other decks, but during night they cut off the trickle of electricity. No need to waste it while folks should be sleeping.

Which was what the entire crew seemed to be doing. Sleeping. Or that was how Ballantine found them. Knocked cold where they had dropped, small handmade darts sticking out expertly from their necks. Whoever was on board, they knew how to use a blowgun.

Too bad for them, Ballantine knew how to use real guns. Which he raised and took aim as a hunched shape crept slowly from the hatch at the end of the corridor.

"Do not shoot me, Ballantine," Ronald whispered. Or tried to whisper. His voice was too deep and powerful to really be considered quiet. "I know you are ready to."

"Ronald," Ballantine sighed, but the sigh was one of relief, not exasperation at having to play hide and seek on his own ship. "I almost pulled the triggers."

"You were half a second from doing so," Ronald said as he stretched to his full height, the top of his hairy head scraping the corridor's ceiling. The compact spaces of a ship were not ideal for a gigantopithecus. "I could hear the tension in your finger and smell the surge in adrenaline."

"You could smell me that fast from that distance?" Ballantine asked. "Impressive."

"Not particularly," Ronald said, but did not elaborate as to why. "Are you the only one awake?"

"I'm afraid so," Ballantine said, walking towards the Bigfoot-like creature that was quite possibly smarter than ninety-nine percent of the human population on Earth. "How did you escape the attack?"

"I didn't," Ronald replied. "I took three darts to the jugular. They obviously have experience with non-human creatures.

Unfortunately for them, my kind can burn through neurotoxins at a highly accelerated rate."

"Were you in Gunnar's lab?" Ballantine asked as he reached Ronald, tucked a .45 under his armpit, and extended his right hand.

"I was," Ronald said, enveloping Ballantine's hand in his own and giving it a healthy shake. "Boris, Gunnar, and Lisa are still there. I checked their vitals and they are stable, but will probably be unconscious for several more hours. I have secured the lab and the intruders will not be able to harm them."

"Have you made it to the upper decks?" Ballantine asked, retrieving the pistol from his armpit and wincing at the moistness on the grip. He was not as calm and cool as he had thought. That bothered him. "Have you found any of the rest of the crew?"

"I have not, to answer both questions," Ronald said. "As soon as I took care of two of the intruders, I came looking for you." He tapped his wide-nostrilled nose. "You were not hard to find."

"Took care of two intruders?" Ballantine asked. "Any chance they are available for interrogation?"

"I'm afraid not," Ronald said, shaking his massive head. "While I may be a highly rational being, I am also a creature of great emotion. Seeing Boris fall to the ground, along with my new friends, may have stirred the more primal inclinations in my behavior."

"You tore them apart," Ballantine stated.

"Yes," Ronald nodded. "Yes, I did."

"Good for you," Ballantine said. "Uninvited guests on my ship must not be allowed to go unpunished."

"I have to say I didn't particularly enjoy the actions," Ronald admitted. "Made me feel dirty, like I cheated."

"Kind of like bringing a couple pistols to a dart fight?" Ballantine asked, a smug sneer on his face. "We do what we have to, Ronald."

Ballantine and the Bigfoot stood there for a second.

"I'm going to have to rely on your senses," Ballantine said. "I'm pretty sharp myself, but I believe you should guide us to the main deck."

"Of course," Ronald said as he turned back towards the hatch he had just come through. "There are six more on board, if my senses are correct."

"I am confident that they are," Ballantine said.'

"We should encounter three shortly," Ronald said, his head cocked. "I believe they may even be able to hear us and are coming this way right now."

"Hear us?" Ballantine asked. "Are they on this level?"

"No, they are not," Ronald replied.

"Then how can they hear us?" Ballantine asked. "I know sounds can carry and echo on a ship, but we are speaking quieter than a normal conversational tone. Even with the vent system they shouldn't hear us."

"Oh, of course," Ronald chuckled. "I forgot to mention that our intruders do not appear to be *Homo sapiens*. At least, not anymore."

"Is that so?"

"Yes, it is so," Ronald said. "I am only guessing here, but I would wager that they are in the Cro-Magnon family. Possibly Neanderthal. I must apologize for my inability to say for sure. You'd think my knowledge of hominids would be sufficient to tell, but there are too many anomalies with these intruders."

"Yes, I was afraid of that," Ballantine said then saw the look on Ronald's face. "No, not at your confusion. I was afraid that more than just simple animal life had appeared on the island."

"I would hardly call the creatures that we have seen simple, Ballantine," Ronald responded. "But then I am sure you are only being your reductionist self."

"That I am, my friend," Ballantine said. "That I am."

"So, is our plan to engage the intruders or avoid them?" Ronald asked.

"Hmmm, good question," Ballantine said. "I say we avoid them and check on the rest of the crew as we make our way topside."

"Fine plan," Ronald said. "I do not relish another encounter where I must rip more limbs off. I enjoy it too much, I believe."

"You and me both, Ronald," Ballantine said. "You and me both."

***

The raft quietly bumped against the hull of the Beowulf III as Darby secured it as tight as she could with a set of magnetic clasps specifically designed for situations where a drop ladder was not available.

"Where's the other raft?" Max whispered. "Did they board on the port side?"

"No," Darby replied, nodding back towards the island. "They went back."

"They passed us in the bay?" Max asked. "How the hell did they do that?"

"They are good," Darby said and left it at that.

"Well, shitty shit shit," Max said. "I guess we'll have more company soon."

"I guess we will," Darby said. "You up for climbing?"

"I was born up for climbing," Max said as he craned his neck and looked at the railing that was quite a few meters above them. "If I'm not up for it, you'll mock me forever and that's just no fun."

"Fun for me," Darby said. She leaned in and gave Max a kiss.

"That was a surprise," he said. "Usually you are all business on an op."

"This is not a usual op," Darby said. "And I'm getting very sick of business."

"Don't let Ballantine hear you say that," Max laughed.

"Who do you think I plan on telling him next?" Darby said.

"Well, shut my mouth and call me Lenny Bruce," Max smiled. "My killer ice queen is thawing right out." He swallowed hard. "I just totally ruined the moment with the ice queen thing, didn't I?"

"Yeah," Darby replied.

"I did preface it with killer, though, so that should get me points," Max said in a pleading whine.

"You are so far in the point hole that it barely matters," Darby said.

"Point hole," Max snickered.

"Climb, dumbass," Darby ordered.

"You talk so sexy," Max responded, giving her an exaggerated wink.

He did as he was told and placed his palms to the ship's hull, letting the magnetic properties of his compression suit activate until he had a solid grip. Hand over hand, foot over foot, Max climbed quietly up the hull until he reached the bottom of the railing. Slowly, trying to match the rhythm and rocking of the ship, Max peeked over the edge.

Two shadows crouched across from him, hunkered down by the superstructure. If Max hadn't known the ship as well as he did, having spent every moment on it for over a year, he probably would have missed the crouched figures. But to his trained sniper's eyes, they stood out as if they had neon arrows flashing and pointing down at them.

When Darby reached him, he nodded in the figures' direction and she turned. He knew she saw them. She was Darby.

They dipped down in unison and moved hand over hand sideways until they were behind the figures' lines of sight. Darby raised her chin at Max and he rolled his eyes, but obeyed and climbed up over the railing first.

The figures were waiting for him.

"Oh," he said. "Hi there."

They stood a couple meters away, their dark eyes locked onto Max, their heavy brows furrowed, their muscled bodies tense and ready to strike.

"I'm guessing you guys have the same parents," Max said, trying to act casual as he straddled the railing, giving Darby time to do whatever Darby was going to do. "Are you brothers? I bet you're brothers. You know, I have a brother. Some folks think we're twins, but we aren't."

Max didn't know what made him jump off the railing and roll across the deck. That sniper's instinct that could feel crosshairs trained on him. Or maybe he just got spooked and didn't want to wait for the Brow Bros to make a move. Whatever the reason, he tucked his shoulder and hit the deck just as several darts flew past where he had been sitting.

The Brow Bros had him by the arms before he could even roll to a stop. They picked him up as if he was a child, lifting him high into the air, and started moving in opposite directions.

"No make a wish!" Max yelled. "No make a wish with Max!"

Two shots rang out and the Brow Bros dropped Max. He hit the deck hard and scrambled away, grabbing a pike that was strapped to the railing. He was up and brandishing the pike, making sure the hooked end was between him and the Brow Bros. Not that it mattered.

The Brow Bros fell to their knees, most of their heads missing. They collapsed face first, revealing Darby standing behind them, a Desert Eagle gripped in her hands.

"What the fuck?" Max asked.

"Lake has these stashed all over the ship," Darby said. "After the Monkey Balls incident, he said he didn't ever want to be more than five feet from a firearm at all times."

"You know where another is?" Max asked.

Before she could answer, she spun about and fired three times up towards the bridge. There was a scream, guttural, primal, and a body fell fast and hard, its limbs snapping and twisting as it hit the deck a couple feet from where Darby stood. It had a blowgun clenched in one fist and the weapon snapped as easily as the body's legs.

"What's with the blowguns?" Max asked.

There were shouts from below and Max pulled his eyes from the broken body and looked at Darby.

"Hello, where's another pistol?" Max asked.

"Lifeboat," Darby said, nodding behind Max. "Not a pistol."

Max didn't wait for her to clarify as he ran to the lifeboat and pulled back the cover. There, in all its beautiful glory, was a classic Winchester 30-30 repeating rifle. Max nearly cried when he saw it. It was like an old friend had showed up to help kick some ass. Memories of the years he and his brother had spent shooting his dad's rifle flooded his mind.

As poignant as it was, Max didn't let the memories slow him down. He grabbed up the rifle, chambered a round, and put the butt to his shoulder. He methodically moved the rifle back and forth, scanning the rest of the ship for threats, but saw none. When he reached Darby, the two were ready to take on whatever came at them from below.

The shouts from the hatch that led below turned from angry surprise to terrified fear. A heavy-browed woman burst from the hatch, wearing nothing but a pair of tattered shorts, her hairy breasts bouncing up and down as she sprinted free of the opening and headed right for Darby and Max.

Max started to squeeze the trigger, but he hesitated as an even hairier form sprang from the hatch and grabbed the browy, hairy woman by the back of the neck. Max let the rifle dip slightly as he and Darby watched Ronald snap the woman's neck and toss her right off the ship, her thick body flying end over end out into the water. Ronald turned on them, his teeth bared like fangs and started to growl then straightened up and smoothed down his bristled hair.

"Oh, hello," he said. He smiled then frowned. "Shouldn't you be on the island?"

"We were," Darby said. "But things got weird."

"What she said," Max agreed.

"Yes, well, we seem to be having some weirdness of our own," Ronald said. There was a shout from behind him and he smacked his forehead. "Dear me. How stupid."

He disappeared back into the hatch while Darby and Max waited. There were a few shouts, more than a few growls, a couple of screams, and then silence. After a minute, a body came flying out of the hatch followed by a second one. Both bodies were similarly browed and hairy like the corpses that lay on the deck by the superstructure.

"There," Ronald said, reappearing. He wiped his hands together. "That's the last of them. I would have much preferred to talk it through with them, perhaps learn more about their nature. But they are brutish things and were apparently focused only on violence and killing."

"Then why use the blowguns?" Max asked. Darby gave him a quick appraisal and he frowned at her. "What? I can ask smart questions too."

"Yes, that is a puzzle," Ronald said. "Why did they use blowguns that incapacitated their targets instead of just killing them? I may have been too rash in dispatching the intruders. We might have learned something if I had left one alive."

"There are more coming," Darby said, hooking a thumb over her shoulder at the island. "At least one went back for reinforcements."

"Is that so?" Ronald asked, moving towards the railing, his eyes studying the bay and the island beyond. "Oh, yes, I see it now. Filled to capacity. I count a dozen, at least."

"Man, you have to give credit to those Zodiacs," Max said. "They are some workhorse rafts."

Darby shook her head.

"Come on," she said. "Let's get to the armory. We'll need more ammunition if we're going to pick them off."

"No need," Max said, grinning. "We don't have to pick them off. We just have to sink the raft. Workhorse or not, put some holes in the thing and it'll be bye bye in seconds. Especially loaded down with the cast of Captain Caveman."

"I have seen that cartoon," Ronald said. "Not a very accurate portrayal of prehistoric man."

"Nope, but it's a hell of a lot of fun to watch when stoned out of your fucking gourd," Max said.

He walked to the railing and took aim with his rifle.

"Anytime now," Darby said.

"Hold on, hold on," Max said. "Don't push me. This isn't a sniper rifle. Doesn't have anywhere near the range or punch to it."

He sighted down the barrel and waited until the raft was in perfect range. Then he squeezed the trigger and sent one round flying at the raft, putting a good-sized hole in the heavy duty plastic.

There was a lot of shouting and yelling and waving of hairy arms, but the raft didn't go down.

"Did you think Ballantine would have rafts that sink after one shot?" Darby asked.

"Yes?" Max replied. "Shit."

Darby bumped Max out of the way with her hip and took aim with the Desert Eagle. It was a heavy duty pistol, shooting .50 caliber rounds, but it wasn't meant for long-range targeting. Darby squared her shoulders, spread her legs and set her feet. With both eyes open she aimed out at the raft that was approaching at a steady clip despite the occupants not using the motor.

"Man, they sure can paddle with those beefy arms," Max said.

"Hush," Darby said.

She fired until the massive pistol clicked empty. There were several screams followed by a lot of splashing.

"Not so hard," Darby said and ejected the magazine. "I'm going to go reload."

"You do that," Max said.

He watched as the Zodiac sank in the middle of the bay while some of its former occupants started to swim and others floated, their bodies ripped apart by the heavy caliber slugs. Max was about to join Darby when he noticed something happening.

"Oh, shit," he said. "Are you seeing that?"

"I'm sorry?" Ronald asked, glancing over at Max. "I was studying the stars. Such a beautiful night."

Max pointed out at the bay. "Check that shit out."

Ronald refocused his attention on the sunk raft and the attackers that flailed about in the tropical bay. His eyes widened and he smiled, showing his large canines.

"I believe those are similar to the Clidastes of the late cretaceous period," Ronald stated. "Although there are some obvious differences."

"Obviously," Max said as he watched the four-meter-long water creatures snap and grab the attackers, pulling them under the surface one by one until all that were left were the floating corpses of Darby's casualties.

Then the corpses began to disappear as well and the island's bay became a peaceful picture of nocturnal tranquility. Until the waters started to turn black with blood.

"Way to ruin a view," Max said and clapped his hands together. "I need a toke. My head is killing me." He gingerly touched his stitched scalp. "Ow. You up for sharing a joint, Ronny my man?"

"Maxwell," Ronald sighed. "I have expressed this to you before, but I would rather you did not refer to me as Ronny. I have a hard enough time being taken serious as the species I am. Your giving me the nickname of a twelve year old does not help."

"Dude, who are you trying to impress?" Max laughed. "Everyone on this fucking ship is a twelve year old. We play with guns and shoot impossible monsters instead of getting real jobs and actually contributing to society."

"One might argue that we protect society, which is part of the more heroic of professions," Ronald said.

"For my uncle, yeah," Max nodded. "But I have to be honest and say I do this because it's a fucking blast and beats getting a regular job."

Max walked to the hatch, stepping over the corpses of the broken intruders.

"Maybe we should toss these guys overboard?" Max asked.

"No, I would like to study them," Ronald said. "Perhaps you could assist me in carrying the bodies down to Gunnar's lab?"

"Nice try," Max said as he walked through the hatch, giving Ronald a quick wave. "But that would be a regular job."

"Maxwell!" Ronald called. "You are being very rude and inconsiderate!"

"Regular job, dude!" Max called back.

Ronald waited, but when Max did not return, he sighed and proceeded to gather up the bodies. Darby reappeared and frowned.

"Where's Max? Why isn't he helping?" she asked.

"He said this work would be too much like a regular job which is apparently something he has been avoiding most of his life," Ronald replied, easily hefting three corpses into his arms at once.

"I'm going to smack the shit out of that lazy ass," Darby said as she turned and stomped back through the hatch.

"Uh, hold on, please," Ronald called, but there was no response. "Never mind. I can get these myself. Thank you for offering."

"Ugh... Who are you talking to?" Mike asked as he pulled himself up by the railing next to the bridge. He looked down at Ronald and grimaced. "Damn... What the hell happened?"

"Hello, Michael," Ronald greeted. "I was completely unaware that you were up there. Is anyone else with you?"

"No, I was relieving Lake when I heard something," Mike replied. "Next thing I know, I'm down on the deck and hear you talking to someone." He paused and stared at what Ronald held in his massive, hairy arms. "Are those cavemen?"

Ronald sighed. "For lack of a better term, yes," Ronald said. "Although I plan on discovering a better term. Do you feel up to assisting me down to the lab with these?"

"Not a chance, man," Mike said. "Sorry. I would like to, but I'm still seeing double."

"Yes, you have been affected by some type of non-lethal neurotoxin," Ronald said. "I do not know the duration of the after affects. I apologize for not having more information. If you would accompany me then I can take some blood samples and compare them to the others. That will give me a range of data to process and I might be able to tell us all more about our attackers and their motives."

Mike stared at him for a second. "You just need me to come down to the lab so you can draw blood?" he asked.

"Yes," Ronald answered.

"That I can do," Mike said.

"Excellent," Ronald said. He shifted his grip on the corpses, looked at the narrowness of the hatch to below decks, and shook his head. "This may take a bit. Would you mind going below and telling Maxwell, Ms. Darby, and perhaps Ballantine that I could use some help?"

"Sure," Mike said. "But what about everyone else?"

"They were attacked the same as you," Ronald said. "So they will not be of much use."

"Gotcha," Mike nodded. "I'll send up anyone I find that can handle the job."

"Thank you," Ronald said as Mike ducked into the bridge.

The hairy hominid tilted his head and looked up at the stars once again.

"Things would be so much simpler without people," he sighed. "It is a lovely night, though."

***

Gunnar grumbled as Ballantine handed him a cup of coffee. The smell was both enticing and repulsive. His stomach grumbled as well, hungry for the liquid while his throat started to close at the idea of swallowing.

"Drink up, all of you," Ballantine said as he set a large pot of coffee aside and took a seat at one of the lab tables. He smiled at the folks assembled around him. "Blood samples have been taken, so now you can get back to your normally alert and productive selves."

"Fuck productive," Max said as he and Darby carried in the last corpse. They set it on an empty table and Max stretched, pushing his hands into the small of his back. "And fuck work. Can I go grab my stash now? These bastards are a lot heavier than they look and I don't want to cramp up."

"Lift with your back," Darby said as she walked by him and slapped his ass. Hard. "And the answer is no, you cannot go get your stash. We need to return to the beach and the base ASAP. We have teammates lost on that island."

"Darby is correct," Ballantine said. "Returning to the island as soon as possible is the best course of action."

"What about those?" Dr. Morganton asked, her hands wrapped about her coffee mug as if it was all that was keeping her from falling off her stool. She nodded towards the corpses then shuddered and began to list to the left.

"Hold tight there, Dr. Morganton," Boris said, putting a hand on her shoulder and keeping her in place. "Do not exert yourself.

Once she was steady, Boris stood from his stool and stretched. He smiled at everyone, but did not receive any smiles in return. Instead, he received a few glares.

"How the hell are you so chipper?" Gunnar asked.

"I am unsure," Boris said. "No reason that I can think of." He placed a finger to his chin. "It could be that I have spent years experimenting with several different psychoactive compounds."

Ballantine frowned. "That wasn't part of your research directive."

"Research? Oh, no, no, no," Boris said, grinning from ear to ear. "That was recreation. It does become monotonous while cooped up without any human companionship. The psychoactives helped pass the time."

"Eh-hem," Ronald said, looking from a microscope and over to Boris.

"Oh, oh, my apologies, my good friend!" Boris exclaimed. "I did not mean to belittle our relationship. Not that we had a relationship in the romantic sense. No, no, no. That would fall well outside normal parameters."

He glanced at Gunnar and Mike.

"But then you two are gay and in a relationship which falls outside the normal parameters," Boris said. "Or does it? Perhaps not. I'll think upon that for a moment."

He proceeded to think upon that for a moment then held up a finger.

"I have concluded that it doesn't," Boris said. "There is ample evidence of homosexual behavior amongst many species, and it is well documented in human history that being gay is a normal part of human civilization. I would almost conclude that the perception of it as an aberration is actually what falls outside the parameters."

Everyone just stared at him.

"Yeah, you might want to quit while you're way, way behind," Max said, leaning close to Boris's ear as he walked by towards the lab's hatchway. "If you need me, I'll be grabbing a joint from Lucy's quarters. Back in two secs."

"Max!" Darby called.

"Sorry, sugar buns of sexy love!" Max replied, his voice echoing back from the corridor. "Maxey need smokey tokey or Maxey gonna explodey splodey!"

"You sleep with that?" Mike chuckled.

"See, right there," Boris began. "One's physical and romantic connections are highly complex as well—"

"Thank you, Doctor," Ballantine interrupted. "We get it. People are weirdos and pervs. Now, let's move on. Ronald? What do you have for us?"

"Not much, Ballantine," Ronald replied. "As I have only had about forty-five minutes to accomplish any work while all of you have crowded around in here, making spectacular distractions of yourselves."

Ballantine gave everyone an exaggerated "yikes" look then grinned. "Our apologies."

"For the fucking record, this is my lab," Gunnar said. "I get to be as distracting as I want."

"However," Ronald continued, ignoring Ballantine and Gunnar. "I have been able to determine that the intruders were human at one point."

"Were?" Gunnar asked. "What are they now?"

"A genetic soup of human, Cro-Magnon, and Neanderthal," Ronald said.

"Croanderthals," Mike said from a seat in the corner.

"Not a name I would choose," Ronald said. "But it does fit considering the mix of species. The only reason I am able to tell you the mix at all is because I do have extensive experience in identifying all three genetic codes. Even with the limited equipment our less than operational lab contains, I could see right away that these former people went through some type of accelerated mutating process."

"*My* less than operational lab," Gunnar muttered.

"Accelerated mutating process?" Boris asked. He moved next to Ronald and looked excitedly at the microscope. "May I?"

"Of course," Ronald said and stepped aside.

Most everyone went back to hanging their heads and trying to pretend they didn't feel like hammered shit. Ballantine stood in the middle of the lab, checked his watch, looked to the hatchway then over to Boris and Ronald. Finally, he glowered at Darby.

"I'll go get him," she said and left.

"Gentlemen?" Ballantine asked Ronald and Boris. "Can we continue?"

"I'm afraid there isn't much more I can tell you," Ronald said. "Like I said before, the lab—"

"Don't," Gunnar warned, holding up his middle finger.

"The human capacity for rudeness is mind boggling," Ronald muttered.

"Be that is it may, my capacity for patience has run out," Ballantine said. He clapped his hands loudly and everyone jumped, even Ronald. "Time to get to work, folks! Rest time is over! I need to know what we are dealing with and I need to know now! Dealing with dinosaurs is one thing, but mutated humans that can think and reason enough to steal a Zodiac and then come attack the B3 is a whole other matter. A matter I am not cool with."

There were a few groans. Ballantine clapped again. Louder.

"Jesus, stop that," Gunnar complained.

"Gunnar, Lisa, Boris, and Ronald," Ballantine said, addressing the scientists in the room. "You will be working around the clock to figure out what the hell went wrong with these people. I want to know everything about them, especially why they wanted our ship."

"How the hell will we find that out?" Gunnar asked, pointing at the corpses. "Can't really ask them."

"That sounds like an excuse, Dr. Peterson," Ballantine replied. "Do you think I like excuses?" He opened his eyes wide and leaned towards Gunnar then said in an exaggerated whisper, "I do not. Nope. Not a fan of excuses."

"I will make sure we get as many answers as we can with the resources we have," Ronald said.

"Will you shut the fuck up about my lab?" Gunnar snapped.

Ballantine pointed at Gunnar. "Do I need to put you in time out?"

Gunnar only sputtered, unable to form a response.

"Good," Ballantine nodded. "Play nice, science folks. I have to attend to other matters. Mike?"

"What did I do?" Mike asked.

"Why does everyone think I'm reprimanding them when I call their name?" Ballantine sighed. "When we finally get a chance to rest and relax, I am calling a family meeting."

No one responded.

"That's a joke," Ballantine said. He pointed at Mike. "You are coming with me to the Toyshop. We're going to kick the elves into high gear. Containment nets and exploding rounds are not good enough. We need serious firepower if we're going to rescue our friends."

"You think they're still alive?" Mike asked. Gunnar whipped his head about and glared. "What? It is a valid question, Gun. Very valid."

"Very valid, indeed," Ballantine agreed. "And yes, I do think they are still alive. I have the utmost confidence in Team Grendel. They are all survivors, each and every one of them. But, survivors or not, I am also confident that they could use some assistance."

"What kind of firepower are we talking about?" Mike asked as he got up and followed Ballantine out of the lab.

"Whatever firepower they have," Ballantine said. "As long as it's big."

"I like it big," Mike said.

"That's what he said!" Boris cried out, turning and grinning at everyone. No one grinned back. "I thought it was funny."

He was met with Gunnar's hungover frown and extended middle finger.

***

The surface was cool, but rough against Kinsey's cheek. It took her several long seconds before she was able to drag herself up into consciousness and realize she was lying down and her face was pressed against rock. She moaned and rolled over slowly, her head protesting and her stomach lurching at the small movement.

"Whoa, whoa, whoa," a voice said. "Hold still there."

Kinsey's eyes shot open and she scrambled as far away from the voice as she could. Her back jammed against more cold stone and she felt pain everywhere. Before she could get a look at who spoke to her, Kinsey's stomach rebelled and she turned her head and vomited. Only thin liquid came up, mostly yellow bile, and she wiped her mouth with the back of her hand before trying to focus once more on the voice.

"Who are you? Where am I?" she asked.

"You don't remember?" Dr. Logan asked, sitting on an upturned log close to a small, guttering flame that seemed to be coming right off the rock wall next to him. "Dr. Will Logan. I found you by the *Brocchinia gargantua*? Does that ring a bell?"

"Bronchitis plant, right," Kinsey said, but she didn't relax. "You were hiding in the bushes. Showed up when that thing puked me out."

"Yes, that is an apt description," Dr. Logan replied. "By the way, how did you get it to, uh, puke you out?"

"Containment net," Kinsey said. "I burned its belly."

"This?" Dr. Logan asked. He held up the containment net's black box. "Interesting device. It is no longer operational,

93

unfortunately. It would be handy to have in this environment. You wouldn't happen to have another, would you?"

"Not on me," Kinsey said.

The two fell silent as Kinsey studied the man.

In his early forties, or maybe late thirties, Dr. Logan was handsome, but in a soft way. He didn't have a rugged bone about him, yet he looked like he could take on a challenge or two. There was something in his eyes, how they bore into Kinsey and shone with the promise of knowledge or the promise of adventure finding the knowledge. He reminded her of a mix between Darren and Gunnar.

But there was something else there, as well. Something...

"Can I check your vitals?" Dr. Logan asked, pulling Kinsey from her thoughts. He held up a stethoscope. "Just want to make sure you're on the mend. The *Brocchinia gargantua* nectar isn't something we take for granted around here."

"Where is here?" Kinsey asked, her eyes studying her surroundings quickly before locking back on Dr. Logan. "Is this a cave? Am I in a cave?"

"Yes, you are in a cave," Dr. Logan said. "And you are safe. No one here wants to hurt you. Quite the opposite. We need you to help us."

"Help you? How?" Kinsey asked.

"Help us get the hell off this island," Dr. Logan said. "It stopped being a place of discovery a long time ago and is now just a place of nightmares. I would like to leave these nightmares."

"No shit," Kinsey laughed dryly. "Who is us? How many of you are there?"

Dr. Logan set the stethoscope aside. "Military. Of course. I guess I need to go through an examination from you before I can be allowed to do my own examination of you. I have met more than a few soldiers for hire in my day and every last one of you has trust issues." He filled the cave with his own dry laugh. "Which is ironic since you are trained to obey orders without question. What mind is conditioned that way?"

"I have trust issues for a lot of reasons, not because I'm military," Kinsey said. "And I'm not a soldier for hire."

"You aren't?" Dr. Logan asked, looking Kinsey up and down. "Then what branch of the military are you with? I'd say Special Operations Forces, but I'm not familiar with your uniform. Is that some type of chain mail?"

Kinsey looked down and was surprised to see her compression suit still on. Dr. Logan grinned at that surprise.

"If I was a bad guy, I'm pretty sure I would have stripped that off you," Dr. Logan said. "If for no reason other than to put you in a compromising position of weakness. Nudity tends to undermine aggression, in my experience."

"I was a Marine. I could give two shits about being naked," Kinsey said. "Cocks out and all that shit."

Dr. Logan raised an eyebrow.

"No, I do not have a cock," Kinsey said.

"Good to know," Dr. Logan responded. "I have seen stranger things on this island."

"Who is the us?" Kinsey asked again.

"There is myself, Dr. Harley Werth, and Dr. Lucas Sales," Dr. Logan said.

Kinsey waited, but when Dr. Logan didn't add any names she shook her head. "That's it? Three of you?"

"That's it," Dr. Logan replied. "Three of us. We recently had a fourth, but he's been missing a while. I'm not holding out hope."

"Are you all that survived the explosion?" Kinsey asked.

Dr. Logan grimaced and shifted uncomfortably in his seat. "Well, that is hard to explain."

"Try me," Kinsey insisted.

"How about this," Dr. Logan proposed. "You ask a question, I give an answer, then I take a reading. I need to check your heart, your lungs, make sure you don't have any cerebral damage—"

"Do I sound like I have cerebral damage?" Kinsey asked. Her head hurt like ten kinds of split fuck, but she wasn't going to admit that. "No deals. You answer my questions. If I decide not to kick your ass when you're done then I'll let you examine me."

"What if you die while asking your questions?" Dr. Logan responded. "Which is a very likely outcome considering what you have been through."

"If I was going to die then I would have died," Kinsey said. "Trust me. I've woken up from more near death experiences than I can even remember."

"Overdoses," Dr. Logan said. It was a statement, not a question. "That's the survivor I'm looking at. I thought you had more going on than just a grunt."

"You don't like military, do you?" Kinsey asked.

"Not really," Dr. Logan admitted and held up a hand. "I have my reasons, trust me. But those reasons are personal and off limits. You want to ask questions then ask questions about this island, not about my past."

Kinsey pursed her lips and struggled with the hundred snarky, personal questions that came to mind. She focused on one, unable to just blindly obey the man.

"Were you a junkie too?" she asked.

Dr. Logan grinned and nodded. "How could you tell?"

"You recognized me," Kinsey replied. "Takes one to know one."

"That it does," Dr. Logan said.

Kinsey sat there and thought for a minute then extended her arm.

"Come and do your poking and prodding," Kinsey said. "But I am going to ask you a fuck ton of questions while you do."

"That works for me," Dr. Logan said as he grabbed his stethoscope again and stood up. "But no poking and prodding. Just listening."

"I'm keeping this suit on," Kinsey insisted. "So you better be able to listen through this."

"I can," Dr. Logan said. "I've checked you a couple times since we brought you here. Sorry if that breaks any consent issues you may have, but I'm claiming Hippocratic oath and basic human decency on that one."

"Then your answers better be really good," Kinsey said. "Or I kick your ass."

Dr. Logan paused. "I have the feeling you are only half kidding."

"I have the feeling I'm not kidding at all," Kinsey replied, but there was a small smile teasing her lips.

"Yes, well, we'll leave that statement there for now," Dr. Logan said.

He had a small smile teasing his lips as well, but the way it didn't meet his eyes troubled Kinsey slightly. She couldn't put her finger on it, but she had a distinct feeling that ex-junkie may not have been correct. The guy smelled like he was still using. But using *what* was what Kinsey couldn't figure out.

Chapter Six- Better Choose Now

The air was thick with the smell of copper. It was a smell that Thorne knew too well.

"Fuck," he muttered as he tried to open his eyes. The pain in his head was almost too much to deal with, but he willed his lids to obey and quickly wished he hadn't. "Double fuck."

He was hanging upside down by his ankles, his hands bound together and hanging below his head, which was the only reason he was able to wake up since most of his blood was pooling in his arms and hands instead of his head. Thorne had done his share of stringing people up over the years and knew that even with the blood rushing to his extremities, he didn't have long before cerebral hemorrhaging began and he'd be dead as fuck.

"Uncle Vinny?" Shane whispered and Thorne looked to his right.

"Shane," Thorne sighed. "How do you feel?"

Even hanging upside down, Shane was able to shrug sarcastically. "Oh, you know, just hanging out."

"Oh, for fuck's sake," Lucy groaned. "He made that joke when I asked him the same question. Then again when Darren woke up."

"Stick with a good one when you find it," Shane replied. "And, fuck, man, when will I get another chance to use a pun like that again?"

"Probably the next time Ballantine sends us to our deaths," Darren said.

Thorne rotated his head slowly, already feeling the pressure start to build to lethal levels.

"Injury report," Thorne ordered.

"We're good," Darren replied. "Except for the obvious."

"We haven't been hanging for too long," Shane said, his voice serious for once. "My vision is good. Hasn't started to darken yet."

"Mine is," Lucy said. "We have what, five minutes before we bleed out our ears?"

"Probably," Thorne grunted. "What do we know?"

"Modern facility," Darren said. "Metal walls, metal and tile floors, halogen lights above us. There used to be tables in here, so I'm guessing it was a lab."

"Messy lab, considering the drain in the center of the floor," Shane said.

Thorne looked over and spotted the drain. He also spotted the dark stains around the drain. There were similar stains directly underneath him.

"We aren't the first they've put in here," Thorne said.

"Yeah, we know," Shane said.

"Any sign of who brought us in?" Thorne asked.

"Not so far," Darren replied. "But we've only been awake for a few minutes."

Thorne looked about and tricked his brain into righting the images. It was a skill every SEAL learned since hanging upside down while keeping your wits was definitely in the job description. Darren was correct- metal walls, metal and tile floor, scuff marks and outlines where table legs used to be. They were in a former lab. But it was much more than that.

"Abattoir," Thorne said.

"Oh, man," Shane said.

"A what?" Lucy asked.

"Slaughterhouse," Darren said. "We're the meat."

"Are you fucking kidding me?" Lucy nearly shrieked. "What the fuck?"

"Yay," Shane said. "I get to be a Reynolds burger. I always thought I'd go out in a blaze of glory, not as part of someone's bowel movement."

"It's not over yet," Thorne said. "They'll be back to get us soon. Letting us hang upside down like this is actually spoiling the meat. This is intimidation, not torture."

"Gonna have to argue with you on that point, Uncle Vinny," Shane said. "Gravity is shoving my balls up into my brains, so I'm going with torture."

There was a rattling at the door and Thorne grinned.

"We're about to find out," Thorne said. "Hurry. Weapons?"

"Pretty sure we're stripped clean," Darren said. "Except for our boots. My arms are dead asleep so I haven't been able to check."

"Me neither," Shane said.

"Same," Lucy added as the door opened and six figures came lurching into the room.

Figures that Thorne could only describe as mutants of some kind. They certainly weren't human. If he'd been on the B3, he would have heard Mike's naming suggestion.

Croanderthals.

The lead croanderthal grunted and more lights began to flicker and come to life as someone hit the switch.

"Ballantine," the lead croanderthal said.

Thorne had no idea how to respond. He didn't know what he was responding to, let alone how to form the words.

Shane, on the other hand, had no problem.

"Holy shit," he said. "It's the fucking mutant Flintstones."

There were several snarls and hisses from five of the six, but the lead croanderthal only raised a thick lip to reveal a couple very sharp teeth.

"Ballantine," the figure said.

Recognition slammed into Thorne's brain and he realized he knew the figure. It was the same face he saw as he was paralyzed in the jungle, before unconsciousness took him.

"What about Ballantine?" Thorne asked.

"Ballantine come here," the lead croanderthal, a woman by the anatomy that peeked out from the tattered remains of the dirty rags she wore. "Ballantine come you."

"I don't think my uncle and Ballantine are close enough for Ballantine to come him," Shane said.

"Jesus H. Christ," Thorne snapped. "Seriously?"

"I plead defense mechanism," Shane said. "Or too much blood to the brain."

The croanderthal woman motioned and four of the other croanderthals, all men by their obvious anatomy, moved to the wall behind Thorne and company. Thorne felt his bonds lurch then the floor was racing up at him. He hit hard, but most of his body was numb anyway, so he didn't feel too much pain. That would kick in later, he was more than sure of it.

"I would totally beat the living shit out of you caveman fucks," Shane said as he lay in a helpless heap, half his body draped over Lucy. "But that would mean moving. Which isn't happening."

"Wait until the pins and needles hit," Lucy said. "Abattoir or not, this is about to turn into a torture chamber."

"Good point," Shane said. "Hey, Grog and friends, you guys got more of that numbing shit we can save for later? I really hate it when my leg falls asleep then wakes up. That shit hurts like a mother—"

One of the croanderthal men grabbed Shane from behind and slammed a heavy, hairy fist into his head a few times until Shane's eye rolled up and he was out.

Thorne felt guilty for all of a split second at the brief relief that his nephew was finally silent. That relief turned to rage almost as fast, though, and Thorne focused back on the woman.

"Why do you think Ballantine will come here?" Thorne asked.

"Ballantine like that," the croanderthal woman replied, shrugging her huge, hairy shoulders. "Ballantine like tidy."

"She's right about that," Darren said. "He does like tidy. No loose ends."

"No ends," the croanderthal woman agreed, nodding her heavy browed head. "He come. He find. If not dead."

"If not dead?" Thorne asked. "Why would he be dead?"

"No tell," the mutant woman said. "Not front them." She pointed at Darren, Lucy, and even the unconscious Shane. "Just you. Leader talk. Me. You. Talk."

"Leader talk," Thorne agreed. "But my Team stays here. Whatever you want to say to me, you say to them too."

"No," the croanderthal woman said. She shook her head and snapped her thick fingers. "No."

The croanderthals behind Team Grendel grabbed up Darren, Lucy, and Shane. There was nothing any of them could do about it.

Their limbs were still completely asleep and numb. Thorne could barely keep his head upright.

He was forced to watch helplessly as Darren and Lucy shouted and screamed at the mutants that dragged them out of the room. Two of them carried Shane, making sure his head smacked against the door jamb at least once on the way out.

That left the croanderthal woman, and a croanderthal man that stood back by the door. The croanderthal woman walked closer to Thorne and crouched close to him. But not too close. Despite his obvious incapacitation, and the binds that still held his wrists and ankles, she kept out of reach. Thorne made a mental note that the woman may have been physically mutated, but intellectually she appeared sharp, despite the stunted speech pattern.

"Leader talk," the croanderthal woman said.

"Fine," Thorne replied. "Leader talk. Leader have a name?"

"Liu," the croanderthal woman said.

"Liu? I know that name," Thorne said.

"Ballantine only name care about," the Liu croanderthal snarled. "Talk. Now. Leader me, leader you. Talk Ballantine."

"Like I said before, *fine*," Thorne said. "We talk Ballantine."

***

"It's been a year since the explosion?" Kinsey asked. "And you've been surviving in this cave since then?"

"Not quite," Dr. Logan said as he placed the stethoscope's disc against Kinsey chest and listened for a second. "We were in a different facility for several months. This is recent."

"Recent? Why? What happened to the other facility? Did it explode as well?" Kinsey asked as the disc was moved about her chest.

"Hold on," Dr. Logan said. "Stop talking and give me a couple deep breaths. This suit is not easy to hear through."

Kinsey reluctantly let the questions drop and breathed in and out several times until Dr. Logan nodded. He removed the stethoscope from his ears and draped it across his neck in that classic motion all doctors use.

"Alright. Breathing sounds good from what I can tell. Slightly thick, but that is to be expected after your encounter with the nectar," he stated. "Heart rate is elevated, but once again, it is expected considering you are in a fight or flight situation."

"No flight," Kinsey said.

"Understood," Dr. Logan said and nodded. "Your abdomen sounds good as well, which was what I was more worried about in case you had ingested any of the nectar. That stuff will eat you from the inside out, believe me."

"You've seen it happen?" Kinsey asked.

"I have," Dr. Logan said, his face a sudden mix of anger and somber resignation.

"Okay, okay, I'm getting confused," Kinsey said. "You weren't in the facility that exploded? You were in a different facility? Why? What's the difference?"

"I was in charge of the Alpha, which was command and observation," Dr. Logan said. "Dr. Ann Liu was in charge of Omega, which was where the matrix facilitator was housed. The two facilities needed to be on opposite ends of the island so readings were clean and not influenced by their respective power grids. It took years to build and was all gone in seconds."

"What's a matrix facilitator?" Kinsey asked.

"You don't know?" Dr. Logan asked. "I'd assumed that was why you were here."

"We're here because Ballantine brought us here," Kinsey said.

"Aren't we all," Dr. Logan chuckled. The look on Kinsey's face stopped the chuckle quickly. "Yes, well, the matrix facilitator is a machine, a connected hive of machines, actually, that takes genetic codes and rebuilds them into fully fledged life forms. Basically, a 3D printer for life."

"And what could possibly go wrong with that?" Kinsey sneered.

"Really, not much," Dr. Logan said. "There were safeguards upon safeguards upon safeguards. Nothing in that facility should have had the power needed to produce an explosion of that size. It was designed to specifically avoid any catastrophes. Everything was small scale, tiny. The matrix facilitator couldn't produce a life form larger than a small dog. Everything that has happened, should not have happened."

"Said every scientist in the world right before they fucked up," Kinsey said.

"Believe me, I am very aware of that," Dr. Logan sighed.

"So, you were in the Alpha facility and this Dr. Liu and her team were in the Omega facility," Kinsey said. "Omega goes boom and everyone dies. Then you find out, what? That your matrix hoodickey has grown some dinosaurs that are a lot bigger than small dogs?"

"No," Dr. Logan said. "You are getting ahead. Let me explain events in order, otherwise you won't be able to understand where you are."

"I'm in a fucking cave," Kinsey said.

"Funny," Dr. Logan said. "Do you want me to keep talking or not?"

"Talk," Kinsey said.

***

"How did you become the leader?" Thorne asked the Liu croanderthal.

"Always," she replied. "How you?"

"Always too," Thorne said.

"Not always," the Liu croanderthal said, shaking her head. She pointed at Thorne. "You soldier. Soldier follow. Lead later."

"I've been leading a very long time," Thorne said. "So pretty much always."

The Liu croanderthal nodded as if that made sense to her.

"Ballantine come. When come, me, leader, kill," she said. "You, leader, not stop. You stay. You help me leader."

"Why would I do that?" Thorne asked.

"Me leader, kill you friends," the Liu croanderthal said. "You stay. You help. Friends live. You fight me leader, friends die. You die. Everyone die."

"That includes you," Thorne said. "If I fight you, you will die. Trust me. This soldier leader knows how to survive."

"This me leader survive too," the Liu croanderthal said. Her face broke into a wide grin and Thorne did everything in his power not to recoil from the size and shape of her sharp teeth.

***

"Human flesh," Ronald said as he held up a microscope slide.

Gunnar and Dr. Morganton gaped at it, both blanching visibly. Boris just nodded.

"These things eat people?" Gunnar asked.

"Yes," Ronald replied. "They also eat each other." He held up another slide. "This is mutated flesh."

"Great," Gunnar said. "Cannibals."

"Are they cannibals because they eat each other or because they were once human and eat us?" Boris mused. "This is something to ponder."

He tapped at his chin a few times and shook his head. Everyone waited, but it didn't look like he was going to come up with an answer anytime soon.

"Doesn't matter," Gunnar said. "They eat people, they eat each other. They also eat a lot. Let me show you this."

He led them to a lab table where one of the attackers was vivisected. The mutant's torso was completely split open. On a cart next to the table was its stomach and the contents were spread out.

"The stomach is twice the size of a normal person's," Gunnar said. "And it was full. I mean stuffed to capacity full."

"But these things moved fast and fought hard, right Ronald?" Dr. Morganton asked.

"They fought hard, yes," Ronald replied. "They are very strong and very fast. Just not as strong and fast as I am."

"Good for you," Gunnar said. "What Dr. Morganton is getting at is that if they were this full then they should have been sluggish, lethargic as their blood flow diverted to digestion. It is never recommended to do battle after eating a big meal. This asshole just ate the biggest of meals and then decided to come pick a fight." He waved his hand around at the lab and the other occupied tables. "All of them did."

"I understand how digestion works," Ronald said. "It appears it works differently for them than it does for you."

"How does digestion work for you?" Dr. Morganton asked.

"Slowly," Ronald replied. "A single meal can last me days, if I so choose."

"Does a large one make you lethargic?" Dr. Morganton asked.

"No, not particularly," Ronald replied. "I may not be at full capacity, but it does not have a significant slowing effect."

"Then these guys are more like you that way," Gunnar said, following Dr. Morganton's lead. "Why would you eat a large meal like this?"

"If I was unsure when the next meal might be," Ronald replied. "I sometimes would do that when I knew I had a very long work session ahead of me. I would go days before eating again in order to make sure I didn't miss any observations and my data was complete."

"These guys don't look like they were getting ready for a work session," Dr. Morganton said. "Unless fighting us was the work session."

"I don't think it was," Gunnar said. "I think they were getting ready for a trip."

"A trip? Where?" Dr. Morganton asked.

"Wherever this ship could take them," Gunnar said.

"That seems plausible," Ronald agreed. "It would also explain why you all were incapacitated and not killed. Killing you would mean needing to store your bodies. Incapacitating you would keep you alive and fresh. Ready and waiting for when their bellies were finally empty enough to need refilling."

"Hold on," Dr. Morganton said. "Are you telling me you think these things, these primitives, have the intellectual ability to take over and run this ship? That is hardly believable."

"Look at me, Doctor," Ronald said. "With all you know about prehistoric hominids, would you think I would have the intellectual capabilities that I do? I am a living example of hardly believable."

"He's right," Gunnar said.

"I know I am," Ronald said.

"You two," Dr. Morganton said. "You're on the same side, remember?"

***

"Our mission was to try to recreate prehistoric biospheres as accurately as possible," Dr. Logan said. "Just on a small scale. Keep them manageable, controllable. Safe. We've all seen Jurassic Park. We knew exactly what could go wrong if we recreated things at full size."

"So you were already fucking with stuff," Kinsey said. "Making it smaller. Fighting nature. How did you expect to recreate anything if it wasn't natural to begin with?"

"Nothing on this island is natural," Dr. Logan said. "Nothing."

He swallowed hard and continued.

"Small scale, that was Ballantine's directive. Apparently, he had had issues with other programs that worked at full scale."

Kinsey snorted then waved her hand in apology. "Sorry, sorry, go on."

"Are you familiar with any of his other programs?" Dr. Logan asked, cocking his head at Kinsey. "How deep are you in with Ballantine?"

"How deep am I in?" Kinsey asked. "I'm not in jack shit with that man. If there is any depth to him then I want to stay as far away from it as possible. Ninety-five percent of what has gone wrong these past few months has been because Ballantine does not share intel. He keeps everything to himself. I don't even think Darby knows what the fuck he has planned."

"Darby is still with him," Dr. Logan stated. He shook his head. "What is it about Ballantine that instills such loyalty?"

"Don't know, don't care," Kinsey said. "Now, what the hell happened with your matrix factory?"

"Facilitator," Dr. Logan corrected.

"Yeah, I know," Kinsey replied. "I also don't care. Just finish your very long story."

"Fine," Dr. Logan said, annoyed. "Dr. Liu was running some basic tests on the equipment. Simple, run of the mill tests done every day since the facility was set up. Then the world was on fire. But it wasn't fire."

"What was it?" Kinsey asked.

"Raw energy," Dr. Logan said. "The stuff that made the Universe. Pure, raw energy. It enveloped the island. We were shielded in Alpha, but Omega wasn't. As far as we can tell, Omega was the source of the energy."

"I guessed that," Kinsey said. "I saw the ruins. That place really blew."

"No, it didn't," Dr. Logan said. "Or not yet."

"What does that mean?" Kinsey asked.

"It means that the energy surged from Omega, but didn't touch any of it," Dr. Logan responded. "Or didn't touch it any more than it touched everything else. It washed over the island like a wave. But nothing was damaged. Nothing was destroyed. Not yet."

"Get to the yet," Kinsey said.

"As soon as the energy dissipated, I sent out an advance team to check on Omega," Dr. Logan said. "They never made it there. I was talking with the team leader on his radio when he started yelling. The rest of the security team began to shout as well then the radios went dead. We tried for hours to reach them, but there was no answer."

"Did you send another team?" Kinsey asked.

"We didn't have another team," Dr. Logan said. "Stupid, I know, but this island was supposed to be safe. We were off the books, according to Ballantine, and no one knew we existed. There was almost no native animal life on the island and certainly no predators. It was why the island was picked. Safe, secure, easy to manage."

"Until the energy wave," Kinsey said.

"Exactly. Until then," Dr. Logan said. "I tried contacting Dr. Liu, but Omega wouldn't respond. I waited twenty-four hours then decided it was time to take a trip to Omega myself and find out what had happened."

"How far did you get?" Kinsey asked.

"All the way," Dr. Logan said. "I made it all the way to Omega without any trouble. Once I was there, that's when the trouble started. The staff, everyone at that facility, were changed. They weren't *Homo sapiens* any longer. They were something new. Cro-Magnon, Neanderthal, early hominid species. They pulled from it all. But they were not primitive. Primal, but not primitive. They still knew how to operate the Omega facility and were in complete control of all of its equipment."

"I am guessing they weren't still working on the research," Kinsey asked.

"No, no, not at all," Dr. Logan answered. "They were butchering my staff."

Kinsey frowned and started to open her mouth then closed. She opened it again then closed it.

"Yeah, that was my reaction," Dr. Logan said. "They had bodies, or what was left of them, strung up on the walls of Omega. Skins and meat out to dry. I knew exactly what I was seeing when I broke from the tree line and approached the facility. Everyone there stopped and looked at me. I looked at them. I saw the changes. My brain didn't put it all together right away, but it put enough together to know to turn and run as fast as I could. So I did. I ran all the way back to Alpha."

"What about the rest of the island?" Kinsey asked. "The staff at Omega changed, but what about this prehistoric jungle and the dinosaurs?"

"I got back and locked down Alpha," Dr. Logan said, as if Kinsey hadn't asked anything. "I locked us down tight. If there were research teams out in the field then they were stuck out there. I changed the facility codes and made it so no one could override my commands." He looked at her with sad eyes. "The others tried to argue with me, but when the research teams came pounding on the doors, everyone saw quickly why we couldn't open up."

"Omega followed you," Kinsey said.

"Yes," Dr. Logan said quietly. "That and the island came at us. One team was taken by the Omega folks. Everyone shouted at me to open the doors so we could go help them. I refused. The next team arrived and that's when the arguing stopped. They were bloody, they were haggard, they were exhausted from running. It was only a couple minutes after they arrived that what they were running from arrived as well."

"One of the big dinosaurs?" Kinsey asked. "With the huge heads and all the teeth?"

"It wasn't as big yet," Dr. Logan said. "But it was big enough to rip into that team and shred them in seconds. They never stood a chance. From that moment on, everything we had come here for was thrown out the window. Twenty-four seven we watched the security cameras and saw how the island environment changed and grew. Small ferns became large ferns became giant ferns. Small animals became large animals became giant animals. And the Omegas changed also."

"Wait, what do you mean it all grew?" Kinsey asked.

"It grew," Dr. Logan said. "The jungle you see out there was small scale at first, mixed in with the natural habitat. Small like it was designed to be. Then it grew and overtook everything. The biospheres we had been trying to create were let loose. They were no longer in Omega's controlled labs, but out in the wild. Everything. Animals, plants, insects, everything. From a dozen different ages and epochs. All intertwined. And the Omegas were just as intertwined. We watched them become more and more primal, their features devolving until all traces of humanity were lost. External microphones picked up how even their speech changed to something more like early man. Few words, short syntax. It was terrifying."

"Because you were waiting for it to happen to you," Kinsey stated.

Dr. Logan started at the insight then nodded. "Yes, we were. The paranoia began to take hold of everyone. Even me. With every sneeze, every twitch, every groan, we all thought the same changes would happen to us. We were safe in Alpha, but we didn't know it."

"Somebody cracked and opened the doors, right?" Kinsey asked.

"Yes. That is precisely what happened," Dr. Logan said quietly. "I woke one morning to screaming. The facility was chaos. Blood was everywhere. I have no idea how I got out, but I did. I ran and ran until I couldn't run anymore."

He waved his hands around.

"I found this cave," Dr. Logan said. "Over the next week, I also found some of my staff. I brought them here and we set up base. Food, water, basic survival were all we could think about, but once we knew we weren't going to starve, that's when I decided we needed to go on the offensive. Alpha was gone, locked back up tight. But Omega was a whole other thing."

Realization dawned on Kinsey's face. "You blew up Omega."

"Yes, but only once I realized what that facility was doing," Dr. Logan said.

"How do you mean? What was it doing?" Kinsey asked.

"It was making everything grow," Dr. Logan said. "The matrix facilitator had created the energy wave and it was still creating them, just on a sub-particle scale that couldn't be observed directly. I wanted to shut it down, but it was too far past that point. So I blew it up."

"Did that make things better?" Kinsey asked.

Dr. Logan looked down at the ground. "No. No, it didn't."

***

The Zodiac hit the beach hard. Max, Darby, and Mike rolled out onto the sand, each taking a kneeling stance, very large rifles to their shoulders. They waited a few seconds, their goggled eyes scanning the beach, the tree line, the darkness beyond. When nothing came for them, and they were sure they were alone, they stood up and moved towards what was left of the FOB they had created.

It was shredded. Everything destroyed. And defiled.

"Something shit and pissed on all this," Mike said. "Jesus. That stinks."

"Claws," Darby said. "Look at the tracks. The animals had very large claws."

"Maybe the sand just makes it look like they have very large claws," Max said, a hopeful look on his face. Darby shook her head at him and he shrugged. "I would like to believe that the sand makes it look like they have very large claws."

"You do that," Mike said.

Max sighed and muttered, "Damned fucking large claws…"

"Objective is to find any trace of the rest of Grendel," Darby stated. She nodded at her rifle. "Are you two both clear on how these work?"

"Plasma is default," Mike said. "Should punch a five-inch hole in anything a blast hits. We can switch to stun with this switch and to self-destruct with this switch."

"Max, what is self-destruct for?" Darby asked.

"For last resorts only and shouldn't be used unless absolutely necessary," Max replied.

"What's it not for?" Darby asked.

"It's not for blowing shit up just because it looks cool," Max said. "Jesus, I make one joke and suddenly I'm on a training leash."

"One joke," Mike laughed. "Right. Just the one."

"Why the hell didn't they give these to us in the first place?" Max asked, ignoring Mike. "Would have been handy the first time we set foot on this beach."

"They weren't perfected yet, according to Carlos," Mike replied. "Ballantine had to be very persuasive to get Carlos to hand them over. I gotta say as crazy as Ballantine is, watching him be persuasive is like watching art happen."

"Obscene art," Darby said and then moved towards the tree line. "I'm on point. Max, you have the rear. Mike, take center and keep your eyes open."

Max hefted the rifle and frowned. "I miss my Win Mag. This thing just feels all bulky and clumsy. Not sexy and sleek like my .300."

"If you shut up about your sniper rifle then I'll be sexy and sleek for you later," Darby said.

"That's a fucking deal," Max chuckled.

"If we live," Darby added.

"And there's the Darby I love," Max said. "Couldn't just leave it at the sexy talk, always bringing the delicate balance of our mortality into things."

"How stoned are you?" Mike asked.

"Just stoned enough," Max said.

"Silent from here on out," Darby said as she stepped into the deep shadows of the jungle. "Eyes open, ears open, mouths shut.

Kill whatever isn't friendly. No exceptions." She tapped her com. "You with us, Ballantine?"

"In your ears like a nasty, nasty worm," Ballantine chuckled. "What kind of worm would I be, I wonder?"

"Silence goes for you as well," Darby ordered. "Monitor only. Watch the beach in case hostiles try to take the Zodiac."

"I have all six senses trained on that island, Darby," Ballantine said. "Don't you worry."

"Six senses?" Max asked.

"What did I say?" Darby growled.

"Right. Sorry," Max whispered.

Darby slid further into the jungle shadows with Mike and Max right behind.

***

"So, to make sure I have this right," Kinsey said. "Freak energy wave hits the island. Probably comes from the Omega facility. It basically turns everything into a giant lab and recreates the biosphere experiments across the whole island. Except, instead of being on a small scale, the biosphere—"

"Biospheres," Dr. Logan corrected. "Multiple."

"*Biospheres*," Kinsey continued. "The biospheres grew, are still growing, and now we are dealing with dinosaurs and carnivorous plants that are larger than even the originals they are based on. Is that it?"

"Plus the cannibal mutants that used to be my colleagues," Dr. Logan said.

"Cannibals? I don't remember you saying they are cannibals," Kinsey snapped. "You said butchering, not eating."

"Didn't I? Oh, yes, well, they are cannibals," Dr. Logan said. "I apologize for leaving that out."

"Fuck me," Kinsey said.

Kinsey looked at Dr. Logan. Dr. Logan looked at Kinsey. They shifted uncomfortably for a second.

"Are you waiting for me to say something?" Kinsey asked. "Because I have no fucking clue what to say."

"I was hoping you would say you have a way off this island," Dr. Logan said.

"I might," Kinsey replied. "But we have to get to the beach. How far is it?"

"The beach? If you mean the beach at Golden Bay then not very far at all," Dr. Logan said, grinning. The grin quickly left his face. "But the beach is always watched. Either by Liu and her people or by some of the creatures. There is a pack of raptors that lives close by. They are also a lot larger than normal raptors."

"There's such a thing as normal raptors?" Kinsey asked. "Don't bother answering that. I don't care."

"There is also a different creature that has claimed the area from Omega to Golden Bay as its territory," Dr. Logan said. "We would be wise to avoid that creature."

"I think I know which one you are talking about," Kinsey said. "The mutant T-Rex looking thing? We ran into it when we first arrived at the island and went to look at the Omega facility." She looked about the cave. "Weapons?"

"Ah, yes," Dr. Logan said and shook his head. "No. No weapons. We had a pistol, but our missing colleague took it with him when he left. He wasn't supposed to."

"Leave or take the pistol?" Kinsey asked.

"Either. Neither. Both," Dr. Logan said.

Kinsey stood up and stretched. It hurt, but she ignored the pain. She studied the cave, noticed a few crates that looked suspiciously like they held weapons. But they could have held anything. That feeling like Dr. Logan had some secret, something he wasn't sharing, crept back into Kinsey's mind, but she shook it off. He was her shot out of the cave and down to the beach. A beach which held the Zodiacs.

"Let's get moving," Kinsey said.

"What? Now?" Dr. Logan asked. "It's the middle of the night."

"And we'll be harder to see during the day?" Kinsey asked.

"Well, no," Dr. Logan responded.

"Then we should use the dark while we can," Kinsey said. "We get to the beach and meet up with my teammates. If they are still there. We have rafts. We'll get you to safety and then come back here with some serious firepower, find the rest of my Team, and kill everything that gets in our way."

"It won't be that simple," Dr. Logan said.

"Never is, man," Kinsey sighed. "But whoopty fucking shit. Life isn't simple. If you want to wait for simple then you'll be dead before you've done a damn thing."

"That's pretty insightful for a soldier," Dr. Logan said.

"Fuck you," Kinsey said.

"No, I didn't mean to insult you," Dr. Logan apologized.

"Tough shit," Kinsey responded. She glared then shook her head. "You have a radio?"

"Yes, but…"

"But, what?" she asked. "Dr. Liu is monitoring?"

"We think so," Dr. Logan said. "Like I said—"

"Primal, not primitive," Kinsey said. "We bring the radio. I have a way to contact my Team without Dr. Liu knowing."

"You do?" Dr. Logan asked. "How?"

"I'm a professional, Doctor," Kinsey said. "You let me handle the soldiering. You introduce me to the others and pack up whatever supplies are useful. We move out now."

"You are a complex person, Kinsey Thorne," Dr. Logan said.

"Not really," Kinsey said and pushed past him towards the rest of the cave.

***

Thorne stared at the Liu croanderthal for several seconds. He weighed his answer very carefully. The ideal approach would be to respond in a diplomatic tone. Maybe tell her what she wanted to hear then figure out a way later to get free. But the way she studied him, the way her eyes belied an intelligence that her caveman-like features didn't, told him that bullshit would be detected instantly and that he would pay for it with his life.

"Won't happen," Thorne said finally. "Ballantine won't let you off this island. Odds are he won't let you live. You already know that. I just spent a year working operations that we thought were legit missions, but turns out were probably just Ballantine's way of cleaning up his messes. This place is a mess, but I don't think he knew that when he first brought us here."

"Ballantine always know," the Liu croanderthal said. "Now Ballantine here. Protocol. Destroy island if mess. Destroy me leader. Destroy me people. Clean up mess."

"Shit," Thorne said.

"Yes," the Liu croanderthal said. She grinned her sharp-toothed grin. "Ballantine not destroy island if you here. Ballantine not destroy me leader, me people, if you here. You make sure no destroy. You make sure me leader live. Me people live."

"Like I said, that's not going to happen," Thorne said. "It's not up to me."

"You useless," the mutant woman said. "Done talk."

"Hold on!" Thorne shouted.

Her fist hit Thorne hard between the eyes. He slumped, but didn't pass out.

"You meat," she snarled as she hit him again. Thorne went completely limp. "Stupid, stupid meat."

She dragged him to the door and the other croanderthal that had remained with her yanked it open so she could pull Thorne out into the corridor beyond. She tossed him out there and pointed at the other croanderthal.

"Kitchen," she ordered. "With others. Kill. Dress. Dry. Need food store. Ballantine no give in."

The other frowned at her. "No give in?"

"Make give in," the mutant woman growled. "Me leader. Me make Ballantine give in. Me take ship. Me leave island. Ballantine stay. Stay in mess. Die in mess. Ballantine loose end."

She lurched off down the corridor and the other croanderthal grabbed Thorne by the ankles and dragged him in the opposite direction. The long trail of dried blood on the corridor floor showed that Thorne wasn't the first body to be dragged that way. But he may have been the first living one.

Chapter Seven- Stand And Fight

After the second huge beast lumbered past, its spiked tail just missing where Mike stood pressed against a palm trunk, Max began to think the elves had actually done something miraculous. He looked down at himself and saw his usual body, his usual gear, his usual everything. Although it was tinted green by the new NVGs he wore.

What he didn't see was the cloaking effect that Carlos swore would keep them from being detected. As long as they remained still and silent in the presence of a threat. Carlos had glared at him for an extra second when he'd said those words. Max wanted to tell him to fuck off, but the guy did have a point. Unless he was in a sniper hide, he had a tendency to not be as quiet as needed on ops. Shane was the quieter of the two, which wasn't saying much.

The strange dinosaurs moved through the jungle, following a narrow trail cut through the foliage and trees by countless other species of giants. The three operators waited until they were sure the coast was clear then Darby moved back onto the path, her hand up and waving them forward. Mike fell in line behind her with Max taking the rear position.

They kept moving, plasma rifles swinging this way and that, ready for the attack they knew would happen eventually.

Max wanted to light up the whole jungle, just blast the fuck out of the trees and ferns and whatever the hell the weird swaying flowers were. And those thorn bushes. Yes, he really wanted to waste those. They looked nasty. He wanted to burn it all down and call it a day. Fuck whatever science project Ballantine had been conducting. He could care less. Seriously.

But there was the whole not knowing where the rest of the Team was and all that crap. Can't burn down the jungle if everybody was trapped in the jungle. Although, Ballantine was fairly certain he knew where they were now. Something about protocol with his researchers. He didn't elaborate, just gave Darby coordinates and made sure she understood that loose ends were not ideal. Darby had nodded at the orders, but Ballantine hadn't looked too pleased with her less than enthusiastic response.

At some point, Max knew, he would have to ask her exactly what her relationship with Ballantine was and why it seemed like she was pulling away from the mysterious bastard. Not that that was a bad thing. Distance from Ballantine was probably in everybody's best interest considering the man was a certified psychotic whacko. Max had been wondering lately whether or not Ballantine was the good guy in the scenario they had found themselves in or if he was maybe the—

He was ripped from his thoughts as a snapped twig got his attention. He did a quick snap of his fingers, which he was surprised he could do considering he was wearing the modified cloaked compression suit. He would have to let the elves know he was impressed with the tactile abilities the suit allowed. Those little tech scamps were getting better and better at their jobs.

Darby and Mike moved up next to him and he pointed off in the direction of where he heard the twig snap. There was no movement, no sign of anything out there in the thick of the jungle, despite his goggles being able to sense infrared and different light spectrums. They waited, but no sound presented itself.

Then, just before they started to move again, there was a clicking in their ears. The com. It was a short set of clicks. Not an SOS, but obviously an intentional signal. One, two, three, four.

A twig snapped again. Not once, but four times. In the exact same rhythm as the clicking over the com. Max looked at Darby and she shook her head. He grimaced and pointed at his ear then pointed out towards where the twig snaps had come from. The sounds repeated themselves, both in the jungle and over the com. Max stared through his goggles at Darby, since that was the only way to see her, until she acquiesced and nodded.

Max moved forward, one step at a time, making sure he didn't make any noise as he slipped off the path and into the thickness of the jungle. He made it about ten yards before he saw a thick grove of what he guessed were rhododendrons. Their flowers were massive, each bloom about the size of his head.

But it wasn't the flowers he was interested in, it was the heat signatures that were inside the grove, hidden behind thick leaves and fragrant blossoms. Max stopped and watched the grove then put two fingers to his lips and gave a long, low whistle. The whistle was instantly returned and he grinned, pulling up the goggles so he could see his cousin in real life, not as a green lit ghost.

"Hey, Sis," he whispered, becoming visible as he deactivated his suit. "It's good to see you guys. We thought we'd have to…"

He trailed off as instead of the rest of Team Grendel coming from between the rhododendrons, three rough looking strangers appeared behind Kinsey. Two men and a woman stood there, eyes wide and scared, body language saying they were ready to bolt and run at any second.

"This is my cousin Max," Kinsey said, whispering at the three strangers. "Max, this is Dr. Logan, Dr. Sales, and Dr. Werth. They used to work for Ballantine here on the island. Until it all went to shit."

"I don't think everything going to shit gets you out of your contracts," Max said, nodding at the three. "But we'll ask Darby on that point."

"Darby is here?" Dr. Logan asked.

Dr. Werth, a mousy-looking woman with short, bobbed black hair and skin so white it glowed in the darkness, took a few steps back. Dr. Sales, a man that had obviously weighed considerably more only a short time before, as evidenced by the hanging jowls and fleshy look to his body, grabbed Dr. Werth by the elbow and held her in place. Although, he looked about as ready to take flight as she did.

"Kinsey said Ballantine was here to help," Dr. Sales said. "Darby won't hurt us."

"I won't," Darby stated, turning off the cloaking mechanism as well. "Not my mess. Ballantine can clean up his own crap now."

"I heard that," Ballantine said over the com.

"Good," Darby said.

"Good?" Dr. Logan asked. Darby tapped at her ear. "Oh. Is that him?"

"Yes," Darby said and glanced to the side. "Dr. Logan, Dr. Werth, and Dr. Sales are here, Ballantine." She looked back at Dr. Logan. "Anyone else?"

"Not with us," Dr. Logan said.

"Let's get back to the beach and out of here," Kinsey said. "Dr. Logan can explain once we're safe on the ship."

"Where's everyone else?" Max asked.

"We don't know," Kinsey said.

"We have an idea," Dr. Logan said.

"Ask if Alpha facility is safe," Ballantine said to Darby.

"Is Alpha safe?" Darby asked.

"No," Dr. Logan replied. "Dr. Liu and her, uh, people have it. That is probably where the rest of your team are being held."

"Being held?" Mike asked, making the newcomers jump. He switched off his cloaking. "Sorry. What do you mean by being held? You know we're talking SpecOps here, right?"

"Doesn't matter," Dr. Logan said. "Dr. Liu and her kind are not like anything you have dealt with."

Max snorted. "Dude, you have no idea how wrong you are."

"Kinsey, take them to the beach," Darby said. "Get them in the raft and back to the ship." She studied Kinsey for a second and shook her head, tapping at her NVGs. "Have Gunnar check you out. You're readings don't look great."

"She was captured by a—" Dr. Logan started.

"Don't care," Darby said. "Get to the beach and back to the B3. You hear me, Ballantine?"

"I'll alert Gunnar right now that we have guests and an operator that will need full work ups," Ballantine replied. "Send them my way."

"I want to help find Grendel," Kinsey said. "Dr. Logan has told me what we are up against."

"We've already dealt with them," Darby said. She quickly recounted the beach attack as well as the fight on the ship. "We aren't taking prisoners."

"They may still be able to be helped," Dr. Werth said quietly.

No one replied.

"If Gunnar gives the okay then bring the raft back and sit tight," Darby said. "You secure the beach and wait for us to return. We'll get the rest of Grendel. I promise."

The tone in Darby's voice left no one with any doubt as to her sincerity.

"I'm coming back whether Gunnar says it's okay or not," Kinsey said.

"I figured," Darby replied. "Now, go."

She took out a 9mm from her belt and handed it to Kinsey. Max grabbed his and handed it over as well, plus two magazines. Mike started to give his up, but Kinsey shook her head.

"These'll do fine," she said.

There was a massive roar from somewhere in the jungle.

"Go!" Darby hissed.

Kinsey racked the slide on one of the 9mms and motioned for the doctors to follow her. They fell in line like ducklings and were lost from sight in seconds.

"Alpha facility is this way," Darby said. "From this point on, we don't stop."

"Lead on, hot stuff," Max said.

***

The air in the kitchen was stifling. It was thick and humid, a miasma of smells and stenches that hung over everything, choking Team Grendel as they stood against the wall, their hands bound over their heads by ropes that were hung on a row of hooks. Despite the fact that their compressions suits, and all clothing, had been removed, each member of the Team was sweating profusely, the perspiration streaming down their naked bodies in long rivulets.

Despite the oppressive temperature, the Teammates knew where the real threat lay. They did their best to ignore the discomfort of the heat and instead focused on the four mutants that worked casually at one of the kitchen tables, laying out various knives, checking their blades, sharpening the ones not up to snuff.

Darren drew his eyes from the glinting metal and glanced over at Thorne. The commander looked dazed, not from the heat, but from the quickly swelling lump on the side of his head. Whatever had struck him had done a number on the man and Darren worried that Thorne might have a serious concussion. The way the older man's eyes swam in their sockets seemed to support his fear.

"Vincent?" Darren whispered. "Hey. Vincent. You keeping it together, frogman?"

Thorne turned his head slowly and the fire that burned inside all SEALs showed itself. His eyes focused and narrowed.

"I'm keeping it together, Chambers," Thorne replied. "Don't you worry about me."

"NO TALK!" one of the croanderthals yelled. "No talk!"

"Fuck you, Lumpy Joe," Shane spat. "My friends will fucking talk if they want to fucking talk!"

The croanderthal growled and stalked over to Shane. He got right up close and grinned, his huge, sharp teeth only an inch from Shane's face. His tongue darted out quickly and licked the tip of Shane's nose then the croanderthal took a deep breath, his wide nostrils spreading even wider, become huge chasms in the mutant's face.

"Not ready," the croanderthal said and the other three at the table grunted in disappointment.

The croanderthal moved over to Thorne and sniffed, shook his head, and moved down to Lucy. Despite her body being completely naked, the mutant didn't give her a second look. At least not with his eyes. He lowered his nose to right between her breasts and breathed deeply, moving up her chest, around her neck and then nearly jammed his wide nostrils right inside her mouth.

"Close," the croanderthal said. "She close."

The three at the table grunted with approval.

"Keep your sniffer away from me," Darren protested when it was his turn to be olfactorily molested.

The croanderthal ignored him and took a long sniff up and down Darren's body. The smell seemed to please the man-thing and he stood back quickly, his hands clenching and unclenching in anticipation.

"He ready," the croanderthal said to the others. "No residue."

"Residue is a big word," Shane snapped. "Looks like someone has been watching Reading Rainbow."

The croanderthal hissed at Shane, but didn't move to harm him. Instead, he turned and took the large chef's knife that was offered to him by one of the others. He approached Darren, the blade before him, and smiled his sharp toothed smile.

"Back the fuck off, asshole!" Darren shouted.

He was about to shout again, but a hard jab by a hairy fist to his diaphragm stopped the words before he could get the breath to push them out. He gasped and struggled for breath as the croanderthal reached over him and slashed the rope holding his hands on the hook. Darren instantly collapsed to the floor, his legs and arms, nothing but pins and needles.

Two croanderthals rushed him and grabbed him under the shoulders, lifting him to his feet like he was made of straw. They dragged him over to one of the tables and tossed him up onto the cool metal. Despite the obvious danger, Darren shivered with relief at the feel of the cool stainless steel.

The relief left him quickly as the croanderthal with the chef's knife appeared over him, the tip of the blade tracing an invisible pattern from his sternum down to his groin.

"Get the fuck away from him!" Lucy yelled. "You want a piece? Come get me! What? You don't like lady meat? Come on, you fucking faggots!"

"I am totally telling Gunnar and Mike you said that," Shane whispered. "That is so not PC."

"Shane," Thorne growled.

"I was kidding," Shane said. "I know she's just pushing buttons."

The croanderthals ignored the rest of Team Grendel as the teammates shouted for Darren to be left alone. The sound of their voices faded into the background. Darren focused on the hairy, heavy faces that loomed over him. And the blade that was getting closer and closer to his skin with each breath.

"You don't want to do this," Darren said. "You really don't want to do this."

"Yes," the croanderthal with the blade said. "We want."

"Cut there," one of the other croanderthals said, pointing at Darren's belly.

"No. Scars," the croanderthal with the knife replied. "Hard cut. Tough meats. Cut out when done."

"Don't go wasting my buddy now!" Shane yelled. "You cut him up, you better use all of him!"

"Not helping!" Darren yelled.

"Mouthy one next," knife croanderthal growled. "Ready or not. He next. Shut him up."

The others nodded.

The tip of the knife nicked the skin below Darren's sternum, but he didn't react. He didn't flinch or gasp or show any sign he felt the steel cut into his skin. His eyes locked onto those of the knife croanderthal's and stayed there as the steel slid in a millimeter at a time. The thing was obviously enjoying playing with Darren and Darren wasn't going to give him the satisfaction of showing he was being played with.

"No scream like others," the knife croanderthal grumbled. "No fun."

"No fun," the others agreed one by one.

Darren saw the look on the knife croanderthal's face change and knew he was about to die. That blade was going to be thrust up under his ribcage, pierce his heart, and it would be all over from there.

Except he was saved by the bell. Or some type of alarm.

The croanderthals backed away from the table and looked towards the door. A red light flashed above it and they grunted and gnashed their teeth, anger and violence rippling through them.

Darren didn't hesitate. He knew he wasn't at peak condition, so he drew deep and brought up as much rage as he had inside him, letting it flow through his body and fuel his actions.

He sprang from the table, grabbed the knife croanderthal by the wrist, twisted the blade around, and jammed it between the thing's fifth and sixth rib, making sure it was angled correctly. The croanderthal gasped, coughed blood, then collapsed to the kitchen floor, its life gone before it hit the industrial tile.

The other croanderthals whirled around and jumped at Darren, but he had already rolled back across the table and was scrambling under it as the things came down right where he had just been. He cleared the table and pushed up onto his feet just as the croanderthals adjusted their attack, spinning about at speeds that made Darren dizzy.

"Jesus," Darren muttered as the things sprang once more.

He stumbled back, his ass bumping into a second table. He heard the clatter of metal and reached back, gasping as his fingers found a wicked sharp blade. He moved down the blade, grabbed the handle, and whipped the knife forward as a croanderthal lunged at him. Darren may not have been as good with a blade as Gunnar was, but he knew his knife skills well enough to make sure he didn't lose that one. He slashed once, twice, then threw himself over the table and rolled backwards to the other side.

The croanderthal stood there, his belly wide open and steaming intestines pooling in its hands. The two other croanderthals shouted and yelled at the sight of their ally's entrails. But neither made a move for Darren, their eyes focusing to the blade he held firmly in his right hand. Then their eyes moved to the couple of blades that rested on the table between them.

They were fast, but Darren was ready.

One reached for a sturdy-looking fillet knife, but yanked its hand back as Darren slashed it across its knuckles. The second one made its move, thinking Darren was distracted, but it howled in pain as Darren took a chunk out of its wrist.

"If you knew the games I used to play with my best friend then you'd know you can't win this," Darren sneered. "You can try, but you won't win."

The first one went for the fillet knife and Darren stabbed it right through the hand, let go of his knife, and snatched up the fillet knife. A sly smile on his face, Darren shrugged at the croanderthals in an 'I told you so' way. There was a lot of angry growling.

"Too bad you guys were so fixed on D!" Shane yelled. "Because now we're free!"

The croanderthals whipped about then roared as they saw that Shane, Thorne, and Lucy were still securely bound. They tried to turn back to Darren, but he was already up and onto the table, his fillet knife slashing out across the sides of their necks, opening their jugulars wide, sending geysers of blood spurting across the kitchen.

For good measure, Darren stabbed each in the back, piercing their lungs. The croanderthals groaned and gurgled then dropped dead to the floor, joining the other corpses.

"Nice one, Ditcher," Shane cheered.

"Really?" Darren said. "I save your asses and you still call me Ditcher?"

"Forever and always," Shane laughed. "Plus, I think I saved us with my quick thinking distraction there."

"I don't fucking think so," Darren said.

"Boys, stop comparing dicks and get us out of here," Lucy said. "Thorne has you both beat anyway."

"Grower, not a shower," Shane said. "And good for you, Uncle Vinny. A man your age should be proud to still represent."

"Fucking shut it," Thorne said. "Darren? Cut us down."

"That's what I'm doing," Darren said as he stepped past the bodies and hurried to Thorne.

He sliced the ropes then made sure Thorne wouldn't collapse before he moved to Lucy then Shane. The four of them hurried about the kitchen, naked as could be, and grabbed up whatever weapon they could find.

Thorne and Lucy each had long knives in one hand and large pot lids in their other. They held the lids like shields and moved to the kitchen doors. Shane grabbed up a meat tenderizer. It was a good-sized mallet, flat on one side and ridged on the other. He found a heavy duty, cast iron frying pan and took that in his other hand.

"D? You just gonna keep the fish sticker?" Shane asked.

"Yeah," Darren said, gripping the fillet knife tighter. "I want to have a hand free and this thing is light and fast."

"Just like your sex life," Shane replied.

"I wouldn't talk, shrinkage," Lucy said, nodding at Shane's crotch.

"I just said I was a grower not a—" Shane started, but shut up as Thorne gave him a harsh growl. He sniffed and puffed out his chest. "I got nothing to prove."

"Obviously," Lucy chuckled.

"Dammit," Shane said. "I really need my brother here to back me up."

"From what Darby has said, he has nothing to worry about," Lucy said then looked at Thorne before Shane could reply. "What's the plan, boss?"

"We don't know which way is out," Thorne said. He looked up at the flashing red light. The alarm still blared. "But I have a feeling everything in this place is heading that direction right now."

"That isn't good," Shane said.

"Depends on what the alarm is for," Thorne said. "Could be one of those giant monsters trying to get in."

"Dinosaurs, Uncle Vinny," Shane said. "They're called dinosaurs."

"Dinosaurs are extinct," Thorne said. "I'm calling them giant monsters because that's what they are."

"Whatever," Shane replied. "I'm calling them dinosaurs."

"You do that," Thorne said.

He looked at the kitchen doors then over at Darren.

"Go at this head on?" he asked.

"I think it's our only option," Darren replied. "I doubt we'll be able to do much stealth with this alarm going off."

"Head on then," Thorne said. "I'll take point. Lucy behind me, Shane then Darren at the rear." He held up his knife and pointed it at Shane. "Not a word."

"No fun," Shane muttered.

Thorne nodded to each of them as they got in position. They nodded back and he shoved through the kitchen doors.

***

"What the fuck?" Max snapped as alarms echoed through the jungle. Bright strobe lights flashed everywhere, but his goggles filtered out the debilitating effects they would have had on his eyes. "How'd they know we were here?"

"Cameras," Darby said. "They saw us coming."

"Cameras?" Max asked. "Since when do cavemen use cameras?"

"Since when do cavemen do anything?" Mike responded. "I don't think we know the rules yet."

"One rule," Darby said as she stalked towards the pile of boulders that concealed the way into the Alpha facility. "Everything can die."

She checked the reading on the side of her plasma rifle, made sure it glowed green and was ready for action, then kicked at a spot on one of the boulders. A small panel slid open and she crouched down, her fingers flying over the number pad that was revealed. The keys flashed red then green and one of the boulders started to swing outward.

"Override code worked," Darby said.

"Good to know," Ballantine replied over the com. "That means I'll have some control when you get inside. I like it when I have some control."

"I'll have the control," Darby replied. "Unless you want to come join us."

"I'm good here on the ship," Ballantine responded.

"That's what I thought," Darby replied. "Stay on the com and do not go anywhere."

"I wouldn't dream of it," Ballantine replied.

The second there was enough room to squeeze through the opening the boulder provided, Darby moved. Then she retreated quickly, her plasma rifle barking out blasts at the opening to the facility. Max and Mike backed up, their own rifles joining Darby's in the barking.

Dozens of croanderthals streamed out of the opening, brandishing clubs, knives, steel rods, and blowguns. Darby dropped three before she had to turn and run. She sprinted back towards the trees, escaping the quickly filling clearing around the boulders as fast as possible. Max and Mike were right on her heels, their rifles done with the barking.

As soon as she was in the cover of the trees, Darby turned sharply to the right and activated her suit. She shimmered for a second then was lost from sight. Mike and Max did the exact same thing, their goggles able to track Darby as she ran through the jungle, circling back around to the boulders.

To their sides, the croanderthals crashed into the foliage, ripping through ferns and small palms, tearing after enemies they could no longer see. None of them even slowed as they roared and screeched for blood. Dozens after dozens sped past and in seconds the clearing around the boulders was empty as Darby slipped inside the facility, Max and Mike right behind her.

The three of them froze and flattened themselves against the wall of the huge corridor they found themselves in as another two dozen croanderthals hurried past and out into the jungle. Darby waited until she was sure no more were coming then started walking down the corridor, her suit still active, her plasma rifle up and aimed at every shadow before her. She glanced back and got nods from Max and Mike. She noticed that the light outside was brightening and that dawn was approaching quickly. That would make things hard for Kinsey and the scientists since she knew the croanderthals were all heading to the beach. That seemed to be their default location.

Hopefully, Kinsey would get the scientists into the Zodiac and off that beach ASAP. If not then there was nothing Darby could do.

"I have eyes on Kinsey and company," Ballantine said over the com, as if reading Darby's mind. "They have just broken the tree line and are heading to the raft. We'll get them taken care of and send the raft back as soon as we can."

Darby gave a quiet grunt as an acknowledgement, very aware of how sounds seemed to carry in the metal-walled corridor.

The three operators kept moving, diving further into the belly of the Alpha facility.

***

The sun had started to come up and Ballantine watched as Kinsey squinted into the light that reflected off the bay as she and the doctors stepped from the safety of the jungle and out onto the open beach. Having anticipated the situation, he leaned on the railing outside the bridge, a sniper rifle steady in his hands, his eye to the powerful scope.

"You sure you know how to use that thing?" Lake asked, leaning against the hatchway, a cup of steaming coffee in his hands. "I'd hate for you to take out our Kinsey because you're a bit rusty."

"I maintain my skills just like everyone else on this ship, Captain Lake," Ballantine replied, his eye never leaving the scope, his hands relaxed around the grip and stock of the rifle. "And to answer your question specifically, yes, I know how to use this thing."

"Okay," Lake said. "I sure as hell hope so. I wouldn't want to be you if you fuck up. Thorne will destroy your ass."

"That is debatable," Ballantine chuckled. "But I plan on avoiding any reason to prove that."

"There," Ingrid said from inside the bridge. "I finally have the console back up and running. We still don't have functional engines, but at least we have active sonar and radar."

Lake twisted around, but stayed leaning on the hatchway, and looked over at where Ingrid stood with a heavy tool belt and several devices and tools that Lake didn't recognize strewn across the bridge's floor.

"We may be a sitting duck out here, but at least we aren't a blind sitting duck," Lake said. "Thanks, Ingrid."

"No problem," Ingrid said. She stifled a yawn with her hand which held a thick screwdriver.

"Go get some sleep," Lake ordered. "We'll handle the island."

"Are you sure?" Ingrid asked. "Carlos wanted me back in the Toyshop as soon as I was done here."

"Go sleep," Ballantine said from the railing. "Take an hour. If we need you, you will know it. If we don't then when you wake up go tell Moshi to do the same thing."

"What about Carlos?" Ingrid asked.

Ballantine gave an almost imperceptible shrug.

"I swear. You two need to make up," Ingrid said. "You're nicer to me than to him and I betrayed you all." She blushed at the admission and started to speak, but Lake held up his hand.

"We've all yelled at you for that enough," Lake said. "Frankly, the subject bores the shit out of me. Go grab some shut eye."

Ingrid smiled and nodded, gathered up her tools, and hurried from the bridge. Lake watched her go then turned back to Ballantine.

"Why do you bust Carlos's balls so much?" Lake asked. "Every time I think you two are getting along, you get grumbly with him. The guy is an ass, but so are most of us on this ship."

"Would you prefer we hugged it out, Captain?" Ballantine asked. "That we held hands and sang happy campfire songs instead?"

"Fuck and you, Ballantine," Lake said and slipped back into the bridge. He walked over to a thermos, popped it open, and poured fresh coffee into his mug. "You want any coffee, smart ass?"

"I'm fully caffeinated," Ballantine said. "But thank you for asking. Courtesies like that go a long way."

"A long way to what?" Lake asked.

"Making it all worth it," Ballantine responded.

"If you say so," Lake said and sat down in his captain's chair. He smiled at the readings that blinked, flashed, and shown in front of him, glad to have his console operational again.

The smile left his face quickly and he leaned forward.

He was about to alert Ballantine to what he saw, but he stopped when the sniper rifle cracked.

"Shit," he swore as he got up and hurried outside the bridge to see what Ballantine was shooting at.

***

Kinsey felt the shot more than she heard it as the bullet whizzed by her head. There was a wet thunk and a loud grunt as she whirled about to see one of the croanderthals toppling to the sand, his head mostly gone. Dr. Werth screamed and Kinsey spun around to see two more croanderthals have their heads blown to bits of brain and bone.

"Come on!" Kinsey shouted, grabbing Dr. Werth by the elbow and yanking her towards the Zodiac that sat waiting in the beach. "Hurry!"

"Someone is shooting at us!" Dr. Werth screeched.

"Bullshit!" Kinsey yelled. "Someone is shooting around us! Now move!"

She wondered who was making the shots since the Grendel snipers were otherwise occupied in the jungle and in the Alpha facility. She didn't waste too much time on the musing and looked back to make sure Drs. Logan and Sales were following closely. They were.

So were several dozen croanderthals as a mob broke from the jungle and came right for them.

"Shit," Kinsey muttered. "We aren't going to have much time."

She shoved Dr. Werth at the Zodiac then stopped and faced the croanderthals, both pistols up and aimed at the mob.

"Get the raft in the water!" she yelled at Dr. Logan. "Start the motor!"

"What about you?" Dr. Logan shouted, but did not slow down.

"I'll buy us some time!" Kinsey called after him. "Don't worry about me!"

Kinsey didn't wait to see how the scientists handled the raft. Her focus was on the mob that was quickly closing the distance.

She opened fire, barely even thinking about her aim. She knew the shooter on the ship was still helping as more heads exploded where she wasn't pointing. Whoever it was, they had adjusted their sights to take out the ones starting to flank Kinsey, making sure the mob didn't surround her.

There were fifteen cartridges in each 9mm. Kinsey made sure that all thirty shots counted as she methodically squeezed the triggers over and over. Not every shot was a kill shot, but they all did the job and dropped a croanderthal. Then her 9mms clicked empty and she took a deep breath as what was left of the mob reached her.

The first croanderthal swung an axe at her head. It was an actual axe, a red and silver fire axe yanked from the wall of Alpha. Kinsey noticed how shiny the blade was as it missed her nose by only an inch. As the croanderthal's momentum took the axe past her, Kinsey slammed a pistol into the thing's face, cracking its wide nose, and then followed that with a blow to the thing's throat with the second pistol.

The mutant dropped, choking and gagging, and Kinsey put the toe of her boot right in its temple. Only when it was flat on its back and out did Kinsey see it was a woman. She couldn't have given a shit.

A croanderthal about to throw a heavy pipe at her stumbled back a couple steps as its chest was ripped open by sniper fire. Then its head became mist and the corpse stood there for a second, arm and pipe raised, before collapsing into the sand.

Kinsey dove and rolled to the side as a croanderthal swung a heavy club down at the spot where she had been standing. She lost one of the pistols to the fine beach sand, but that freed up a hand to grab a magazine from her belt and slam it into the remaining pistol. Fifteen more shots were at the ready as she racked the slide and jumped back up onto her feet.

A croanderthal went headless and skidded to a stop a foot in front of her as three more rushed her position. Kinsey took those three down and was about to whirl to her left, instinct telling her trouble was coming, but she barely got turned before the pistol was knocked from her grip. Her forearm sang with pain as a heavy club impacted through the compression suit, nailing bone.

Kinsey immediately ducked and struck out with a sweeping kick, knocking the attacker to the sand. She kicked again, connecting with the croanderthal's face, but the thing was able to recover and roll away, club still in hand. Kinsey scrambled to grab the fallen pistol, but there were too many croanderthals coming at her and being on the ground was not a defensible position.

She moved hand over hand, her feet sliding under her, as she retreated towards the Zodiac. The air cracked around her as bullets flew from ship to beach, but she didn't stop to see what kind of damage they did. Grunts and yelps of pain told her that at least some of the bullets were finding marks. But several loud growls and grunts also told her there were plenty of marks on her ass as well.

"Come on!" Dr. Logan yelled as the Zodiac bobbed in the waves a few yards from shore. "Run!"

Kinsey swallowed the nasty response she wanted to shout. The man wasn't a pro like her and didn't know that coming on and running were pretty much what she was trained to do. She dug deep, careful that her feet didn't slip out from under her as she sprinted across the beach, and headed for the water

She pushed thoughts of what things were in the water out of her head as she dove into the surf. She stroked hard and fast, closing the distance between her and the Zodiac in a matter of seconds. Hands reached out and grabbed her, yanking her up into the raft.

"Go!" she yelled as she fell to her back onto the bottom of the Zodiac. "Go, go, go!"

"More," Dr. Sales said, some of the few words Kinsey had heard him speak since meeting him. "How?"

Kinsey looked up at the scientist, her eyes squinting into the ever brightening sky, and frowned. That's when it hit her that there were way too many croanderthals on that beach. If the staff of the Omega facility had changed, transformed into those things, then there should have only been a couple dozen total on the whole island. There were more than that lying dead on the beach.

"Anything you guys want to tell me before we get to the ship and Ballantine has a chat with you?" Kinsey asked. "Because if you've been lying to me then I can't help you once Ballantine gets his hooks into you. And trust me, he will get his hooks into you."

Drs. Werth and Sales looked at Dr. Logan as he piloted the craft towards the B3. He frowned and sighed, but didn't offer any information.

"Okay," Kinsey said. "Don't say I didn't warn you."

***

"Well, that was fun," Ballantine chuckled as he stepped into the cool shadows of the bridge and set the sniper rifle aside. "Remind me to join the Reynolds and Lucy the next time they practice shooting. I missed a lot more targets than I would have cared to."

He saw the look on Lake's face as the captain stared at the radar screen on the ship's control console.

"Right," Ballantine sighed. "You were calling to me about something."

"That," Lake said, pointing to a blip. "It's heading right for us."

"Is it now," Ballantine said.

He stood next to Lake and the two men studied the blip, watching its progress across the green and black screen. After a minute, Ballantine rubbed his face and looked up at the ceiling of the bridge as if to ask why him.

The sound of the approaching Zodiac drew the attention of both men to the bridge windows.

"Go help winch them up," Ballantine said.

"We have crew for that," Lake said as he saw two members of the crew already running towards the winches.

"I need space to think," Ballantine said.

"My bridge," Lake replied.

"Not debating that, Captain," Ballantine responded. "But do you know what is coming for us?"

"Nope," Lake said. "And I sure as fuck won't learn by helping winch up the Zodiac."

"I'm asking as a favor," Ballantine said.

"Fine," Lake grumbled as he got up and walked out of the bridge. "Next time I won't agree, Ballantine."

"Noted," Ballantine called after Lake, his eyes never leaving the constant blip.

It was good-sized, probably a ship close to the Beowulf's dimensions, maybe bigger, if the radar was correct.

"Darby? We have company coming," Ballantine said. "Extract and get back here ASAP."

"That is the plan, Balla—"

Darby's voice cut out and a loud squeal ripped into Ballantine's ear before he killed the com.

"That is not good," Ballantine said to himself. "None of this is good."

He looked up at the ceiling again and stuck his tongue out.

Chapter Eight- Running In Circles

Sadly, or fortunately, it was not the first time Darren had to engage in combat while stark naked. So he was prepared for the awkwardness of having his dick hanging loose while two croanderthals came at him. Despite the risk, Darren did exactly what he did the last time he had to fight in the nude.

He thrust out his hips and waggled his dick at the attackers.

"Come for a piece of this, boys?" he called out in a high falsetto.

Both croanderthals stopped in their tracks, eyes wide and confused as Darren walked casually towards them. It was too late for them to recover by the time Darren was close enough to get to work with his fillet knife. The two croanderthals fell to the floor, blood spilling from their necks as Darren spun about to see how the others were doing.

Pretty damn well, by the looks of it.

Shane slammed his mallet and frying pain on either side of a croanderthal's head so hard that one of the thing's eyes popped right from its socket. Shane drew the mallet back quickly and let it fly once more, dropping the croanderthal to the floor. Blood poured from the thing's crushed skull and Shane blew him a kiss as he stepped over the corpse.

Lucy shoved two croanderthals back with the pot lid and slashed out with her knife. One of the croanderthals slipped on a pool of blood and kicked out with his foot as he fell, nailing Lucy in the knee. She cried out and fell as well, but not before thrusting her knife up and out, catching the other croanderthal in the chest. The thing screamed and stumbled back, taking the knife with it. Lucy swore under her breath, lifted the pot lid up over her head, and brought it down hard onto the fallen croanderthal that had kicked her.

The thing's ribs cracked like gunshots, over and over, until it lay there, suffocating from its pulverized chest and lungs. Bright red bubbles of bloody spittle coated its face and Lucy grimaced at the thing as she stood up, careful of her tender knee. She spat on the thing then went and retrieved her knife from the chest of the other croanderthal. It took some tugging, having gotten wedged between two ribs, but she managed to get it free and wiped the blade clean on the tattered remains of the thing's pants.

Standing next to a pile of corpses, Thorne smacked his knife against his pot lid to get Team Grendel's attention.

"Move," he ordered. "We have no idea where the exit is and we won't ever find it if we keep standing around staring at the dead."

"I gotta catch a breather," Shane said then shook his head and smiled at the look Thorne gave him. "Just kidding, just kidding. I am good to go."

"Better be," Lucy said, smacking his naked ass with the flat of her knife.

"Ow," Shane complained as he tried to look back and see if there was a mark. "Damn. That fucking hurt."

Darren shook his head and moved up next to Thorne.

"The fact we haven't seen any stairs or elevators is starting to weird me out," Darren said.

"You noticed that too?" Thorne asked. "Hard to believe there is only one level. But then Ballantine never ceases to surprise me. I wouldn't put it past him to have this facility spread out over half the island."

"Under half the island," Shane said. "We're underground. I can smell it. If there is only one level then it stretches under the jungle for a very long ways."

"But only one way in and one way out?" Lucy asked. "Doesn't make sense. What about emergencies or fires?"

"Fires count as emergencies," Shane said.

"So does that toothpick dick of yours," Lucy replied.

"Damn! You are not letting up!" Shane exclaimed.

"Nope," Lucy said. "When will I get another chance to make fun of your junk? I'll take every cheap shot I can get in."

"I'll give you a cheap shot," Shane said and grinned. Then frowned. He hung his head. "I wish Max was here."

"Do you?" Max asked, suddenly shimmering into sight as he came around the corner, his plasma rifle glowing at the end of the barrel. "That is so damn sweet, bro. I would hug you, but, uh, you don't have any clothes on. Um…none of you do. Hey, guys? What happened to your clothes?"

"Doesn't matter," Darby said, joining him. She was covered from head to toe in bright blood while Mike, who came up only a few feet behind her, looked spotless. Everyone stared. "What?"

"Turns out that plasma blasts don't blast things as much as they pop things," Max said, grinning from ear to ear. "It is so cool to watch."

"Fuck you, Maxwell," Darby said.

"Let me see one of those," Thorne insisted.

All eyes turned from Darby to Max.

"Ah, man," Max whined. "Why you gotta take all my toys, Uncle Vinny?"

He reluctantly handed the plasma rifle over to Thorne. Thorne hefted it, turning it over this way and that in his hands then sighted down the barrel. He nodded and gave it back to Max.

"Yay," Max said. "Toy is back!"

"You have an extra one of those for your favorite brother?" Shane asked Max.

"Where the fuck would I have an extra one?" Max replied.

"Shoved up your ass," Shane replied.

"Just because you hide your clothes in your butt, doesn't mean I'm hiding a plasma rifle in mine," Max said. "I don't play those assdeer games."

"Nothing wrong with a little anal play every once in a while," Lucy said.

It was the Team's turn to stare at her. She just put her hands on her hips and stared back.

"Okey doke," Max said. "On that note…"

"How are we not all dead?" Thorne mumbled.

"Because I'm here to save your asses," Darby said. "Exit is this way."

She turned to go back around the corner then stopped.

"Fuck," she said, backing away from the corner.

Mike looked over his shoulder and frowned.

"Where the hell are they all coming from?" he asked, backing up with Darby.

"I don't know, I don't care," Darby said. "Everyone get behind us. Move to the end of the corridor. This is going to get messy."

Darby, Max, and Mike were halfway down the corridor when the first wave of croanderthals hit the corner and came screaming at them, a multitude of weapons raised and ready for battle.

That first wave never made it more than three feet before they were obliterated and turned into flesh chunks splattered against the walls.

"Come on!" Darby called.

Team Grendel followed her around the corner then skidded to a stop. Their way was blocked by a hundred croanderthals. At least.

They swung around to go back towards the kitchen, but that corridor was suddenly filled by another hundred croanderthals.

"Where are they coming from?" Shane asked.

"Deeper," Thorne growled as he turned and ran the only way that wasn't blocked by sneering, hissing, grunting enemies. "We have to go deeper!"

"No," Darby snapped at Max.

"Come on," Max whined. "It was so easy. He set it up perfectly."

"No," Darby said again.

"Your girlfriend is a total joke kill, bro," Shane said.

"So is your dick, Reynolds," Darby said.

"That's my girl!" Lucy said and raised her hand. "High five on that." Darby smacked it as she sprinted past.

***

Ballantine walked into the infirmary, his hand held out, a big smile on his face.

"Will, it is good to see you safe and sound," Ballantine said as Dr. Logan, Dr. Sales, and Dr. Werth all sat on exam tables while Gunnar moved back and forth from each, taking blood samples and checking their vitals. "I can only imagine what a nightmare you have been put through."

"Ballantine," Dr. Logan said, shaking the man's hand. "It certainly has been a nightmare."

"I am sure," Ballantine said. "My apologies for not meeting you on the deck, but there is a situation that has come up."

"Situation?" Kinsey asked as she leaned against the far wall. "What situation? Have you found the rest of Team Grendel?"

"Sorry to say, we have not," Ballantine replied. "But Darby, Max, and Mike are on that right now, as you know."

"I'm done here," Kinsey said. "I'm taking the Zodiac back and going to join them."

"Not yet," Ballantine said. "I need a word with you in a minute. Would you mind waiting up on the bridge?"

Kinsey began to protest, but Ballantine gave her a look that stopped the words before she could speak them. She nodded and left the infirmary.

"Those Thornes sure are emotional," Ballantine said, grinning at Dr. Logan. "So, Will, fill me in on what happened."

The doctor did. He told everything to Ballantine as he had to Kinsey. Ballantine stood there and took it all in, nodding at the appropriate times, acting shocked at other times, making sure he looked mournful at the mention of the lives lost.

It was a sad story and Ballantine felt bad about it. Felt responsible. Felt like it was entirely bullshit.

"You're lucky to be alive, Will," Ballantine said. "All of you are. And you say that Dr. Chen disappeared and you have no idea where he is?"

"None," Dr. Logan replied. "He was gone the other morning and we haven't seen him since."

"So sad," Ballantine said. "So, so sad." He glanced over as Gunnar was studying a blood sample under a microscope. "Dr. Peterson? May I have a word in the corridor?"

"Right now?" Gunnar asked. "I'm in the middle of—"

"Won't take long," Ballantine insisted.

"Fine," Gunnar nodded. He nodded to his new patients. "I'll be right back."

"Take your time," Dr. Logan chuckled. "We aren't going anywhere."

Ballantine gestured for Gunnar to follow him. He closed the hatch to the infirmary as they stepped into the passageway

"Is that necessary?" Gunnar asked.

"Yes, if I want to make sure they can't hear me," Ballantine said. "Let's step aside so they can't read our lips through the porthole."

"Seriously?" Gunnar replied. "Have you gone nuts? These people have been surviving in a jungle cave for weeks and weeks. Because one of your many secret projects went boom. What could you possibly have against them?"

"That is not Will Logan," Ballantine said. "I know Will Logan. I have known him a very long time. That is not him."

Gunnar stared at Ballantine then started to peer through the porthole into the infirmary, but Ballantine grabbed him by the shoulder and yanked him back.

"A little discretion would be appropriate at this time," Ballantine said. "I would rather we didn't tip them off that we know their secret."

"But that looks like Dr. Logan, right?" Gunnar asked. "It's not some stranger pretending? It's actually someone with Dr. Logan's face?"

"Exactly," Ballantine said.

"Okay. Just wanted to clear that up so I know what we're dealing with," he said. Gunnar was silent for a second. "Uh…what are we dealing with?"

Ballantine clapped Gunnar on both shoulders. "That's what you get to find out. Doesn't that sound like fun?"

"You do know that I have only maybe ten percent of the equipment I need to do any sort of analysis, right?" Gunnar grumbled. "The rest is fried and the elves haven't had time to fix any of it."

"Then go use their equipment," Ballantine said. "They have redundancies of most of the machines you need down in the Toyshop. They probably have things that work even better than what is broken in your lab. Of course, anything will work better than broken machines." Ballantine chuckled at his own joke. "Ah, broken machines. The sorrow of our age."

"You are so fucked up," Gunnar said.

"As you constantly remind me, Gun," Ballantine chuckled. "And I thank you for that. It's good for me to hear. I think it's why I like you and Team Grendel so much, plus all the crew on the Beowulf III. You never cease to hand me my ass when you feel like it. Others have always kissed my ass, even my most dangerous enemies. You guys? Never. Refreshing."

"Glad I could be of help," Gunnar said then looked at the infirmary hatch. "What do I do with them while I'm in the Toyshop figuring out who they are?"

"Leave them here while I go talk to Kinsey on the bridge," Ballantine suggested. "I'll be right back and they'll stay put like good little doctors."

"You want them here? Unsupervised?" Gunnar asked.

"No one is unsupervised on this ship," Ballantine said.

"God, you really know how to turn up the creep," Gunnar said. "Fine. I'll show them down there and then go see the elves about some working equipment."

"Good man," Ballantine said, clapping him on the shoulders again. "The second you have any insight, please come find me."

"Where will you be?" Gunnar asked as Ballantine walked off.

"On the bridge with Kinsey and Lake," Ballantine said. "Watching our company get closer."

"Okay," Gunnar said and reached for the infirmary hatch. Then he stopped and turned quickly. "Hold the fuck on. Did you say we have company? What company?"

Ballantine just gave him a wave and walked up the steps towards the bridge.

***

Team Grendel turned left so many times that Thorne thought they had to be going in circles, but with every turn came a new corridor, one he knew they hadn't been in because Darby had been making sure to mark each corner with some of the blood and gore that stuck to her suit. It left a trail for the croanderthals to follow, but it also kept them from returning to corridors they had already gone through.

But that many lefts without going in a circle made no sense.

None of what they had been through made any sense. Dinosaurs, both small and gigantic, living cavemen/cavewomen, a massive hidden island that Ballantine was certain couldn't be found, basically everything they had been through as a Team for the last two years.

It was all madness in the making.

"Stop," Thorne said. "Just stop."

Everyone slowed up and turned to the commander. Darby was obviously itching to keep moving, but even she stopped and waited to see what Thorne wanted.

"Does any of this feel right to you?" Thorne asked, making eye contact with each Team member as he caught his breath. "We should have found a way out by now. Why haven't we? And why are we always turning left?"

"We're crossing the island," Darby said. "These corridors are scorched. You can smell it."

"She's right," Shane said, tapping his nose. "I could smell the damp of being underground, but there is something else. What is it?"

"Fire," Darby said. "These walls have just been burned. Something very hot happened here and I have an idea I know what. We keep turning left because we are skirting the island."

"They herded us this way," Thorne said. "Why?"

No one had an answer.

"Their leader, that woman," Thorne said. He snorted at calling the Liu croanderthal a woman. "She wanted my help. She wanted to make a deal to get her and her people off this island. I told her Ballantine wouldn't allow that. Loose ends. She knew what I meant."

"Ballantine doesn't care about these loose ends," Darby said. "These loose ends are insignificant to what else is out there."

Everyone waited for her to continue, but Darby only stood there. Max cleared his throat.

"Um, deadly death muffin, I think you need to elaborate," Max said.

"All of this is not a loose end," Darby said. "It was supposed to be a new beginning. A refuge for us to rest up in until we were at full strength."

"Full strength for what?" Thorne asked.

"The real mission," Darby said. "Wiping every one of Ballantine's enemies off the face of this planet. There's a few of them, so we really needed the rest."

"But we ended up at the island that time forgot instead," Shane said. "And naked, I may add. Awesome."

"Great story," Thorne said. "One I'll revisit with Ballantine later. But for now, none of that helps us get out of here."

"No, it doesn't," Darby said. "But neither does standing still. If you will shut up and follow me, I'll get us out of here."

"How?" Thorne asked. "Do you know where we're going?"

"I have an idea, yes," Darby said. "The smell tells me a lot, but the fact that woman wanted your help and is sending us this way then I think I know why."

"We're going to that other facility, aren't we?" Shane asked. "The one that blew up and was being squatted on by the giant T-rex-looking motherfucker."

"I believe so," Darby said. "But we'll only find out if we keep going." She looked to Thorne. He nodded. "Come on. We can't slow down."

*　*　*

Kinsey did not like the look of the blip on the radar screen. Sure, it was only a green dot that showed up every couple seconds when the equally green line rotated past it, but it was still a green dot where Ballantine had assured them there would be no green dots.

"What is it?" Kinsey asked. "A ship?"

"Yes," Ballantine said. "A good-sized one."

"How can you tell that?" Kinsey asked.

"Ingrid got it all working," Lake said, pointing to a computer monitor that was streaming data. "The system is analyzing the radar and calculating what type of vessel it could be. Right now it looks like it's about twice the size of the B3."

"Military?" Kinsey asked.

"Can't tell," Lake said. "Not enough info yet. When it gets closer, we'll know for sure."

"If it gets close enough, we can just look through the binoculars and tell for ourselves," Kinsey said. She glanced at Ballantine. "But I'm guessing you don't want it to get that close first, do you?"

"I do not," Ballantine said. "Which is what I need you for. I'd like you and Ingrid to take the mini-sub and go have a closer look. You can drive while she takes readings and surveils the craft."

"Mini-sub? What fucking mini-sub?" Kinsey asked. "Marty? Since when do we have a mini-sub again?"

"Fuck if I know," Lake sighed. "I'm only the captain of this goddamned ship."

"Oh, stop being such a baby," Ballantine said. "I had the elves fix one up. It's not the same as the Wiglaf was since we don't have the manufacturing capabilities to put something that large together. But it'll do the job."

Kinsey thought about how cramped their former mini-sub had been before it was lost to the ocean depths because of one of their many encounters with giant sharks. There wasn't exactly a lot of elbow room in that thing.

"You'll be fine," Ballantine said, seeing Kinsey's hesitancy. "All you have to do is get it close enough for Ingrid to get as much info as possible then come back here on the double. I'm taking as much of a risk as you are."

"How's that?" Kinsey asked.

"Well, for starters, that man down there isn't Dr. Will Logan," Ballantine said. "I don't know who it is, but it's not Will."

"What are you talking about?" Kinsey asked.

"Why even ask anymore?" Lake said and reached down to open a mini-fridge by his feet. He pulled out a beer and popped the can, took a long drink, and sat in his captain's chair. "At least Ingrid fixed the fridge too. Nice."

"How can you drink when Ballantine just said we have strangers on board?" Kinsey asked.

"Seems like the perfect time to drink," Lake said. "And when don't we have strangers on board? As far as I can tell, this ship has

an open invitation to assholes. Present company included." He
looked right at Ballantine.

"Thank you," Ballantine smirked.

Kinsey's shoulders sagged and she looked out the bridge
towards the island.

"We'll find them and get them back to the ship in one piece,"
Ballantine said. "But to do that, I need to know what's coming at
us so *we* can stay in one piece. If it is military then we are horribly
out gunned. If it is something else then we may be out gunned in
other ways."

"You aren't doing much to boost my mood, Ballantine," Kinsey
said.

"It's not a mood, it's an adventure," Ballantine said and winked.
He clapped his hands together. "Alright. Good talk. You can find
Ingrid in the specimen bay waiting for you. I'm going to go get
Ronald and ask for his assistance with my interrogation of the
doppelgangers. Captain Lake? Do you need anything before we
get too busy?"

"Got beer," Lake said, holding up the can. He reached down to
a shelf and pulled out a Desert Eagle. "Got pistol. Get lost."

"As you wish," Ballantine said. He pointed at the radar screen.
"Keep an eye on that."

"Aye, aye, asshole," Lake said.

"He really doesn't like you," Kinsey said to Ballantine as the
two left the bridge.

"What do you mean?" Ballantine asked. "That guy loves me."

***

The corridor finally came to an end and Team Grendel
gratefully stopped to catch their breath. They leaned against the
soot-covered walls, coughing at the acrid taste of the air. Darby
started searching the wall at the end of the corridor for a latch or
some mechanism that would open a door for them. After a few
minutes, she gave up and kicked the bottom the wall as hard as she
could.

"That couldn't have felt good," Max said.

"Wasn't supposed to," Darby said.

"Com still out?" Shane asked.

Darby tapped at her ear and nodded. "Went out almost as soon as we entered the facility. They must have a jamming device in place. Makes sense. They'd want to limit outside interference as they take sensor readings."

"Sensor readings of what?" Lucy asked. "I still don't know what this island is."

Darby narrowed her eyes then shrugged. "Fuck it. I'll tell you what I know."

She proceeded to fill them in on the purpose of the island. The experiments performed, the scientists and researchers hired to perform those experiments, and the reason Ballantine decided they should come to the island in the first place.

"It's shielded? Like cloaked?" Shane asked.

"The same as our new suits?" Max asked

"Wait, what?" Shane responded, looking at Max's suit. "That's not just a compression suit?"

"Nope," Max said. "It cloaks us so we blend into our surroundings. Bends light and other sciencey shit."

"Dude," Shane exclaimed. "I thought I was just trippin' when you showed up."

"There's a generator on this island that powers a device that keeps this entire place hidden from satellite and other electronic surveillance," Darby said.

"Then how could we see it when we showed up?" Max asked.

"Are your eyes electronic?" Darren asked. "Pay attention."

"I wish my eye was electronic," Shane said, tapping his eye patch.

"X-ray," Max said.

"Totally," Shane agreed.

"Shut the fuck up, you two," Darren said then frowned at Thorne. "Sorry. I should have let you say it."

"They sure as fuck don't listen to me," Thorne said.

"Ah, come on, Uncle Vinny," Max smirked. "We listen, we just don't do what you say."

"Yeah, we are totally listening," Shane said.

Darby pointed at the Reynolds. "Do I have to castrate you boys?"

"Listening and shutting up," Max said.

"Totally shutting up," Shane said.

"This island is beyond off the books," Darby said. "Part of Ballantine's personal holdings. He has slowly been amassing them over the years."

"Them? How many fucking islands does he have?" Max asked.

"I didn't say his holdings were all islands," Darby said. "But there are a few more. This was supposed to be the safest. We rest here then start striking. Didn't work out that way. Never fucking does with that man."

"Chaos junkie," Thorne said. "I've learned a lot about junkie behavior. He shows it in spades."

"In spades. That saying has always—" Shane started then screamed and dropped to his knees, his hands covering his crotch.

"Keep going," Lucy said.

"Did you just flick him in the dick?" Darby asked.

"Yes," Lucy said.

"Nice," Darby said and smiled. The smile lasted one second. "Ballantine has been walking a razor's edge for a long time. He needed Team Grendel to keep him on that edge. First to clean up the giant sharks that had gotten loose. Then to deal with some of the various mistakes made by South American regimes. Finally to wipe out the last bits of his past. He broke from the company a long time before he put this Team together."

"They have been hunting him all this time?" Thorne asked.

"Hunting Ballantine?" Darby laughed. It was a terrifying sound. "He's been hunting them. The company is a broken shambles."

"But I heard him talking to a man on the inside," Thorne said. "Back on the beach in American Samoa. He was pretty upset that he had been cut off. He even told us as much."

"He told you what he wanted you to hear," Darby said. "Ballantine lies. About everything. The only truth with him is that he never tells the truth."

"Why are you saying this?" Darren asked. "What's the point of telling us now?"

"Because he can't keep it going without getting some or all of us killed," Darby said. "And I like you people. I like being part of this Team. I don't want any of you to die."

She grinned wide and it was genuine.

"Plus, look at you idiots," Darby chuckled. "Half of you are naked and holding kitchen tools as weapons. You really fucking need my help."

"So, what do we do after this?" Shane asked. He stood up and made sure he was as far away from Lucy as he could get. "If we live through this shit and get off this island, then what?"

"Then we have a chat with Ballantine," Darby said. "And things change."

"You ever going to tell us all of your story?" Thorne asked. "Where you came from and why you have been so loyal to Ballantine?"

"You ever going to tell me all the pain in your life, Commander?" Darby responded. "Just going to lay your soul out on the table for everyone to poke at?"

"Good point," Thorne said. "I just need to know I can trust you."

Darby nodded then walked up to Max, grabbed him by the back of the head, and kissed him long and hard. There was no doubt that she wasn't faking her passion for the Reynolds brother.

"You can trust her," Max said when Darby finally broke away and he could catch his breath. "That's not Little Max talking. She's legit."

"Fine," Thorne nodded and held out his hand. "Let's make this formal. Welcome to the family."

Darby took his hand and shook it.

"Now, I need to keep looking for a way through this wall," Darby said.

"I guess I'm the only one that isn't family in some way," Lucy said. "Max and Shane are brothers. Darby is with Max. Thorne is their uncle. Darren was married to Kinsey who is Thorne's daughter. All family."

"You flicked my dick," Shane said. "You count as family." He cupped his crotch again. "But don't do it again, okay?"

Lucy gave him a wink then walked over to help Darby.

***

The mini-sub looked like a sleek missile that tapered from the front to the back. It was nothing like the bulky yellow mini-sub they used to have. Kinsey eyed it warily as it bobbed up and down in the water that filled half the specimen bay at the belly of the B3.

"We're going to be ass to nose in there," Kinsey said as Ingrid set a case down on the deck next to her. "How will we even move?"

"Not ass to nose," Ingrid said. "Belly to back. You'll be underneath piloting the sub and I'll be basically right on top of you taking readings. There's a metal grate between us, so I won't be literally right on top of you."

"Not that that wouldn't be nice to see," Carlos said.

"Did you just go there?" Kinsey asked as she turned on the tech. "Do you want to die that badly?"

"It was a joke," Carlos grumbled. "No need to get pissy. All the crap you operators put me through and you can't take one joke. You guys are always joking. It's all you ever do is joke."

"Make it funny next time," Kinsey said. "Better yet, how about there just not be a next time?"

"Get in the sub," Carlos said and then flinched at the look he received from Kinsey. "Please."

"You're fucking A right please," Kinsey said.

She stepped onto the narrow plank that led from the deck to the back of the mini-sub where a very small hatch stood open. It took her a second to get across the plank then wiggle down through the hatch and into the sub. It became very obvious that Ballantine did not intend any of the men to pilot the sub. It was only big enough for her or Darby.

Kinsey worked her way through a thin slot in the grate that separated the two levels of the sub and lay down on her belly in front of the meager control station. Ingrid climbed in after her and settled on the grate above.

"I'm locking us down," Ingrid said as she closed the hatch and turned the wheel until it was sealed. "Carlos is already starting the purge process."

"He is?" Kinsey asked. "I don't even know how to pilot this yet."

"Oh, it's simple," Ingrid said. "Basically the same as the other mini-sub. Steering is there. Throttle is there. You'll figure it out on the go. The real reason Carlos is purging already is he has to open the bay doors manually and then he'll have to pump out the excess water manually once we're gone."

"Oh, shit, really?" Kinsey laughed. "Maybe I shouldn't have been so hard on him."

"It's not like he has to do it by himself," Ingrid said. "Cougher and some of the crew are helping."

"Oh, then fuck him," Kinsey replied.

"Yeah, fuck him," Ingrid laughed.

Ingrid pointed out what everything did and Kinsey settled into her spot as they felt the sub start to move back and forth.

"Specimen bay is flooded," Ingrid said. "Doors are open. We can leave whenever you are ready."

Kinsey stared out the small window that sat over the control console. She aimed for the open water, pushed the throttle forward, made sure her rudders were straight, and piloted the sub out of the B3.

"What's this thing's name?" Kinsey asked.

"I don't know," Ingrid said. "We haven't named it yet."

"We'll have to work on that," Kinsey said. "Bad luck for it not to have a name."

"Ballantine usually likes to name things himself," Ingrid said.

"Fuck Ballantine," Kinsey said. "Is he cramped in here with us?"

"Nope," Ingrid replied.

"Then we name it," Kinsey said.

"Cool," Ingrid said and grinned as the sub worked its way out into the depths.

***

"Doctors," Ballantine said as he walked back into the infirmary. "I'd like to introduce Ronald. He was stationed at one of our other islands. The one that dealt with recreating individual genetic specimens as opposed to the work you all have done recreating entire biospheres. His work, as well as Dr. Boris Kelnichov's, was instrumental in what you have achieved." He cleared his throat. "And then promptly lost control of."

Drs. Werth and Sales slunk back away from the gigantopithecus, but Dr. Logan stayed steady. After a couple of seconds of awe, he extended his hand.

"Good to meet you, Ronald." Dr. Logan said.

"You as well," Ronald said, shaking the man's hand. He smiled down at the scientist and showed him his very, very large teeth. "I am sorry, but I did not catch your name."

Dr. Logan glanced at Ballantine who just stood to the side, his arms folded across his chest.

"Ballantine didn't tell you?" Dr. Logan said. "Ah, well, I'm Dr. Will Logan. This is—"

"No, your real names," Ronald said. "Not the names you have taken to match your appearances." Ronald tapped his nose. "I can tell you are lying, so don't try to keep the ruse going. Your real names, please."

"Ballantine? What is this?" Dr. Logan asked.

"An interrogation," Ballantine said. "Interrogation by Bigfoot."

"Ballantine," Ronald growled. "You know I do not like that name."

"Sorry," Ballantine said. "I apologize. It was just too good not to say. Interrogation by Bigfoot has a ring to it. I do like a good ring."

"Ballantine, listen, you have lost your mind," Dr. Logan said. He hopped off the exam table and took a step forward, but a hairy hand to his chest stopped him in his tracks.

"Ballantine is listening," Ronald said, easily pushing Dr. Logan back onto the table. "As am I. What is your real name?"

"This is ridiculous," Dr. Logan snapped. "You know exactly who I am. Quiz me. Go ahead."

"What's your father's mother's maiden name?" Ballantine asked.

"My what? Are you joking? I don't think I ever learned that," Dr. Logan said. "If I did, I've forgotten it. She passed away years ago."

"Not bad," Ballantine said, clapping lightly. "Very plausible response. But the wrong one. You see, Dr. Logan, her maiden name is your last name. Dr. Will Logan's father was raised by an unwed, single mother. It is part of why the real Will Logan was driven to succeed. He wanted legitimacy his own father never had. So, you lose. Ronald? Rip his arms out of his sockets, if you please."

"I do please," Ronald said. The toothy grin was back. "I have been needing to tear arms off. I get stuck in my head so much as a researcher that I sometimes need a return to the primal."

"Wait!" Dr. Logan yelled before Ronald even took a step. "Okay! Okay, okay… I'm not Will Logan. I look like him, but I'm not him."

"Are any of you who you say you are?" Ronald asked. "Please be honest. As much as I want to tear your arms off, I prefer honesty. It's much more civilized."

"Ronald is very civilized," Ballantine said. "More so than me."

Ballantine walked over to a tray with medical tools laid out in a row. He picked up a pair of heavy duty forceps.

"I bet these could rip some eyelids right off," Ballantine mused. "What do you think, Ronald?"

"I think that would be a misuse of perfectly good equipment," Ronald said. "It would be easier to use my nails." He showed the three doctors his long, sharp nails.

"They are who they say they are," Dr. Logan said. "You can do DNA testing. That is Dr. Harley Werth and that is Dr. Lucas Sales."

"And you are?" Ronald asked.

"Timothy Norris," Dr. Logan replied. "Dr. Timothy Norris."

Setting the forceps down and leaving them behind, Ballantine frowned and moved forward until he was only a few inches from the man that called himself Dr. Logan.

"Timothy?" Ballantine said, looking the man over. "What the fuck happened?"

"You know this man, Ballantine?" Ronald asked.

"I do," Ballantine said. "He was Dr. Logan's assistant for years. I suspect he wrote half the man's papers."

"More than half," Dr. Logan, nee Dr. Norris replied. "Will wasn't the greatest writer so I did most of that work and he would go over it, change what he wanted to change, then approve it and put his name on it."

"Did you kill him?" Ballantine asked bluntly.

"What?" Dr. Norris gasped. "No! I would never have hurt Will! Yes, he could be an ass, but he wasn't that much of an ass."

"Then why are you him?" Ballantine asked.

"Do you still need me?" Ronald asked. "I'd like to rejoin Boris and Lisa in the lab. We have been having a fine time studying the primitives' corpses."

"Primitives' corpses?" Dr. Norris asked. He looked back at the other doctors and they blanched. "You have them here? On board this ship?"

"Yes," Ballantine said. "They attacked us and tried to take the ship. We stopped them. It's what we do."

"It seems to be all we do," Ronald said. "I do miss my time on the island with my lab and specimens."

"The pirate's life isn't exactly Ronald's cup of tea," Ballantine said.

"Do you have tea?" Dr. Werth asked, her eyes hoping and expectant.

"Yes, quite a nice selection," Ronald said.

"The corpses, take me to them," Dr. Norris said. "I need to show you something. It's something you'll miss unless you are looking for it."

"Does it have to do with why you look like Dr. Logan?" Ballantine asked.

"One hundred percent," Dr. Norris said. "It's how I can prove that taking Will's face was the only path. Everything else led to destruction."

"Seemed that happened anyway," Ballantine said.

"Not nearly on the scale it could have been," Dr. Norris replied.

Ballantine studied the man for a full minute then nodded.

"My bullshit detector isn't going off, so yes, you may see the corpses," he said. "Ronald? Will you show Drs. Werth and Sales to the mess and get them some tea?"

Ronald groaned. "But, Ballantine, I would much prefer to be in the lab when—"

"Please?" Ballantine asked. "Come on, big guy. When do I ever say please? If I'm saying please then I must really mean it."

"Yes," Ronald said. "Of course. Doctors? This way."

Ballantine watched them leave then turned to Dr. Norris. "I have to say the resemblance is uncanny."

"It should be," Dr. Norris responded. "This is a perfect clone of Dr. Logan's body."

"Clone? This isn't surgical?" Ballantine asked.

"No," Dr. Norris replied.

"Jesus," Ballantine said. "He did it then. He applied the science to humans, not just to the prehistoric DNA. Perfect replication."

"He did," Dr. Norris said and nodded. "Then it killed him. If I hadn't taken his place, we'd all be dead. It was the only way I could keep control of Alpha and then get her to attempt it as well."

"Get who to attempt what?" Ballantine asked.

"Dr. Liu," Dr. Norris said. "She drank her own Kool-Aid, Ballantine. And it did very bad things to her." He shook his head. "It'll do bad things to me, too, but I can live with that. Or perhaps not live, as the case may be."

"Come on," Ballantine said, eyeing the man for a couple of seconds. "We'll talk as I take you to the lab. I'm not liking the sound of Kool-Aid. If anyone gets to dispense Kool-Aid on one of my islands, it's me."

Chapter Nine- Should We Stay Or Should We Go Now

The wall slid to the side and Team Grendel jumped back, plasma rifles, kitchen knives, and various weapons up and at the ready. The smell of smoke and damp intensified, which wasn't a surprise. What was a surprise were the halogen lights that shone brightly in the corridor beyond.

And the sound of machinery running.

"This can't be the other facility," Shane said. "That one was blasted all to shit."

"He's right," Darren agreed.

"I know," Thorne said. "I saw it as well."

"This is the other facility," Darby said. "The distance we traveled and the course we took means there is no other option."

"There has to be another option," Max said. "We just spiraled around and around for hours. We could be anywhere on this island."

"But we aren't anywhere," Darby replied. "We're at the Omega facility."

"Omega?" Thorne asked.

"I've read the files," Darby said. "I've read all the files. Ballantine pretends like I haven't because it was a breach of his trust." She hefted the plasma rifle and aimed it at the lit corridor beyond. "Fuck that. He can trust me or not, I don't give a shit anymore."

She moved forward before Thorne could give the okay. Everyone fell in line behind her, trusting her illicit knowledge to keep them alive. Or at least give them a fighting chance.

"Sounds like your girlfriend is having an existential crisis," Lucy whispered to Max.

"Big word for someone without clothes," Max replied.

"What does that mean?" Lucy snapped.

"I don't know," Max said. "Sorry. My girlfriend is having an existential crisis."

He glanced at Lucy.

"Nice abs, by the way," Max said. "You have to show me what core routine you do. I just can't get that cut."

Lucy laughed quietly.

"You need a joint to focus," she said. "Your brain is starting to wander."

"Good call," Max said, fishing a joint out of a pocket on his vest. He sparked it and drew deep then handed it over to Lucy. She took a huge toke, reached forward, and tapped Shane on the shoulder. He looked back and his eye went wide.

"What the fuck?" he said. "Where were you hiding that? Do I even want to know?"

"Dude, I had it," Max said.

"Oh, right, my bad," Shane replied, taking the joint and nearly killing it in one draw. He exhaled and grinned from ear to ear. "There it is. The sweet spot."

"I hear that," Max said.

"Boys," Thorne hissed. "If we all die because you're getting stoned instead of paying the fuck attention, I'll fucking kill your ghosts."

"If we all die then you'd be a ghost too, Uncle Vinny," Max said.

"You think my ghost wouldn't be able to fucking annihilate your ghosts?" Thorne asked.

"Good point," Shane said.

Darby held up a fist and everyone stopped. All thoughts of ghosts and joints and dying were gone. Team Grendel was instant business. Darby pointed at a set of double doors where the machinery sounds were the loudest. Before she could move forward, the doors started to slide apart.

"Back!" Darby hissed. "In there!"

There was a second set of double doors behind them and to their right. Max slung his plasma rifle and gripped the gap between the doors, pushing as hard as he could to get them open. Lucy shoved her pot lid into the gap and pressed it back, using it as a wedge so everyone else could get their hands inside and push.

The doors slid far enough apart that each operator could just barely squeeze through. Darren, being the largest, almost didn't make it before figures started to come out of the other set of doors, but he got inside and was yanked back into the shadows by the others just as the figures passed the doors.

A long line of croanderthals lumbered past, nearly moving in unison as their long, hairy arms swung back and forth and their thick legs shuffled them along. Males and females were interspersed. It took several minutes for the line to finally thin out.

Before anyone moved, Darby held up a fist and waited. After a few seconds, a croanderthal came creeping back to the gap in their doors. He sniffed the air and furrowed his thick, heavy brow. He reached a massive hand into the gap and was about to push on the doors when there were several loud grunts from down the corridor. The croanderthal grunted back, took a last look at the gap, and then lumbered away.

No one moved for a couple minutes then Darby nodded and they all squeezed back into the corridor.

"Is it me or did they all look the same?" Max asked.

"Racist," Shane responded.

"Fuck you," Max said.

"No, he's right," Lucy said. "Other than the obvious difference between the genders, they do look the same. Or most of them."

"Four males and three females," Darby said.

"There were a few more than that," Shane said.

"I meant that there were four male templates and three female templates," Darby said. "I know how many total there were. I can fucking count."

Shane held up his hands. "Back off, angry lady. Same side."

"I'm not angry," Darby sighed. "I'm tired. I want to get this mission over with and move on."

"What is our mission?" Darren asked. "Vincent?"

Thorne looked at Darby, but she only shrugged.

"Clean up Ballantine's mess, as usual," Thorne said.

"This is a pretty fucking big mess," Max said.

He was about to say more, but they had come to the double doors with the machine sounds. Darby pressed a lever and the doors slid right open, no groaning or protesting. What they saw inside stopped all words from coming out of everyone's mouths.

The room beyond was cavernous and filled with hundreds and hundreds of vats of semi-clear liquid. Inside each vat was some type of creature, from strange-looking dinosaurs to plants of questionable origin. None of the vats were larger than a microwave and they were stacked one upon the other, row after row for as far as they could see.

But what held their attention weren't the prehistoric creatures or tentacled plants, it was the line of fifty vats towards the front that held miniature versions of the croanderthals. And those vats were systematically emptying their contents onto a conveyer belt that moved the seemingly sleeping figures towards a row of shower heads that rinsed them off before dropping them onto a large, bright grey mat.

Once the mat was filled, the vats stopped dumping and the conveyer belt stopped moving. The cavernous room was filled with the scent of ozone and the mat began to crackle and spark with electricity. The miniature croanderthals shuddered and bounced on the mat until the sparks stopped.

Then they grew. They grew to their full size, opened their eyes, and all turned towards the double doors. Which was exactly where Team Grendel still stood.

"We should go," Max said quietly. "Like now."

Team Grendel spun about and were ready to get the hell out of there, but they found their exit blocked by fifty croanderthals.

"Son of a bitch," Thorne grumbled. He sighed and looked at Darby. "Light them up."

Darby smiled and put her plasma rifle to her shoulder. Then she lit them up.

***

Kinsey was impressed with how responsive the mini-sub was, which she and Ingrid had dubbed the Barracuda because of its long shape. Kinsey knew that it looked nothing like a barracuda, but fuck it, she was the one sweating her tits off in the thing, so she was going to name it Barracuda.

Plus, she got to hum the Heart song over and over while she worked the controls, which was cool.

"We've been pinged," Ingrid said.

"That's not good," Kinsey said. "The ship knows we're coming."

"Maybe not," Ingrid said. "Moshi worked her magic on the hull. If what she said would happen does happen then the ship only sees us as a tenth our size. We look like a tarpon or something similar, not like a mini-sub."

"This thing barely looks like a mini-sub," Kinsey said. "Even full size it would be confusing."

"Maybe act more fish like, just in case," Ingrid said.

"What the hell does that mean?" Kinsey asked.

"I don't know," Ingrid replied. "Swim around in circles or dive down then come up. Do what fish do."

"Okay," Kinsey said and started to weave the Barracuda back and forth, hoping she looked like an imitation of a fish swimming through the water.

After a few minutes with no response or apparent reaction from the ship, Kinsey relaxed slightly and got into the rhythm of piloting like a fish. It was somewhat soothing.

Until an alarm rang out in the mini-sub and Ingrid gasped.

"It didn't work!" she cried. "It didn't work! They are opening torpedo bays!"

"Wait, what?" Kinsey shouted. "They have torpedo bays? What kind of fucking ship is this?"

"A really well-armed one!" Ingrid cried. "Ten torpedo bays, six cannons on deck, more than a few machine gun nests, as well as what look like a couple racks of depth charges."

"Holy shit," Kinsey said. "This ship is coming to kill us all, isn't it?"

"Looks like it," Ingrid said.

"How do we evade the torpedoes?" Kinsey asked. "We can't outrun them in this thing."

"We don't need to," Ingrid said. "Keep your current course. I'll handle the torpedoes. But whatever you do, please stay on course. I haven't quite figured out the nuances of the EMP cannon."

"EMP cannon? What the fuck, Ingrid?" Kinsey snapped. "Won't that hurt us too?"

"Shouldn't," Ingrid said as a loud whining filled the mini-sub. "Not in theory."

"Great," Kinsey said. "I love relying on theory."

"Stay the course," Ingrid said.

"Can you see my middle finger?" Kinsey asked.

"Thankfully, no," Ingrid said. "But I've seen it before, so I can picture it in my mind."

"Picture it up your ass if this goes south," Kinsey said.

"Really?" Ingrid laughed.

"Okay, don't picture that," Kinsey laughed as well. "I was trying to sound like my cousins. They always say shit like that."

"I know," Ingrid said. "It's cute. Especially the way Shane says things."

"Don't even go there," Kinsey said. "You do not want to get involved with my cousins. Darby with Max is one thing, but you will find nothing but heartbreak getting with an operator."

"I'm not looking for long term," Ingrid said. "Just a long orgasm. God, I haven't had one of those in a while."

Kinsey shivered. "Okay, okay, enough with the orgasm talk about my cousin," Kinsey said. "You so do not want me to throw up in this thing."

"Sorry," Ingrid said. "But do you think he'd—"

"Nope," Kinsey said. "Just nope. Talk to Lucy or Darby about this, not me."

"Sorry," Ingrid said again. "Three seconds until the torpedoes are in range."

"We disable those and they'll know for sure we aren't a fish," Kinsey said.

"I believe it's too late for that," Ingrid replied. "Here we go."

The whining grew louder and there was a clang, like two pots being smacked together. Kinsey winced at the sound and waited.

"Torpedoes are disabled," Ingrid said. "They are sinking below us."

"Right on," Kinsey said.

Then their world was rocked and everything started to roll.

"What happened?" Kinsey shouted as the Barracuda turned and twisted in the water, all the systems blinking on and off over and over again. "Did we EMP ourselves? Goddammit, Ingrid! I knew this shit would fuck us up!"

"No, it wasn't the EMP!" Ingrid yelled. "It was the torpedoes! We shut down their motors, but didn't disarm them! They went off below us and the concussions have hurt us bad!"

"How bad?" Kinsey shouted as she struggled to get control of the mini-sub. "Ingrid? How bad?"

"Bad," Ingrid said. "We'll sink in about five minutes!"

"Shit," Kinsey said and reached over to her side where a rebreather sat nestled into a small nook. "Get your mustache on."

"My what?" Ingrid asked.

"Your mustache," Kinsey repeated. "And make sure your compression suit is ready."

"Uh..."

"Ingrid? You are wearing a compression suit, right?" Kinsey asked.

"I sort of forgot," Ingrid said. "This is just a regular wet suit. I don't have a compression suit on."

"Okay, that's fine," Kinsey said. "These are tropical waters and we aren't that deep. You'll be fine."

The Barracuda shuddered several times then everything went dark except for the faint light that filtered in through the window in front of Kinsey.

"Mustache now!" Kinsey yelled. "We are getting the fuck out of this thing!"

Kinsey twisted around and watched as Ingrid fit the small rebreather unit under her nose. The woman gagged and choked as black tendrils worked their way up her nostrils and down her throat. Kinsey couldn't help but smile as she knew exactly how uncomfortable that feeling was before the tendrils thickened in position in a person's trachea, sealing off the airway so that no water could get in.

"That really sucks," Ingrid said.

"Welcome to my world," Kinsey said. "Now open the hatch and get us out of here."

Ingrid reached up and hit the emergency release on the hatch above her and the Barracuda was suddenly filling with sea water. Kinsey saw Ingrid panic and she pushed up from her seat and grabbed onto the woman, making sure she didn't thrash about and hurt herself.

"Stay calm!" Kinsey barked, her mustache rebreather converting the vibrations in her voice box to the com system in their ears. "Let the sub fill with water and the pressure will equalize! Then you can just swim right out!"

Ingrid's eyes were huge, but she nodded and stopped thrashing. She looked far from relaxed, but at least she wouldn't hurt herself. Or Kinsey.

Once the Barracuda had filled completely, Kinsey gave Ingrid a hard shove in the small of her back. The tech hesitated, but then moved out of the mini-sub before Kinsey had to shove again. Kinsey was out in seconds then panicked as she realized Ingrid wasn't anywhere around her.

Then she looked up and wanted to scream.

Ingrid was stroking to the surface, swimming as fast as she could to get to the open air above.

"Dammit!" Kinsey yelled into the com. "What the hell are you thinking?"

Kinsey kicked her legs and pumped her arms, hoping to catch up to the woman, but she was too late. Ingrid broke the surface and Kinsey had no choice but to follow.

"You moron!" Kinsey yelled once her head was above water. "They'll be looking for us! With the Barracuda sinking, at least we had a chance of them thinking we went down with it!"

"The Barracuda didn't sink," Ingrid said. She yanked the mustache free and gasped. "Ow. That is really, really uncomfortable."

Kinsey yanked hers out as well and glared at Ingrid.

"What the hell do you mean it isn't sinking?" Kinsey shouted.

"Look," Ingrid said, nodding away from them.

Kinsey turned her body to see where Ingrid had nodded. She saw the top of the Barracuda, hatch wide open, surface and start to spew water. Then the hatch closed as a metal panel slid into place. The mini-sub submerged once again and was lost from sight.

"Where the hell did it go?" Kinsey asked.

"It's going back to the B3," Ingrid said. "Moshi came up with everything. This was really her baby. It self-purges and automatically returns home when damaged. There is a shielded back-up battery that has enough power to get the mini-sub about six miles before it has to stop and wait to recharge."

"Recharge? How?" Kinsey asked.

"Look around," Ingrid said. "The Earth's most powerful engine is all about us. It will let a current push through several small turbines, sort of like power gills, and that will charge the battery enough for another six mile journey until it reaches the B3."

"So why didn't we just stay inside?" Kinsey asked.

"Oh, well, it doesn't work if there are people in it," Ingrid said. "Too heavy and also the whole point of the mini-sub returning is to know what went wrong and salvage any data collected."

"Of course," Kinsey sighed. "Leave it to techs to care about data more than human lives."

"You guys are pretty good at taking care of yourselves," Ingrid said, a little bitterly. "But you suck at taking care of equipment. We were only trying to minimize the constant waste of our creations."

Kinsey was about to argue, but shut up as she realized just how little credit Team Grendel gave the elves. They gave them plenty of shit, but very little credit for the weapons and equipment they made all to keep the Team alive.

"Come on," Kinsey said, pulling at Ingrid's shoulder. "We can't tread here forever."

"Where are we going?" Ingrid asked.

"You want data? Then let's go right to the source," Kinsey said.

She fiddled with her rebreather then strapped it to her belt under the water. She turned and started to swim towards the ship that was getting closer and closer.

"Wait! You want to go towards that ship?" Ingrid cried.

"They're coming for us anyway," Kinsey said. "And what better place to get data than straight from the source?"

"They'll kill us," Ingrid whimpered.

"I doubt that," Kinsey said. Or she hoped.

***

"Clones?" Dr. Morganton asked.

"Clones," the man wearing a copy of Dr. Logan's body replied. "All of them. There are four male variants and three female variants."

"And you're a clone too?" Boris asked. "A living clone? Of Dr. Logan?"

"I am," Dr. Harris said. "That's a long story."

"We'd appreciate hearing it," Boris said.

"Later," Ballantine said. "It has nothing to do with the science and everything to do with Dr. Harris's survival. We'll leave that to later. Doctor? Tell them why you created the clones."

"You were having issues stabilizing the specimens," Boris said before Dr. Harris could speak. "And since each embryo and specimen was slightly different, despite coming from the same original genetic material, you couldn't isolate the problem. So you created clones of the exact same embryo, hoping to be able to focus on one genetic sample and find the problem."

"Uh, yes, exactly," Dr. Harris said.

"That seems like a good solution," Dr. Morganton said. "So what went wrong?"

"In order to keep up the schedule we needed, we may have forced the growth process slightly," Dr. Harris said.

"That is why we rejected cloning as a viable option. The instability of rapid growth presented too many of its own problems," Boris said. "Which I warned against in my notes that I gave to Ballantine and Ballantine should have given to you."

Ballantine nodded. "I did. I passed them on directly to Dr. Logan as well as Dr. Liu." He rubbed at his head. "The rapid growth process is why the biospheres have taken over the island, right?"

"Right," Dr. Harris nodded. "It spread everywhere when Omega exploded."

"But the rapid growth should not have been viable," Boris said, shaking his head. "I was clear on that. The cells degenerate too quickly for accurate analysis."

"Dr. Logan and Dr. Liu thought they could overcome the issues you faced when you attempted cloning," Dr. Harris said to Boris. "Which they did. To a certain extent."

"They did?" Boris asked. "How? Because I can hardly believe that. I am an accomplished scientist and have perfected more than my share of procedures. To think that they—"

"By shortening the lifespan of the subjects," Dr. Harris interrupted. He waited until everyone in the room understood the implications of his statement.

"Oh," Boris said. "Does that include you?"

"It does," Dr. Harris said. "As well as the creatures Dr. Liu and her people have become. Except they think they have found a way around it. They haven't, but that hasn't stopped the woman from going forward with her butchery."

"Cannibalism," Ballantine said. "She thinks if they consume others' life forces she will extend her lifespan."

"Yes," Dr. Harris nodded.

"But that is insane," Boris said.

"Exactly," Dr. Harris said. "And that is what you have to understand. The woman is completely insane. So are her people. Shoving their minds into bodies that are not human warped them. It wasn't easy for me, going from my cerebral structure to Dr. Logan's. Their cerebral structure isn't even human. It's a mix of many species. She thought she could fix all the problems by creating something new. She just made more."

"Oh, dear," Boris said. "How many more?"

"What?" Dr. Harris asked.

"How many more clones did she create?" Boris asked.

"No, that's not what I meant," Dr. Harris said.

"Oh, I know what you mean," Boris said. "I certainly do. That didn't get past me. No, sir. What I want to know is how many human clones she created? Dr. Liu is a smart woman, I have read her work, and insane or not, she would know that eventually she'd run out of a food source. So she must have created more human clones. It would be the only sensible solution. Well, not sensible in that it makes sense from its very concept, but sensible from the viewpoint of a crazy person. True humans would be ideal, but clones may work in a pinch. If you are crazy to think along those lines."

"Yes, Boris, we have established that she is crazy," Ballantine said. Ballantine looked at Dr. Harris. "But Omega was destroyed, so she wouldn't have that option, would she?"

Dr. Harris shifted uncomfortably.

"Doctor?" Ballantine pushed. "Omega was destroyed completely, yes? That is what happened in the explosion. It destroyed the entire facility, right? Changing Dr. Liu and her people into the things they have become. She wouldn't be able to create human clones, correct?"

"You saw it yourself," Dr. Morganton said to Ballantine. "You said it was in ruins."

"I only saw the surface buildings," Ballantine said. "I didn't get a chance to see the sub-level. That was going to be Grendel's next mission once they finished their initial recon and then secured the Alpha facility."

"Oh, dear," Boris said. "If the sub-level is still intact then Dr. Liu could not only be creating her own food source, but also an army of creatures like her. Not to mention whatever else her cuckoo brain can think up. It is quite a brain, I must say. Have I mentioned I've read her work?"

"Yes, Boris," Ballantine sighed. He focused all of his attention on Dr. Harris. "Spill it."

"We tried," Dr. Harris said. "We truly tried. After I was transferred into this body, and Dr. Logan was gone for good, we knew we couldn't let the technology fall into Dr. Liu's hands. I destroyed the transference matrix. Which was much easier to recreate than you would think. It was all a simple matter of—"

"Later," Ballantine snapped. "Focus on telling me what really happened."

"We'd lured Dr. Liu and her people to Alpha as a distraction then set the charges to blow up Omega," Dr. Harris said. "We'd escaped and were deep into the jungle when the charges went off.

But I knew the explosion wasn't big enough. Only half detonated. The ones in the sub-level didn't go off. She must have gotten to them."

"How?" Ballantine asked.

"You have to understand that she had been going insane for a lot longer than any of us knew," Dr. Harris said. "She was highly functional, but far from stable well before the idea of cloning even came up. I think she had an agenda from the beginning."

Ballantine closed his eyes and steepled his fingers in front of his face. He took a couple of deep breaths then opened his eyes and moved quickly towards Dr. Harris. The man was down on the ground, holding a hand to his chin, with Ballantine standing over him, before anyone could even move.

"Is it all bullshit, Harris? Is everything you have told me and are telling us now, just complete bullshit?" Ballantine shouted. "Because it sounds like bullshit! You had me snowed for a while there, but your timeline isn't making any sense. I am a man that understands timelines. I have stayed alive for this long because timelines, and timing, are a specialty of mine. Down to a minute. I can calculate a plan down to a minute. I can calculate a million variant scenarios to branch off from a plan if that minute becomes compromised. Your timeline is compromised and I am not liking the variants that are going through my head."

"Listen, Ballantine, none of us meant for any of this to happen," Dr. Norris began. A swift kick to his face stopped him.

"NO!" Ballantine said. "I think you did want this to happen! I think you wanted all of this to happen! Who are you? Because you are not Dr. Timothy Harris anymore! Just like that thing on that island isn't Dr. Ann Liu anymore either! WHO ARE YOU?"

Dr. Norris wiped blood from his nose and started to speak then shook his head. He cautiously stood up, and Ballantine let him. The two men stared at each other and the scared, helpless look that had been in Dr. Norris's eyes was replaced by something sinister. Something more akin to the look in Ballantine's eyes.

Ballantine watched him for a moment.

"You aren't a human clone, are you?" Ballantine asked. "You added something in there so the lifespan could be extended. What did you do? What are you now?"

"We are gods," Dr. Norris said and grinned. "And there isn't a fucking thing any of you tiny little ants can do about it."

Then he picked up Ballantine and tossed the man all the way across the lab.

"I didn't see that coming," Boris said and grabbed Dr. Morganton's arm, yanking her towards the lab's hatchway. "We should run now!"

"Yes! Run!" Dr. Norris shouted. His form began to change and swell, his muscles thickening and almost doubling in size as his height increased at a rapid rate until his head almost touched the ceiling. "Run! BUT YOU CANNOT HIDE!"

***

Surrounded, Team Grendel looked for the weakest point in the attack and pushed in that direction. Unfortunately for them, it was deeper into the cavernous room.

Croanderthals came at them hard and fast, but Darby, Max, and Mike held them back with their plasma rifles while Thorne, Darren, Shane, and Lucy tried to find a way out of the massive room of tanks.

"What the holy fuck?" Thorne growled as he stood before a row of tanks that held what were obviously humans. Small, miniature humans, but humans for sure. "What the hell place is this?"

"That guy's dick is still bigger than yours," Lucy said to Shane as they passed the tanks.

"Ah, come on! Really?" Shane replied. "No fair with the burns while we're in mortal danger. Save them all up for later."

Lucy didn't have time to respond as about twenty croanderthals came rushing at them from their right, squeezing through the gaps in the tanks. She ducked a swing from one and then jammed both fists into the belly of another. It grunted, but didn't go down. So she jammed both fists into its crotch and it dropped like lead.

"Oh, I have a good one I'm saving!" Lucy called out. "You're gonna love it!"

"I have a feeling no, I am not," Shane said.

He swung out with a powerful right haymaker and the sound of a cracking cheekbone was like a gunshot. The croanderthal that had been grabbing for him screeched and grabbed its own cheek instead. Shane came forward with a headbutt then stumbled back, instantly regretting the action.

"Ow," he muttered, his head fuzzy from the impact. "Big craniums. Remember that."

"Move," Thorne said and shoved Shane aside. He stabbed the croanderthal in the belly and lifted up with the knife, sending guts spilling to the thing's feet. "Stop fucking around."

Thorne yanked the blade free and spun about, slashing at two that had come at his back. He glanced past them as they jumped away and saw a group of croanderthals circumventing the barrage of plasma blasts. Thorne was about to yell a warning, but the words didn't get to leave his mouth as his legs were taken out from under him by a tackling croanderthal.

Thorne's head hit the metal floor hard and he felt blood fill his mouth as he bit down on his tongue. He spat the blood out and hammered at the croanderthal that still had its arms wrapped about Thorne's knees. The thing grunted under the attack, but didn't loosen its grip.

"God dammit!" Thorne shouted. "You are too close to my penis!"

He made two fists, raising the middle knuckle of each hand just above the others, then smashed those knuckles right into the thing's temples. It cried out and its arms loosened slightly. Thorne hit it again and again until it slackened and lay slumped across him.

He shoved it off and hopped to his feet in time to dip his shoulder and toss an incoming croanderthal over his back. He swung about and stomped on the thing's face, wincing as the thing's teeth sliced his heel. The pain didn't stop him, though, and he brought his foot down again and again until the croanderthal's face was nothing but mush.

The plasma blasts stopped and Thorne looked up.

"Empty!" Darby yelled.

"Same here!" Max shouted.

"Fuck!" Mike cried. "I'm done too!"

Darby flipped her rifle around and gripped its barrel then began to swing the weapon like a bat, cracking every skull that got within range. Mike and Max did the same and the three slowly backed up to Thorne and everyone else's position. That's when Thorne looked around and realized Darren was missing.

"Chambers!" Thorne yelled.

"Here!" Darren called from a few rows away. "I found a door! Come on!"

Team Grendel sprinted past the rows, giving up on the fight and looking only for escape. They found Darren spread-eagled in a doorway, his arms and feet stretched out, keeping the sliding doors from shutting.

"Hurry your asses!" Darren shouted. "This is not as easy as it looks!"

"Oh, come on!" Max cried. "Don't tell me we have to crawl between his fucking legs to get out?"

"I won't tell you that," Thorne said. "Because you already know it has to happen."

Thorne got onto all fours and crawled between Darren's legs, followed by Darby, Mike, Lucy, and Shane. Max cringed and joined them.

"Please don't let his junk touch me. Please don't let his junk touch me," he whispered over and over then screeched in a very high-pitched voice. "His junk touched me!"

Once through, Darren let go and jumped away from the doors. They slid closed with a bang and everyone took a deep breath as the doors seemed to hold despite the pounding from the croanderthals on the other side.

"I feel so dirty," Max said.

"Suck it up, frogman," Shane said, clapping his brother on the shoulder. "At least you have a suit on. I almost got some skin on skin action." He held up a hand at Lucy. "What did we agree on?"

"I'd save all the jokes until later," Lucy said, sounding very disappointed.

"Did you shout 'You are too close to my penis'?" Mike asked Thorne.

"Yes," Thorne nodded.

"I thought so," Mike said, grinning. "That was beautiful to hear coming from you."

"I'm glad I could amuse you," Thorne growled. "Now let's stop fucking around and find our way out of here."

"Stairs," Darby said, pointing to a door at the end of the corridor they found themselves in. "They better not be blocked."

The Team ran to the door and Darby got it open, everyone sighed with relief as they felt a breeze of fresh air coming from above. Thorne leaned in and looked up, his eyes studying the spiral staircase that wound for a couple stories before opening up onto what looked like nothing but open space.

"We're going to be exposed," Thorne said.

"Too late," Shane said, motioning to his nudity.

The doors behind them shuddered.

"We can't stay," Darby said to Thorne. "We get up there and then figure it out."

"We have no firearms," Thorne said. "Not until your rifles charge."

"We'll make do," Darby said.

Thorne nodded as metal began to groan. He looked back at the doors. They were beginning to bulge from the croanderthals' weight on the other side.

"Go," he said.

Team Grendel didn't hesitate. They hurried up the stairs to the surface above. The sound of the doors finally giving in echoed up to them all as they stood in the midst of the burned out ruins of the top level of the Omega facility.

"Which way?" Darby asked, looking at Thorne, Darren, and Shane. "You've been here before. Which way?"

"We never got out of the Zodiac," Thorne said. "Ballantine did the recon for us. That lasted all of a minute before he was sprinting back to us."

"I think the river is that way," Darren said.

"He's right," Shane said, pointing at a small mountain peak in the distance. "I remember catching a glimpse of that through the trees as we waited at the dock."

"Then we go that way," Thorne said. "Towards the mountain."

"Not towards the river?" Lucy asked.

"Not unless we want to swim," Thorne said. "I would rather not find out what's in the river. Would you?"

The sound of heavy feet coming up the stairs ended the discussion.

Team Grendel began running through the scorched ruins, making their way past the blackened carcasses of not just equipment, but people as well. Everywhere they looked was nothing but destruction. Even when they reached the edge of the tree line, the palms were stunted and burned. The blast had reached far into the jungle.

They pushed through the destruction and were almost concealed by the shadows of the jungle when they heard the angry screams and murderous grunts from the croanderthal mob.

"They'll catch us," Darby stated. She looked at her plasma rifle and stopped, spinning to face the things. "It's worked up some charge. Go. I'll buy you some time."

"We go together," Thorne said. "You won't buy us nearly as much time as we need."

Darby began to argue, but shut up as the air was split by a deafening roar.

"Oh, fuck," Shane said. "I know that song."

"Where is it?" Darren asked, turning in a circle.

The roar came again, but it was so loud, no one could figure out its direction.

Then the jungle to the side of the ruins split open and a massive monster surged through, its giant head dipping, its mouth opening wide as it scooped up half a dozen croanderthals at once. There were more screams, but no longer of an angry or murderous nature. They were screams of terror as the huge dinosaur gulped down the first bite and went in for more.

"This is our only shot," Thorne said. "Keep running. Head for the mountain. We'll try to find somewhere up there to hunker down in."

Everyone nodded and tore their eyes from the horror that unfolded in the ruins of the Omega facility. It was a long time before their ears found relief as the screams continued until they were thoroughly deep in the jungle, the palms and ferns finally thick enough to block the sounds.

***

The room Kinsey and Ingrid found themselves in was Spartan. From what they had seen after being hauled aboard, so was the entire ship. It was stripped down for combat efficiency, having none of the luxuries that the Beowulf III had.

Yet even with the obvious lack of niceties, Kinsey did not think the vessel was military. At least not officially. Everyone she'd come in contact with stank of private contractors, guns for hire doing a job they were getting well paid for. No one with any authority had come to see them as they stood on the upper deck dripping wet while being stripped down to nothing but their underwear.

Kinsey's were classic grey boxers and sports bra. Ingrid's, on the other hand, were what Kinsey guessed would be called adult Underoos.

"Are you supposed to be Wonder Woman?" Kinsey asked, unable to hold back her curiosity any longer.

"Shut up," a guard barked as he stood by the hatch to the small room, a M4 gripped tightly and at the ready. Kinsey and Ingrid were handcuffed to a metal table in the center of the room, both sitting in cold, steel chairs. "No talking."

Ingrid looked like she was about to pee her Underoos and Kinsey felt sorry for the woman. She'd been sheltered in the sanctuary of the Toyshop for so long that Kinsey figured Ingrid had probably forgotten just how dangerous their lives were on a day-to-day basis. She made a mental note to talk to Ballantine about getting the elves out of their comfort zones and learning some real skills. Skills that would keep them from falling apart like Ingrid looked like she was about to do.

"Hold on," Kinsey whispered. "We're getting out of this. Just keep it together."

"I said to shut up!" the guard barked. "Next time you open your fucking mouth, I'll fill it with this barrel." He waved the M4 at them and sneered. "I will fucking do it."

"Come try," Kinsey responded. Her eyes narrowed and she grinned.

She could feel the old Kinsey, the junkie Kinsey that killed anything that was even close to a threat, start to grow in her. She didn't like that junkie Kinsey was still in her, lurking in the background like a deadly shadow, but at that moment she knew she'd need all of her to get them free if the opportunity presented itself.

"You want me to shut up?" Kinsey laughed. "Then walk that carbine my way and just try to shove it in my mouth. We'll see how well that turns out for you, asshole."

The guard debated then his sneer grew and he took two steps towards the table. But he only got two steps before the door opened and he snapped to attention.

"Clemmons? What the hell were you moving from your post for?" Jowarski asked. "Get the hell out of here before I decide your services are no longer needed."

The guard didn't argue with the man, he did not question leaving him alone with the two women, he just nodded and removed himself from the small room as quickly as possible.

When the door was closed again, Jowarski turned and smiled at Kinsey and Ingrid.

"Hello there," he said and folded his hands in front of him. "Kinsey Thorne. A pleasure to meet you finally. And Ingrid...? I'm sorry, but our records have never included your last name. Ballantine seemed to pluck you and the other, what does he call you, elves? Yes, elves. He seemed to pluck you and the other elves out of nowhere. I'm afraid we have no record of you existing anywhere. Ever."

"He did that?" Ingrid asked, looking genuinely shocked. "He said he could, but I never checked to see if he did. I probably should have. I had access to all the files down in the—"

"Who the fuck are you?" Kinsey asked, cutting off Ingrid before she spoiled the benefits of being anonymous. "You know us, you know Ballantine, but we don't know you."

"Chance Jowarski," Jowarski said, not moving from his spot. "And you will get to know me very well before our time is done, I think. Probably too well, if I have my way."

"God, I hate you black ops fuckers," Kinsey muttered.

"I get that a lot," Jowarski said. "I'd think you would be used to us considering how long you have been around Ballantine.

Speaking of, how about we start there? Tell me everything you know about Ballantine and I promise our time here will be short."

"And if we don't then our time here will be really long because you'll make it as painful as possible, is that it?" Kinsey asked. "Just knock it off and ask your questions."

"Oh, I will," Jowarski said. "I'm waiting for someone to join me. A couple people actually."

Jowarski smiled and didn't say anything else. When the door rattled he stepped to the side, making room for the two people that came through.

"Popeye!" Kinsey yelled and tried to stand, but was caught short by the handcuffs bolted to the table. "You died!"

"Nope," Popeye shrugged as he was shoved against the wall by Jowarski. He didn't even try to resist. "Close, but these assholes found me and fixed me up."

"We did our best," the next person in said. Dr. Dana Ballantine frowned at Kinsey and Ingrid. "Let's get to the heart of the matter, shall we? Is my husband on that ship in the bay? Or is he on the island? I need to know right this second or one of you gets hurt badly. I don't want to hurt you, but Mr. Jowarski does. I'm afraid I cannot hold him back, as much as I would like to."

She looked from Kinsey to Ingrid and waited.

"Well?" she asked.

"Did you say husband?" Kinsey asked.

"Yes, I did," Dana said. "My name is Dr. Dana Ballantine. I am going to ask one more time. Where is my husband? The ship or the island?"

"That's probably how my face looked when she said the same thing to me," Popeye said. "It doesn't get easier to understand, trust me. Just tell the woman what she wants to know or this guy will do some nasty things to you. He's a scary fuck."

It was at that moment that Kinsey wasn't sure she could trust him. It was Popeye alright, but he seemed changed. He seemed beaten. She could see the look in his eyes. Junkie Kinsey recognized that look. It was defeat. It was giving in to those that said they held all the power. Kinsey knew that if she cooperated then she and Ingrid would be dead in seconds. The alternative was not much better, but it meant living.

"Go fuck yourself, bitch," Kinsey spat and readied herself for the pain that was about to come as Jowarski came at her almost before the words were out of her mouth.

Chapter Ten- Make This Bitch Ours

The Harris-Logan thing tore through the passageway, its bulk denting the walls, pushing in metal that was designed to resist major explosives. It roared and thumped its chest, thick, black hair sprouting from its skin. Skin that had started to darken a deep grey, becoming wrinkled and folded across its face.

It ripped the stairs free from their bolts at the end of the passageway, making enough room so it could get to the hatchway beyond. It tore the hatch off, not even bothering to spin the wheel in the middle, and threw it back the way it had come. Its bulk was way too big to get through the hatchway, but that did not stop the Harris-Logan thing.

More metal groaned and splits sped across the surface of the walls as the thing shoved through the too small hatchway and into the passageway beyond. A man, an anonymous crewman that had kept his head down and out of sight during the past few months, screamed as he saw what came at him. He tried to run, but he was caught before he could make it more than a few steps.

The Harris-Logan thing lifted the crewman up by the back of his neck then slammed his whole body down into the floor, literally into the floor, denting the metal and pulverizing the man instantly. Blood and bone sprayed against the walls and shot upward like a geyser to be left dripping from the ceiling, an interior rain of horror.

The hatch at the end of that passageway swung open and Ballantine stared at the monstrosity. One of his eyes was swollen shut and he had a heavy gash across his forehead. He was favoring his left arm and his jaw was set, teeth gritted, against the obvious pain he was in.

"You," the Harris-Logan thing growled. It was a deep, low voice filled with violence and violence only. "You should be dead."

"If I had a nickel," Ballantine said and shook his head. Slowly. It hurt to shake more than just slowly. "I am extremely hard to kill, Harris. Ask everyone that has tried. Not to say I haven't actually been dead now and again, but I give all the credit to the miracles of modern medical science for bringing me back."

Ballantine sighed.

"What the hell, Harris?" He nodded his head at the Harris-Logan thing. "What is going on?"

"Still you want answers," the Harris-Logan thing responded. "Even as you face your death, you want answers."

"I'm an answer man," Ballantine shrugged. He winced at the movement. "Some guys are boob men, some are ass men, some go for exotic eyes or small feet. Me? I get turned on by answers. So, since I am about to die, as you say, how about giving me some? Real ones now."

"You do not deserve them," the Harris-Logan thing said. "You do not deserve anything except for a painful death. You did this to me, Ballantine. You made me what I am."

"Oh, fuck off!" Ballantine shouted then rolled his jaw a couple of times. "Ow. I just found out that loud can hurt. I also found out that while you look like a giant gorilla, or a toddler King Kong, if you will, you are also about as emotionally developed." He waited, but when the Harris-Logan thing didn't respond he sighed again. "You're like a toddler, is what I'm saying."

"That will be the last condescending thing you ever say, Ballantine," the Harris-Logan thing roared. "Now you die!"

Ballantine shook his head as the thing raced towards him.

"God, you are stupid," he said. Ballantine's whole body looked defeated, just flat-out tired. He stepped aside and Carlos and Moshi stepped forward with what looked like a very large cannon on wheels. "Who do you think found me, you fool?"

The Harris-Logan thing saw the cannon and changed its direction just before the weapon fired. A dark blue/black wave of energy seemed to roll through the passageway, but the Harris-Logan thing was no longer there. It had torn right through the wall, ripping the metal like it was paper, and hurried from cabin to cabin until it hit the passageway on the other side of the ship.

"That could have gone better," Ballantine said.

"Don't blame me," Carlos said. "We fired as soon as you got out of the way."

"For once, I won't blame you, Carlos," Ballantine said. "I'm blaming Moshi."

The mostly silent woman raised an eyebrow and Ballantine chuckled.

"I'm joking, of course," he said. "Who could blame Moshi for anything?"

"Well, I do have a list of issues that I want to bring up on her next performance review," Carlos said.

"You, sir, might be the biggest asshole on this ship," Ballantine said. "Even bigger than me." He leaned close to Moshi. "There're no more performance reviews. I only told him there would still be some so he'd shut up. It didn't work."

There were several loud screams and Ballantine limped to the hole in the wall. He watched through the impromptu passage that the Harris-Logan thing created as body parts flew across the opening on the other side.

"We're going to need new crew members after this," Ballantine said. "Where the hell will I find them?"

Carlos and Moshi had followed him and stared in shock at the amount of blood they were seeing.

"The cannon," Ballantine said, walking back towards the weapon. "Bring it along. I know where he's headed."

"Where?" Carlos asked.

Moshi looked puzzled then snapped her fingers and pointed at Ballantine.

"Yep, the engine room," Ballantine said. "The dumb ape thinks he can fix the engines and take the ship. Scientists and their egos, am I right?"

Moshi gave a quick giggle then stopped as Carlos glared at her.

She flipped him the bird as soon as he turned away.

***

Ronald raised an arm to block the table that flew at him as he stood in the middle of the mess, food everywhere, blood everywhere, body parts everywhere.

Strangely reptilian body parts covered in iridescent scales of green and black. And blood. The body parts were certainly covered in blood.

The table went flying to the side as Ronald swatted it away.

"I do not see the point in this!" he shouted and pointed a hairy finger at the scaled and bloody body parts. "I have already dispatched your comrade with ease. Do not think that you will have any better chance at defeating me than he did."

The thing at the far side of the mess, a cross between a hyena and a spider monkey, screeched and hissed at Ronald then picked up another table and threw it.

"Dr. Werth, please stop this," Ronald said. "I do not want to hurt you, if I do not have to. I could help you with your condition. Perhaps find a way to reverse and return you to your normal self?"

"No!" the Werth thing screeched. "This is my normal self!"

The voice was like a grating combination of fingernails on a chalkboard and the yip of a strangled Chihuahua. Ronald winced at the sound, his sensitive ears not caring for the noise at all.

"I would beg to differ with you about your appearance, Dr. Werth," Ronald argued. "While I am hardly the picture of normalcy, I am a complete, contained species. You, however, are not. Something went very wrong when you attempted whatever you tried to attempt."

"LIES!" the Werth thing hissed and spat. Drool matted the fur on its pointed chin and it licked its jowls with a wide, splotchy tongue. "ALL LIES!"

"I have tried," Ronald said as he started to move forward.

A rolling sound from the passageway, like squeaking wheels, became louder and louder until a strange cannon came into view at the mess's hatchway. It rolled by and soon revealed Carlos and Moshi behind it, both struggling with the effort to keep the cannon moving. Carlos didn't even turn to look in the mess, but Moshi gave Ronald a wave.

"Moshi," Ronald said, nodding his head towards the passageway before she was lost from sight.

He started to turn his attention back to the Werth thing, but then Ballantine limped into view.

"Ronald," Ballantine said as he passed by.

"Ballantine," Ronald replied.

Ronald returned his attention to the Werth thing.

"Need any help?" Ballantine asked as he ducked his head back into view. "I'm sure Lake is around here somewhere. You know how he likes his hand cannons. I'm willing to bet he has two Desert Eagles on him right now with at least another four within easy reach."

"No, but thank you for offering to fetch him," Ronald said. "I have this situation well in hand."

"Okey doke," Ballantine said and gave him a thumbs up. "Ow. Damn, even my thumb hurts. I don't know how Grendel does it day after day. Well, carry on then."

"Thank you, I will," Ronald said and closed the distance between himself and the Werth thing. "Gladly."

"Ballantine!" Carlos yelled from the end of the passageway.

Ballantine shook his head and ducked away. "Coming!" he yelled back.

Ronald easily ignored the far off argument that ensued. He was too busy shredding an abomination with the immense strength of his hands. And his jaw. There may have been some biting.

***

"There," Darby said, pointing to a cave at the base of the ridge they had just climbed. She looked back and saw the rest of Team Grendel struggling up the grade. She winced at the sight of the cuts and scrapes on those that were still without clothing. "We'll rest inside until we come up with a new plan."

Several screeches from above made her look up and that time she winced at the sight of the huge red birds that flew in lazy circles over their heads.

"Get inside now," Darby said.

The Team followed her gaze and their pace quickened.

The inside of the cave was dark and cool, a welcome relief to the scorching, tropical sun outside. Darby turned about and took a knee, her plasma rifle trained on the cave mouth, ready for whatever might follow. The far-off sound of a terrible roar made her shiver. It wasn't far off enough for her comfort. In fact, if her ears weren't lying to her, it was getting closer.

"Following our trail," Thorne said, pulling on a pair of sweat pants and a ratty t-shirt that hadn't been washed in some time. Darby raised her eyebrows. "There're quite a bit of supplies at the back of the cave. Crates everywhere. Someone was staying here for a while. More than one person by the looks."

"Will they be coming back?" Darby asked.

"Not likely with that thing out there," Thorne said. He knelt and tied a pair of sneakers then picked up a pistol from between his feet. "Weapons crates. Not hidden at all. Someone didn't think they'd be found up here."

"Ammo?" Darby asked.

"Tight," Thorne said. "We'll have to make each shot count."

"We always do," Darby said. She nodded to the back of the cave. "You should rest. You're going to crash if you don't."

"This isn't my first rodeo," Thorne said. "I know how to manage my adrenaline surges."

The terrible roar sounded again and several winged creatures took flight from the jungle treetops below.

"Closer. Shit," Darby said. "If it is coming for us then it'll be here in minutes at the rate it's moving."

"We can handle it," Thorne said. "Relax."

"Relax?" Darby snapped. "How the fuck can you say that?"

"Hold on," Thorne snapped back. "I'm not Ballantine, so don't take this out on me. I've been watching your patience with him get shorter and shorter over the weeks. I know dealing with your old team brought up some shit, but do not let that shit get in the way of your job. Ballantine is not in charge here, I am. Unquestionably. I am telling you to fucking relax, so fucking relax!"

"We good up here?" Darren asked as he walked up from the back of the cave, pulling on a tank top and some running shorts.

"Fine!" Darby and Thorne yelled.

"Oh fuck that," Darren said. He stomped up to the two of them and jabbed a finger at Thorne. "I can take getting yelled at by you and Kinsey. We have personal history and I deserve it. But technically I am co-leader of Team Grendel, so neither of you gets to speak that way to me. Whatever you are talking about that has you so pissed off, stop talking about it. Right now. Just fucking stop."

"What's up?" Max asked, following Darren. He had on a Hawaiian print shirt and a pair of thrashed and dirty jeans. "Family meeting? Should I get Shane?"

"Someone call me?" Shane asked. He had a bag of potato chips in his hands and was munching away. He offered the chips to everyone. "Want some? They are stale as all fuck, but damn if the salt doesn't taste good."

"What are you going to do when the salt stops tasting good and you are dying of thirst?" Lucy asked, dressed in too tight shorts and a too tight polo shirt. "Did you think of that?"

"Damn," Shane said. "I didn't." He took another handful of chips and stuffed them in his mouth. Everyone stared as he struggled to chew and finally swallow. "In for a penny, in for a delicious pound."

That broke the tension. Thorne rolled his eyes and shook his head. Darby pretty much repeated the same motions while Max and Darren cracked up.

"Is this a good time to tell all the dick jokes I have saved up?" Lucy asked.

A roar from the base of the ridge told her it was not a good time.

Team Grendel filled the mouth of the cave, weapons up and trained on the jungle below. They watched as the trees swayed and shook then began to crack and topple as the massive dinosaur tore into the open. Its muzzle was coated with blood and there were bits and pieces of croanderthals hanging from its lips. It opened its mouth and roared again, sending most of the bits and pieces flying this way and that.

The smell of the meat eater's breath wafted up to the cave and everyone had to struggle not to gag.

"I really wish I hadn't eaten those chips," Shane said. "That smell is making me seriously nauseous." He looked at his brother. "You know what helps with nausea?"

"All out of that medicine, bro," Max said.

"Dammit!" Shane swore.

The dinosaur roared again.

"See? Even he's pissed at us," Shane said. "Is it a he?"

"I don't know," Max said. "Go down there and check under its tail."

"We should send Lucy," Shane said. "She's our expert dick looker."

"Boys!" Thorne roared nearly as loud as the dinosaur.

"Sorry, Uncle Vinny," they replied in unison.

Thorne took a deep breath as the monster scaled the ridge and came for them.

"Alright," he said. "Time to make this bitch ours."

"I like the sound of that," Darby said, taking aim with her plasma rifle.

They waited a couple more seconds, then as the dinosaur opened its mouth to roar again, Team Grendel let loose with everything they had. Bullets slammed into the thing's hide, but being normal rounds, they barely managed to leave a nick. The plasma bolts on the other hand ripped chunks out of the creature's flesh everywhere they hit.

The dinosaur stopped climbing and swayed against the attack. Its new roar was one of pain and no longer anger. A hunk of its shoulder burst into a thick spray of blood and flesh and it cried out. The monster spun around and raced its way back down the ridge, almost diving into the jungle and the shadows it afforded.

"Huh," Shane said. "That was easier than I thought it'd be."

"Move!" Lucy yelled and shoved Shane aside as one of the huge red birds dove at him. The thing's talons slashed across Lucy's cheek and down her neck, sending blood spurting out in a high geyser.

"No!" half the Team yelled as the other half looked up and opened fire, obliterating the circling birds that weren't fast enough to fly away.

Lucy stared up at the sky as hands pressed against her neck. Darby leaned over and filled her vision.

"You won't die," Darby stated. "You die and you leave us with the boys as our only shooters. You want that?"

Lucy gave her a weak grin and closed her eyes.

Darby looked at Darren who had his hands firmly gripped to Lucy's neck.

"I've got her," Darren said. "Someone find me something to close the wound with. We can save her."

Darby handed her plasma rifle to Shane and sprinted into the cave. She was desperate to find a hidden med kit or anything that would save her teammate. She was just as desperate for the others to not see the stream of tears running down her cheeks.

***

Sweat streamed down Carlos and Moshi's faces as they brought the cannon to a stop outside the engine room hatch. The passageway and ceiling were buckled and dented all the way down, but the engine room hatch wasn't even touched.

"Huh," Ballantine said as he looked at the intact hatch. "Was I wrong? I could have sworn he would come here."

Ballantine held up a finger for Carlos and Moshi to sit tight then reached out and knocked on the engine room door.

"What?" Cougher called out.

"Hello, Cougher," Ballantine said. "Could you open up? Only take a second."

The hatch creaked and groaned as Cougher spun the wheel from the other side then yanked the hatch open. He cautiously peeked his head out, looked left, looked right, then leaned back into the room.

"You didn't happen to see a giant ape thing come roaring past here, did you?" Ballantine asked. "Apparently we have a Jekyll and Hyde situation and the Hyde is, well, hiding."

"Yeah, I fucking saw the gorilla," Cougher said. "I was standing here and it came crashing down the passageway. It was about to break in here, shouting about taking the ship for itself or something. I yelled that the engines were hit by an EMP and we didn't have the parts to fix them so it could have the fucking ship, for all I cared."

"You yelled all that before it had a chance to rip your arms off?" Ballantine said.

"I may have hit it with a wrench," Cougher said. "It was a really big wrench. The thing sniffed the air and seemed to believe me. I think it was going to tear me apart anyway, but then it lifted its head like it heard something and took off that way."

Cougher pointed down the passageway at the continuation of destruction.

"This is really going to be a bitch to fix, Ballantine," Cougher said. "I hope you plan on making the rest of the crew handle it. I'm still working on salvaging what I can from the engines, I don't have time to knock dents out of the walls."

"Not to worry," Ballantine said, clapping Cougher on the shoulder. "You just focus on what you're doing. Carry on."

"Fucking whacko," Cougher muttered as he closed the hatch.

Ballantine turned to Carlos and Moshi.

"I think we need to get above decks," Ballantine said. He looked at the cannon. "You two good to bring this up top?"

"No," Carlos said. "Even with the hydraulic lifters, this thing is a bitch to maneuver. I thought we would shoot it a couple times and be done. I do not want to lug this all over the ship."

"Is there anything more manageable?" Ballantine asked. "Perhaps a portable version back in the Toyshop?"

Carlos frowned at the use of the word Toyshop. Moshi only shook her head.

"That's unfortunate," Ballantine said.

There were several loud thunks and the ship shuddered slightly. Ballantine, Carlos, and Moshi all looked up at the ceiling, listening to the new development. After a few minutes, there were some sharp bangs and a couple of far-off shouts.

"Flash bangs," Ballantine said. "We've been boarded."

"Boarded? By whom?" Carlos asked.

"I'm guessing by whoever was on that ship coming towards us," Ballantine said. He smacked his forehead. "I knew I was forgetting something. That giant ape really smacked me around. I'm going to need a long soak in a tub and a nap to get my bearings straight again."

Moshi nodded.

"I know, right?" Ballantine smiled. "Doesn't a soak sound wonderful?"

More bangs, more shouts, but closer.

"Well, they're below decks now," Ballantine said. "We should really go introduce ourselves before they find us and a horrible accident happens."

Moshi squeaked a little.

"Not to worry, Moshi," Ballantine said. He draped an arm across her shoulders and steered her back towards the stairs. "Stick with me and you'll be fine."

"What about me?" Carlos snapped.

"With your attitude?" Ballantine replied, shaking his head. "Not sure what's going to happen to you."

"You are such an asshole, Ballantine," Carlos grumbled.

"That's what I have been told," Ballantine said.

Even more bangs and shouts.

"Man, they should all relax," Ballantine said. "We're actually reasonable people once you get to know us, right Moshi?"

Moshi nodded as they ascended the stairs.

***

Popeye stared at the deck of the Beowulf III and shook his head.

"The place is a fucking mess," he said. "Who has been in charge while I was gone?"

"We've all chipped in to help," Kinsey said, her hands restrained behind her back by zip ties. Her face was puffy and both lips were split. She had a nasty burn mark on her right cheek and her shoulders were hunched forward like she was in pain. She coughed and winced before continuing. "Mostly it's been whatever deckhand Lake can intimidate the most. They just haven't been motivated since you left."

"Damn right," Popeye said, brandishing his prosthetic leg. "Ain't no one to threaten to jam this up their asses."

"This is a lovely conversation on the finer points of employee motivation, but please shut the hell up, all of you," Jowarski said.

He grabbed Kinsey by the arms and shook her. She almost cried out, yet was able to choke it back. Jowarski saw this and shook her again. Hard. Kinsey did cry out that time.

Standing next to Kinsey was a zip-tied, shell-shocked-looking Ingrid. Her eyes were swollen and she had snot dripping from both nostrils. There weren't any marks on her, but her body trembled like a kicked dog waiting for the next blow. She leaned her shoulder against Kinsey, her subconscious mind desperate for some kind of protection even if her potential protector was beaten badly and zip tied.

Men dressed in black body armor swarmed across the deck and filtered down through the hatches to the decks below. Kinsey watched them go and wondered how many Ballantine would kill before he was captured. She hadn't told Jowarski or Dana where she thought Ballantine would be, ship or island. She didn't need to. After a few punches and kicks, Ingrid couldn't stand to watch Kinsey get tortured so she caved, spilling everything she knew.

It was all over in minutes. That pissed Jowarski off. He looked like his favorite toy had been taken away. He wanted more time to tear the truth out of Kinsey and Ingrid went and ruined that.

So he got nasty.

Kinsey had been through worse. Ingrid had not. Glancing at the tech out of the corner of her eye, Kinsey wondered if Ingrid would bounce back. She hoped so. Ingrid was too strong a person deep down to just give in. Fuck that shit.

Several men came hurrying out of one of the hatchways. The man in front rushed over to Jowarski.

"We have him," the man reported. "He was with two nerds. They, uh, got away."

"Nerds got away?" Jowarski growled.

"Sorry, sir," the man replied.

"That's not nice. Nerds are cool," Ingrid whispered and Kinsey smiled. Yeah, she would be just fine.

"Whatever," Jowarski said. "Bring him to me." He tapped at his ear. "Dana? We have your husband secured. You can come over at your discretion." He listened for a few seconds and then nodded. "I won't touch him, I promise." He gave Kinsey a wink. "You get to take care of him yourself."

"You really think you can kill Ballantine?" Kinsey asked. "You're an idiot."

"People have said that," Jowarski replied. "But I am goal oriented. My goal isn't to kill Ballantine, it's to present him to his wife so she can kill him. If she asks me to do it for her then so be it."

Popeye scoffed.

"You agree with Ms. Thorne?" Jowarski asked.

"I agree that you are an idiot, yeah," Popeye said.

"Is that so?" Jowarski replied. "Then I guess you were broken by an idiot. So what does that make you?"

Popeye turned his face away and stared out over the water. He muttered something, but it was lost to the sea wind.

"No need to be pushy," Ballantine said as he was led from one of the hatchways. "I am cooperating." He held up his hands and showed the body-armored men the cuffs he was sporting. "You have me perfectly secured. Big, tough professionals like you shouldn't be scared of a simple pencil pusher like me. Guys, I'm administration, not operations."

"Our men have been fully briefed on your skills, Ballantine," Jowarski said.

Ballantine's entire demeanor changed. The smart ass, devil may care attitude was replaced with pure rage.

"Oh, this just got very interesting," Ballantine said, his voice that of a cold, deadly predator. "You should not have come, Chance. You really, really shouldn't have come."

He glanced over at the ship that was sitting hull to hull with the Beowulf III.

"Is she with you?" he asked. "Is she, Chance? You brought her along, didn't you? Man, you are dumber than I thought."

"This is her mission, Ballantine," Jowarski said. "I didn't bring her, she brought me."

Ballantine watched the man for a couple of seconds then nodded.

"Then where is she?" he asked.

"On her way," Jowarski replied.

Ballantine studied Kinsey, Ingrid, then Popeye.

"Mr. DeBruhl, it is good to see you amongst the living," Ballantine said.

"If you say so," Popeye replied.

Ballantine frowned at the answer then looked at Kinsey and Ingrid, especially Ingrid.

"Ms. Thorne, is our elf going to be alright?" he asked.

"She is," Kinsey said. "She's strong."

"I take it Mr. Jowarski was not polite in his behavior," Ballantine said. It was not a question.

"Nope," Kinsey said. "I took most of the impoliteness, but he did save some for Ingrid."

"The best for last, you might say," Jowarski chuckled.

Ingrid flashed him a look of pure rage and Ballantine smiled.

"Yes, our elf will be fine," Ballantine said. Then he studied Popeye some more. "As for our boatswain, I think you may have done some long-term damage. Was it one of your patented mind fucks, Chance? Or did my wife get her claws in him too? Did she use that machine of hers?"

"Why don't you ask me?" Dana said as she stepped onto a gangplank that bridged the slight gap between ships. She easily balanced her way over and dropped onto the Beowulf III's deck, her eyes steely and locked onto Ballantine. "It is good to see you, Ballantine."

"Even your wife calls you by your last name?" Kinsey asked. "Classic."

"I know, right?" Ballantine laughed. "I'm a man of great mystery and intrigue." He cleared his throat and bowed slightly to Dana. "Hello, my love. You are supposed to be dead. That was part of the bargain. You being here now means you broke our bargain."

"Oh, here it comes!" Dana exclaimed. "Deals and bargains and contracts! Every damn time with you, Ballantine! Every damn time! You know what? Life changes! People change! And when you decide to wipe out the company and take things over for yourself, without even giving me the courtesy of a heads up, then bargains change!"

"You were dead," Ballantine stated. "I can't give a dead person a heads up."

"Oh, bullshit!" Dana shouted. It was loud enough to make even Jowarski flinch. "You knew I wasn't dead! You knew exactly where I was at all times!"

"With him," Ballantine said, turning his attention to Jowarski. "We'll come back to that, Chance. Don't you worry."

"Not worried at all," Jowarski replied. "No need to be. Endgame is over, Ballantine. You failed. In order for your plan to work, you needed to kill us all. Leaving even one splinter of one division was failure. Guess what? You failed!"

"Yep," Ballantine nodded. "I failed."

Jowarski coughed and looked puzzled. "What was that? Did you agree with me?"

"I did," Ballantine said. "I let my emotions overrule common sense. I should have started with you and your division. But I decided to wait and leave you for last. My mistake."

"Yes...your mistake," Jowarski said.

"What now?" Ballantine asked. "You put a bullet in my head?"

"Not yet," Dana said. "The assets of yours we know about are probably only a tenth of what you really have. I want names and locations before I put you out of my misery."

"Okay," Ballantine said.

Dana sighed.

"Dammit, what do you have up your sleeve?" she asked. "I know you, Ballantine. You have something planned. What is it?"

"I actually have nothing planned," Ballantine said. "All plans are done. I'm winging it from here on out. It's the new Ballantine. Footloose and fancy free."

"More bullshit," Dana grumbled. "You never stop."

"If a shark stops, he drowns," Ballantine said. "And you know how much I love sharks."

"That makes no sense," Jowarski said.

"Put him over there against that rail," Dana ordered. "Let him sit in the sun for an hour and then I'll start my little chat." She pointed at Popeye. "You! Time to give us the tour of this ship."

"Are you a tour guide now, Popeye?" Ballantine asked.

"Yeah," Popeye said. "I guess I am."

"Be sure and show them the mess," Ballantine said. "And perhaps the Toyshop? The elves have done some great things to it. Can you do that, Popeye?"

"The Toyshop is your armory, right?" Jowarski asked. "Nice try, Ballantine. I'll send some of my men down there on their own. No need for Mr. DeBruhl to waste his time."

Ballantine shrugged.

"What about these two?" Jowarski asked, yanking Kinsey's arm almost out of the socket.

"Leave them up here," Dana said. "But nowhere near Ballantine. Keep them on opposite sides of the ship."

"You heard her," Jowarski said to the men that stood guard. "And make sure they don't talk to each other."

"Mr. DeBruhl?" Dana said. "After you."

Popeye sighed and limped over to the main hatchway. He glanced over his shoulder at Kinsey and Ingrid then Ballantine. Ballantine responded with a huge smile. Popeye shook his head then was quickly lost from sight.

As soon as Dana and Jowarski were gone, Kinsey looked over at Ballantine. His eyes were averted, looking off into space. But Kinsey knew the man well enough to realize he was telling her something. She rolled her head on her neck and casually looked at the other ship, but not in the direction Ballantine was looking. She made a point of specifically looking in the opposite direction.

For a brief second, she thought the beatings and hot sun were making her hallucinate. But considering all the crazy shit she'd seen since becoming a part of Team Grendel, a huge gorilla with tattered clothes plastered to its hairy body wasn't exactly out of the realm of possibility. In the time it took her to comprehend what she saw, the thing was lost from sight, gone into the belly of the other ship.

Kinsey looked back at Ballantine and that time he was staring right at her. His huge grin was even huger.

But it faltered at the sound of several loud roars that came from the island. All eyes, even the guards', looked across the bay with its perpetually schooling fish things, and watched as far off trees shuddered and shook. Huge red birds circled above the jungle, darting down now and again, screeching their prehistoric screeches.

"You know what?" Ballantine said to the guards. "If you guys are looking for new employment, keep me in mind." He nodded towards the island. "I really do know how to keep the workplace from being boring."

***

"Son of a fuck!" Thorne shouted as he pulled the trigger on the plasma rifle again and again, turning one of the twelve-foot dinosaurs that chased them into a pulpy splat against the wall of ferns to Team Grendel's left. "I really hate dinosaurs!"

On his other side stood Darby, her plasma rifle barking as well. A second dino then a third became bloody gunk. She looked down at her energy readings and snarled.

"Almost out again," Darby said.

Thorne fired off three bolts before checking his. "Yeah, same here."

Behind them, Darren and Shane carried a makeshift stretcher that held Lucy. Her eyes were bright and she held her own hands to her neck, but her skin was almost pure white and her lips had a bluish tinge to them.

"You okay, Luce?" Shane asked, holding the rear of the stretcher. "You hang on, okay?"

Lucy gave him a weak smile.

Behind the stretcher were Mike and Max. Mike had his plasma rifle up, but Max held a sawed-off Mossberg pistol grip shotgun, having given his plasma rifle to Thorne. He pumped the shotgun and fired, sending a slug into the face of a dinosaur that looked like its teeth could shred an aluminum can as easily as slicing a tomato.

"What are you grinning at?" Mike asked, firing at another dinosaur, that one about twice the size of the one that Max just relieved of most of its chest. "You think this is fun, don't you?"

"I'd need to change professions if I didn't," Max said. "And I was grinning because I was remembering that old Ginsu commercial. It slices!" He fired at another dinosaur, shredding half the thing's face. "It dices!" He fired again, taking off a stubby arm from a raptor-looking thing that had just leapt at him. "It even cuts cans!"

He flipped the Mossberg around and whacked a second leaping dino like it was a baseball heading over home plate. Max reached into his pockets and started pulling out shells then shoving them into the shotgun's breach.

Mike fried a dozen creeper vines that lashed out at his face. Half the jungle to his left seemed to shrink back as if it had been hit. Mike blasted that greenery and suddenly hundreds of vines that had been hanging from branches and clung to trunks slunk away, desperate to get clear of danger.

"Remind me to tell Ballantine that I am no longer cool with jungle work," Mike said. "A nice, barren desert would be ideal for our next op. No more greenery."

"There's scary shit in deserts, man," Max said. He blasted two snake looking things, ripping their bellies open. Whatever they had for their dinners spilled out onto the jungle floor. "But I totally hear you."

The Team came to a clearing and Darby halted them briefly. Just for a split second so she could get her bearings. It wasn't hard since they were still on an incline and they could see the bay in the distance.

"Is that a second ship?" Darby asked.

"Yeah," Thorne said. "We'll deal with that later."

A massive roar shook the jungle and half the dinosaurs that were coming in to attack Team Grendel decided they no longer wanted to be anywhere near the area. They rushed off as fast as their clawed feet would take them.

"Oh, piss," Max said. "I think our old buddy is coming to see us off."

A red bird dino swooped down at them and Thorne took it out with a well-placed blast. His plasma rifle beeped and he looked at Darby as they got moving again.

"Six more shots, maybe," Darby said to Thorne. "Make the best of them."

Thorne nodded. He had a pistol on his hip and a knife strapped to his leg, all thanks to the weapons cache they had found in the cave, but as a second roar shook the trees that lined the small clearing, he knew they would be as effective as toothpicks and spitballs against the thing coming for them.

"We do what we can," Thorne said. "We get Lucy and the others to the Zodiac and make sure they can get back to the ship. Understood?"

"Understood," Darby said. She swung to the left and fired into the trees. An explosion of blood and bone filled the shadows and spilled out over the ferns that swayed in the island breeze.

Team Grendel kept moving, kept fighting, kept on surviving as they dove into the jungle at the far end of the clearing.

Chapter Eleven- Company

"What exactly is it you're looking for?" Popeye asked as he was shoved forward by Jowarski. "It's just a ship."

"The Beowulf is hardly just a ship," Dana said.

"Beowulf III," Popeye said.

"Beowulf IV, to be more accurate," Dana said. "But I can see how Ballantine would prefer to forget the very first ship that bore the name. It was not a good time in our marriage. We don't talk about that."

Popeye shook his head. "You people are messed up."

"Just get us to Ballantine's personal quarters," Jowarski said. "He'll have his files stashed there." He glanced at Dana. "You sure you can get his safe open? We have techs on our ship that can crack it in only a few minutes."

"No, I can do it," Dana said. "He hasn't changed the combination. He'd never do that."

"Doesn't seem like a secure way to go about keeping anything safe," Jowarski said. "Amateur, if you ask me."

"I didn't," Dana said.

"I ain't never been in Ballantine's personal quarters," Popeye said. "I didn't think the man needed any since I ain't never seen him sleep."

"Hard to see a man sleep if you've never been to where he sleeps," Jowarski said. "That's called logic, Mr. DeBruhl."

"You can cram that logic up your ass," Popeye said.

The party kept moving down the passageway. Popeye noted the destruction to the walls and ceiling and shook his head. The damage had the guards that flanked Popeye, Jowarski, and Dana, on edge and Popeye looked over to see more than a couple trigger fingers looking mighty itchy.

"Careful," Popeye said. "You start firing in here and we're likely to get killed by a ricochet."

"My men know their jobs, Mr. DeBruhl," Jowarski said. "You just need to know yours. Get us to Ballantine's quarters."

"It's this way," Popeye said and took them through a mangled hatchway and into another damaged passageway. "What in hell did they do to my ship?"

They had gotten to the middle of the passageway when the wall on their left began to shimmer then disappear completely.

"Hello," Ronald said just before he reached out of the Toyshop and ripped one of the guard's head off. "Goodbye."

A second guard spun about to fire at the gigantopithecus, but he stopped in mid turn and let go of his rifle, his hands going to the open wound across his throat. Blood poured from between his fingers and he collapsed to his knees.

"What the fuck?" Jowarski yelled as he pulled a pistol from his hip and fired at Ronald.

Ronald cried out as blood bloomed from his right shoulder. Then the cry turned into a wall rumbling growl of rage.

"Oh, shit," Jowarski said. He turned and ran, leaving the guards to stand there, their mouths wide open as the impossible creature closed on them.

"That's new," Popeye said to Dana.

Two more guards went down with slashed throats before they could get a shot off. The second to last guard was ripped limb from limb by Ronald before the very last guard dropped his rifle and held his hands above his head.

"I don't want to die!" the man shouted, dropping to his knees. "Please don't kill me, Bigfoot!"

"I do not like being called Bigfoot!" Ronald roared as he grabbed them man by the helmet and lifted him up off his knees. One shake, one snap, and it was all over. The body fell to the floor as Ronald opened his hand. "It is rude to call someone of my intelligence and learning the name of a mythical creature."

"I wouldn't say mythical," Gunnar stated as he materialized next to Dana, a combat knife in his hand and the blade pressed to the woman's throat. "I mean, come on, Ronald, you do have family in the Pacific Northwest that get spotted sometimes."

"That does not mean I have to accept the Bigfoot moniker," Ronald said. "I do have dignity."

"Gunnar? That you?" Popeye asked, looking at the suited figure standing next to Dana.

Gunnar pulled back the mesh that obscured his head and face and grinned at Popeye. "Popeye? What the fuck, man? You're dead!"

"Yeah, yeah, I know," Popeye said. "But I ain't."

"I can see that," Gunnar said.

Popeye turned and stared at Ronald.

"Oh, sorry," Gunnar said, the blade still pressed to Dana's throat. "Popeye DeBruhl, this is Ronald. Ronald, Popeye. Ronald joined us when we reached the other island, but you were dead by then."

"Nice to meet ya," Popeye said. He sort of held his hand out. "Do we shake?"

"Of course," Ronald said, enveloping the small man's hand in his massive hairy one. "Decorum doesn't go away just because there are bodies on the ground."

Ronald grinned big and Popeye struggled not to shy away from the huge mouth full of equally huge teeth.

"Since we're doing introductions," Popeye said, nodding to Dana. "This is Dana Ballantine. Our Ballantine's wife."

"Hello, Ronald," Dana said.

"Dana, a pleasure to see you again," Ronald said. "You may remove the knife from her throat, Gunnar. Dr. Ballantine will no longer be a threat."

"Did you say this is Ballantine's wife?" Gunnar asked.

"Yes, and we are old friends," Ronald said. "It was she that introduced me to Ballantine and made it possible for me to take my position with Boris." Ronald smacked his forehead. "Oh, dear me." He turned back to the Toyshop. "It is safe to come out now."

Moshi, Carlos, Boris, and Dr. Morganton all peeked around the various shelves of equipment inside the Toyshop.

"Moshi!" Dana said and held out her arms.

Moshi frowned and shook her head back and forth then disappeared deeper into the Toyshop.

"Dana," Carlos nodded.

"Carlos," Dana replied and glared.

"Whatever," Carlos sighed.

***

All heads turned from the island and towards the other ship as the first screams echoed across the gap.

"Uh oh," Ballantine said to the guards. "Sounds like you may have a spot of trouble over there. You guys go help your friends. I'll keep an eye on the ladies here. What? No? Okay, but don't say I didn't try to help."

A claxon blared on the other ship and the screams increased despite the added noise. Men began to scramble across the upper deck and someone was shouting from the bridge. The sound of metal being ripped apart was almost as loud as the claxon.

"Someone over there is not a happy camper," Ballantine said.

The guards turned to the other ship and raised their rifles. A couple of them took tentative steps towards the gangplank then stopped as they watched crumpled body after crumpled body being tossed out of one of the hatchways.

Then more metal ripped and shrapnel was sent flying everywhere as the Harris-Logan thing exploded out from the lower decks and back into the open air.

"This will be my ship!" the monster bellowed.

"I think he just called dibs, guys," Ballantine said to the guards. "Are you going to let him get away with that?"

"I will take this ship and I will leave this Hell!" the Harris-Logan thing roared.

The guards on the B3 looked at each other then took aim and started firing.

The Harris-Logan thing turned towards them and waved its massive hands like it was batting away annoying gnats. Small dots of red appeared on its massively muscled chest, but it did not seem to affect the beast one bit.

"MY SHIP!" the Harris-Logan thing bellowed as it picked up a hatch door that had been torn free and threw it across the gap to the B3.

Only a couple of guards were able to get out of the way in time as the hatch door flew at them. The rest were ripped in half. Ballantine barely had time to duck and let the bloody door fly over his head.

"Good toss, Timothy!" Ballantine yelled as he stood back up. "Almost got them all!"

The remaining guards got back to their feet and opened fire again. The Harris-Logan thing roared at them then was lost from sight as it dove below decks once more.

"I think he's going back for seconds," Ballantine said.

The two guards left turned on Ballantine, rifles up and smoking.

"What was that thing?" one of the guards asked. "That something you made? Jowarski's going to—"

The guard didn't get to finish as two legs suddenly wrapped about his neck, yanking him over backwards. The snapping of vertebrae wasn't quite loud enough to be heard over the chaos coming from the other ship, but everyone on deck got the gist of what had happened as the guard's head turned at a very unnatural angle.

The second guard spun about and took aim at the owner of the two legs, but he didn't get a shot off as Ingrid rammed him from the side. He stumbled and fell towards Ballantine. All the man had to do was step aside and stick out a foot. The guard tripped and flipped end over end across the railing and was lost from sight. Ballantine nodded when he heard the splash. He smiled when he heard the screams as what was in the water found a fresh meal.

"We do make a fine team," Ballantine said.

Kinsey unlocked her legs from the dead guard's neck and stood up. She turned around and showed her zip ties to Ballantine.

"Your hands are in front," she said. "You think you can get the knife from his belt and cut me loose?"

"My pleasure, Ms. Thorne," Ballantine said.

He started to crouch then dove instead, taking Kinsey and Ingrid out at the legs, sending them falling to the deck. Shots rang out as Jowarski burst from the main hatchway, a pistol in his hand firing wildly.

"What the fuck is going on?" Jowarski screamed as he came to a stop, his eyes locked on the destruction happening on his ship. He spun about and aimed his pistol at Ballantine. "What have you done? How? How can you do these things when you are tied up? What kind of fucking freak are you?"

"I'm the freak that knows how to plan for every contingency," Ballantine replied calmly, his body shielding Kinsey's and Ingrid's as they lay on the deck. "But more importantly, I'm the freak that embraces chaos and has all the faith in the world that it will turn out my way."

"Then that makes you a dead freak," Jowarski said, moving towards Ballantine. "Because this chaos is not going to turn out—"

His chest exploded open and then half his head was gone as extremely loud shots rang out. More of Jowarski's body was lost to the barrage of bullets that crashed into him until there wasn't enough of him left to stay standing.

Ballantine, Kinsey, and Ingrid looked up to see Lake standing at the railing outside the bridge, a smoking Desert Eagle in each hand.

"I'm the captain of this fucking ship!" Lake yelled, his words slurred. "If anyone gets to kill Ballantine it's me!"

He belched loudly then turned and vomited over the railing.

"That is the chaos I'm talking about," Ballantine grinned. "Damn that man is good with those hand cannons. He doesn't even need a double grip."

"Is he drunk?" Ingrid asked as Lake continued puking.

"They didn't think to check the bridge?" Kinsey asked.

"I know, right?" Ballantine said, getting to his feet. "There is just no accounting for professionalism these days."

Lake puked some more then waved his pistols in the air. Right before his eyes rolled up in his head and he passed out.

***

Team Grendel broke from the tree line then stopped as they saw what was before them. The way to the Zodiac was blocked by a hundred croanderthals, all brandishing various weapons and blowguns. The blowgunned few put their weapons to their lips and prepared to fire.

"You have got to be fucking kidding me," Thorne said as he locked eyes with the woman he recognized as the Liu croanderthal. Despite their new discoveries below the Omega facility, Thorne knew she wasn't a clone. He saw the differences in her instantly, his SEAL-trained eyes sizing her up on the spot. "This bitch again?"

Darby grinned at his comment and put her plasma rifle to her shoulder. "We get Lucy and the others to the Zodiac."

"That's the plan," Thorne said.

"What was that?" Darren asked. "No fucking way! No suicide pacts! This is not self-sacrifice day!"

"Every day is self-sacrifice day when you work for Ballantine," Darby said.

"Take them down!" the Liu croanderthal shouted.

Before a single poisoned dart was blown, three croanderthal heads burst open. A half second later, three gunshots echoed across the bay. The Liu croanderthal spun around and roared at the far-off ship.

More shots rang out as croanderthal after croanderthal was dropped. A bullet whizzed past Thorne's cheek and he could have sworn he heard his daughter's far-off voice yell, "Sorry, Daddy!"

The Liu croanderthal began shoving her people about, yelling at them to ignore the guns and go kill Thorne and his Team. She shook with rage and opened her mouth to roar again, but she was beaten to the punch by a considerably more forceful roar that tore through the trees behind Thorne and company.

"Big and ugly is back!" Max yelled. "Go!"

Darren and Shane lifted Lucy off the stretcher and each draped one of her arms over their shoulders. They drug her off to the side, getting as far away as possible from what was about to come out at them.

Mike opened fire on the croanderthals with his plasma gun, running sideways and providing covering fire for Darren and Shane as they struggled to keep Lucy up on her feet.

Max was right beside him, his shotgun barking at the mutant cannibals that came for them, clubs held high, razor sharp teeth showing.

Thorne and Darby simply walked forward, taking careful, well-placed shots with their plasma rifles, ripping holes in the mob of croanderthals. The croanderthals responded in kind by rushing towards the two, rage overriding the fear of what was coming from the jungle.

"Here we go," Thorne said as his plasma rifle powered down. He whipped it about and grabbed the barrel like a bat just as Darby did the same thing.

Croanderthal heads stopped exploding as Thorne and Darby got too close to the targets, but Thorne could tell the firing hadn't stopped completely. Gunshots still echoed across the bay. Either the shooters had found targets far enough away not to hit Thorne and Darby with friendly fire or...

The trees were torn from their roots as the massive, mutated, T-rex-looking bastard burst from the jungle and immediately scooped up four croanderthals in its mouth, crunching down hard and sending blood and guts spewing for several meters across the white sand beach.

Thorne ignored the monster, knowing there was absolutely nothing he could do about it. He just concentrated on bashing in as many protruding foreheads as he could. Croanderthal after croanderthal dropped from his constant swinging of the dead plasma rifle. Almost as many dropped from Darby's swinging as well, but she was taking more careful aim, making sure each swing was a certain kill shot. Thorne admired the dedication briefly then focused back on his mad attack.

Down the beach, Max fired his shotgun into a dozen croanderthals running at him until the gun clicked empty. He tossed it aside and pulled a .45 from his hip, firing until that was empty. A dozen croanderthal corpses lay at his feet, but more were coming at him and his guns were empty.

He picked up a crude club and held it over his head.

"Come on, you Flintstone motherfuckers!" he shouted. "It's time to go clubbing!"

Even with all the distance and violence between them, Max would swear later he heard Darby groan.

He brought the club down onto one skull then another before he was tackled at the waist and sent falling onto his back in the sand.

"Dig in!" Mike shouted and Max covered his head with his arms and closed his eyes.

He felt the heat of the plasma blasts rip around him and the skin on his arms burned and tingled. Then he was covered in croanderthal gore. But at least he wasn't under a prehistoric dogpile anymore. He opened his eyes and gave Mike a thumbs up then wiped as much of the guts off him as he could before getting to his feet.

"Thanks," Max said.

"Yeah, you won't thank me if you get caveman Hep C," Mike said, frowning at Max's appearance. "You're going to need a lot of showers."

Mike's eyes went wide and he lifted the plasma rifle again. Max dropped to a knee as the man fired then looked over his shoulder as two croanderthals exploded into piles of offal.

"These fuckers never give up, do they?" Max asked as he once again got to his feet.

"No, they fucking don't," Mike said.

A few yards away, Darren and Shane still struggled with Lucy.

"Luce? Can you hear me?" Shane asked.

"Yeah," Lucy replied weakly. "But I'm really tired, Shane. Can I sleep for a bit?"

"No," Darren barked. "Keep your eyes open and stay with us. You sleep, you die."

"Way to sugar coat it, D," Shane said.

They turned to their right and headed for the Zodiac that was left all alone a few feet up from the high tide line on the beach. All of the croanderthals were occupied dealing with Darby and Thorne or running and scrambling from the giant dinosaur that was even busier making snacks out of them.

"Lucy? Answer me," Shane snapped as Lucy's head lulled against his cheek. "Lucy!"

"What?" she grumbled in a sleepy voice. "Stop yelling at me. Too loud."

"Tell me some dick jokes," Darren said.

"Really?" Shane responded.

"Whatever it takes," Darren snapped.

"Fine," Shane said. "Hey, Lucy? Remember how fun it was to mock my penis? You got anymore good ones you've been saving up?"

"I have good ones," Lucy replied quietly. "Which is more than you can say, little balls."

"Okay, now we are going after all of my genitalia," Shane said. "Awesome."

"What's two inches and grows to six inches when you stroke it?" Lucy asked, smiling a crooked smile.

"I don't know, Luce, what is two inches and grows to six inches when you stroke it?" Shane asked.

"Yeah, you'd have to ask," Lucy said. "Because you've never made it passed the two inches."

"That was awful," Darren said, laughing. "Tell another one."

"How many dicks does it take Shane to screw a chick?" Lucy asked.

"How many dicks does it take?" Shane asked as they progressively got closer to the Zodiac.

"One," Lucy said. "Just one. Which is more than you have."

"I should let her die," Shane said. "No one should have to suffer jokes this lame."

"I'm dying, asshole," Lucy whispered. "Fuck off."

They got her into the raft and eased her to the bottom then Darren turned to wave the others over.

"Fuck," he said.

Shane looked up and saw Thorne and Darby surrounded by croanderthals while Max and Mike were busy trying to draw off as many as possible further down the beach so the shooters on the B3 could pick them off.

"We can't wait," Darren said and looked at Shane.

"Go," Shane said. "You're a better sailor. You'll get her on board faster than me."

Darren handed him a knife and a 9mm.

"Kill 'em all," Darren said as he started shoving the Zodiac towards the surf.

"That's the plan," Shane said. He turned and looked at the brutal chaos. "Hey, Uncle Vinny! Got room for one more?"

Shane started to run towards a group of croanderthals, but they all spun around and fled. He thought it was because of them then realized the mutant T-Rex was moving fast in their direction.

"Oh, fuck," Shane said as he realized it was coming at him as well. He turned and took off after Darren and the Zodiac. "D! Hold up!"

***

Ballantine pulled his eye away from the rifle scope and looked over his shoulder as he heard voices coming up from the main hatchway. He ignored the look he received from Dana and focused on the person that was last to step through the hatchway.

"Carlos, we need that cannon, now!" Ballantine shouted. "I also need you to focus the beam so it can hit a specific target on that beach!"

"You what?" Carlos snapped then he looked at who was standing at the railing. His eyes went past Kinsey and fixed on Ingrid. "Why does she have a rifle? She can't shoot!"

"The hell she can't!" Kinsey snapped without looking away from her scope. "The girl has a gift! Looks like we have another shooter on this ship!"

"I may assign her to Team Grendel," Ballantine said. "If you don't hurry your ass down there and bring up the cannon right this damned second!"

"If it is heavy then I will gladly help carry it," Ronald said.

"Yeah, it's heavy," Carlos snapped as he turned on his heel and headed back through the hatchway, uttering various curses and insults in a muffled voice.

"I shall return," Ronald said to Gunnar. "Please watch over Dana for me. She is not to be trusted, unfortunately."

"You got that right," Ballantine said, returning to his scope and squeezing the trigger twice before looking back at Gunnar. "Gut her if you have to."

"What the hell?" Gunnar mumbled. "Your relationships need work, Ballantine."

Ballantine only laughed and went back to sniping.

"There is nothing to be done for him," Dana said. She glanced over at her ship and her eyes widened. "Oh my god…"

Blood coated every inch of the upper deck. There were quiet moans and some cries for help. Those stopped quickly as the Harris-Logan thing went from survivor to survivor and crushed their skulls, sending spurts of blood shooting up into the sea air. It looked over at the B3 and roared then grabbed a railing and swung itself up onto the platform outside the bridge.

"What is that?" Dana asked.

"Dr. Timothy Harris," Ballantine responded without stopping his firing. "You remember Timothy, don't you? That kid that kept calling when we lived in Boston? You said he was bordering on being creepy. I think he stepped over the border."

"Everything you touch…" Dana let the words hang there and then just folded onto the deck, her butt hitting the hot metal with an unceremonious whump.

Gunnar held his knife to his side and watched her closely.

***

A jagged hunk of rock tore into Thorne's side and he fell to a knee in severe pain. Darby grabbed him under the armpit and yanked him back up.

"No quitting!" Darby shouted, using her rifle butt to shatter the croanderthal's skull that attacked Thorne. "Fight, goddammit!"

"I am," Thorne said, gasping as the wound in his side stretched and blood squirted out. "I got this."

Darby let him go and blocked an attack from another croanderthal. The thing tried to sweep her legs, but she perfectly timed a stomp and snapped his leg off at the knee. The creature screamed then shut up as Darby crushed his face with her rifle.

A hard blow to the back of her head sent her reeling and she stumbled into a pack of four croanderthals who immediately began to pummel her. At least until one of them was snatched up in the jaws of the giant T-rex that wasn't really a T-rex. The other croanderthals scattered and fled, leaving Darby on her knees, blood pouring from a gash across her left eyebrow and her right ear swelling to an unsafe size.

"Hey!" Max yelled just as the mutant T-rex gulped down another croanderthal and started to turn its attention on Darby. "Hey, you scaly fucker! Over here!"

The beast whipped its head about and roared at Max.

"Shit," Max said as he took a couple of steps back. "I don't think it liked being called a scaly fucker."

The monster faced Max and then began to run full on towards the Reynolds brother.

"Go!" Mike yelled, yanking at Max's arm. "Come on!"

"I guess that distraction worked," Max said, huffing and puffing as he and Mike sprinted across the sand. "Too bad it's going to get me killed."

"It's going to get the both of us killed," Mike said. "Dickhead."

"The thing wanted to munch on my lady and I'm the only one that gets to munch on my lady," Max said.

"Jesus, if that's the last image I have in my head before I die, I am so going to haunt you in the afterlife," Mike shouted.

***

Thorne watched the beast take off after Mike and his nephew. He knew there wasn't a damn thing he could do about it. There wasn't a damn thing he could do about much considering he was surrounded by croanderthals. They encircled him and Darby, their wide brows glowering, their razor sharp teeth on full display.

"What the fucking point is there to any of you?" Thorne snarled. "Bunch of fucking savages jerking off on some deserted island."

"Not deserted," the Liu croanderthal said as she stepped from the circle to face Thorne. "We here. We live. No desert."

Darby took a swing at the woman thing, but her blow was blocked and she was sent falling back against the legs of those that had her and Thorne surrounded. Rough, gnarled hands picked her up and shoved her back in the center.

"What do you want?" Thorne asked. His shoulders were slumped and his chest heaved up and down as he tried to catch his breath. "Just tell me what you want."

"I tell you," the Liu thing said. "Leader want Ballantine. Me break Ballantine."

"He's never going to set foot on this beach," Darby said. "He'll let us die first."

She said it with some venom that the Liu croanderthal couldn't help but smile at. It was a nasty smile. All teeth and blood.

"You hate Ballantine," the Liu croanderthal said. "You hate like leader me hate."

"I hate like Darby me hate," Darby said. "No one else hates like Darby me hates."

"Can we not talk like them, please?" Thorne said. "Have some dignity before we die."

Before Darby could respond, the Liu croanderthal grabbed Darby by the throat and lifted her off the sand. It carried the woman out of the circle and towards the surf, shaking her like she was made of nothing.

"BALLANTINE!" the Liu Croanderthal shouted. "I have friend! I have her! I kill! You come or I kill!"

There was a far-off voice and the Liu croanderthal frowned.

"I no hear!" she yelled.

Then her face exploded and the back of her head opened wide sending croanderthal brains splattering against the mutants that stood and watched. The headless corpse stood there for a second, its grip still strong on Darby's throat, then it toppled over and Darby cried out as she gasped for breath.

Thorne pushed himself to the ground, nearly burying his body in the sand as shots rang out over and over again.

In seconds it was over and as he lifted his head, all he could see were croanderthal corpses piled up three high.

"Darby?" he called, spitting sand.

"Yeah," Darby replied, her voice a harsh croak.

"You gonna live?" Thorne asked.

"Yeah," Darby replied.

"Good," Thorne said.

He began to relax, but a roar down the beach forced him to push up onto his knees so he could see past the piles of corpses.

"Dammit," he said as he watched the mutant T-rex chase Max and Mike.

***

The Zodiac was winched into place and Darren and Shane both stared at who greeted them from the railing.

"Yeah, yeah, I'm alive," Popeye said. "Get over it."

"Okay," Darren said cautiously. "Where's Gunnar?"

"Here," Gunnar said and hurried over to the raft. "What do you need? Are you wounded?"

"Lucy," Shane said as he helped Darren get her out of the raft.

"Again?" Gunnar snapped. "Okay, no more trips to islands for this girl. Jesus Christ."

He checked her pulse and frowned.

"Let's get her to the infirmary now!" Gunnar yelled. "And I need O negative blood ASAP, so get ready to donate, people!"

They carried Lucy's limp body past Kinsey, Ingrid, and Ballantine, who were lowering their rifles and taking deep breaths.

"Good shooting," Darren said to Ballantine then looked at Kinsey. "You too, 'Sey."

"Ingrid was the superstar, 'Ren," Kinsey replied. "She deserves most of the credit."

"Does she?" Shane asked. "Good to know."

A roar from the beach made everyone pause.

"God dammit!" Ballantine shouted. "Where are Ronald and Carlos?"

"We are here, Ballantine," Ronald said, hefting the wave form cannon over his shoulder like it was a rolled tarp. "Please do not yell so much. It is irritating."

"We all second that notion," Shane said.

Ronald set the cannon by the railing and let Carlos make several adjustments to the machine.

"Are we ready?" Ronald asked. "Who will be taking the shot?"

"I can," Ingrid said. "I know how this works."

"And she's found her inner sniper," Kinsey said.

"This isn't a sniper rifle," Ingrid said as she stepped to the cannon and flipped a switch. She smiled up at Ronald. "Can you rotate it twenty-five degrees to the right, please?"

Ronald made the adjustment and Ingrid stared out at the beach across the bay.

"Breathe through the shot," Shane said.

"Shut up," pretty much everyone else replied.

Ingrid breathed through the shot.

***

Max screamed at the top of his lungs as he felt the hot breath of the mutant T-rex on his head. The stench from the giant maw was enough to make him want to puke, but he didn't want his last seconds on Earth to be filled with vomit, so he controlled his gorge and just kept screaming.

Mike was right next to him, but wasn't screaming. He was saying variations on almost every major religions' wrote prayers that he could think of. He also wanted to vomit from the stench.

The giant monster's footfalls made the ground shake underneath them and Max stumbled, stumbled, then fell. He face planted right into the sand and was ready to kiss his ass goodbye when he felt a force press him down against the beach. He thought he was being crushed by one of the thing's feet, yet he didn't feel his bones breaking or his internal organs leaking out his asshole.

What he did feel was about two tons of guts splatter about him, coating everything, from surf to tree line, on the beach in former mutant T-rex. He shoved what he thought was the thing's giant pancreas off his legs and looked around, wiping gore and sand from his eyes.

"Mike?" he called out.

"Here," Mike replied, extending a hand from the middle of a pile of intestines. "I don't want to be here though. Help."

Max got to his feet and staggered over to the pile of dino offal. He tossed looped guts this way and that and finally got Mike free.

The two gore-covered operators stood there for a second then looked down the beach at Darby and Thorne.

"What the fuck just happened?" Max yelled.

Darby shook her head and pointed at the Beowulf III.

"Well, duh," Max replied. "You good?"

Darby gave him a thumbs up.

"Uncle Vinny?" he shouted.

Thorne raised a thumbs up as well where he sat on a pile of croanderthal corpses.

"Ok. Looks like we're all good," Max said. "I'm going to sit down now."

He plopped to the sand and sighed.

"Ah, that feels good," Max said.

"I'm going for a swim," Mike said. "Wash some of this off."

"Monsters in the bay," Max said.

"Son of a bitch!" Mike yelled. "I fucking hate this place!"

Chapter Twelve- Just Another To Kill Ya Sunset

The crew of the Beowulf III sat in deck chairs and faced the other ship. They were wrapped in various bandages, slings, casts, and antiseptic creams. A flask was passed down the line of chairs, making its way three times before it was drained and empty.

"You're sure he'll be alright?" Ingrid asked, leaning forward to look at Ballantine a few seats away.

"That's what he said," Ballantine replied. "And I trust Ronald to know his own limits."

There were the sounds of breaking glass and crunching metal from the other ship then the Harris-Logan thing went flying up from the lower decks.

"NOOOOO!" the thing roared. "This is my ship now! I will leave here and take over the world!"

"He's got a more fucked up ego than you do, Ballantine," Max said.

"Oh, I doubt that," Ballantine replied.

"Have I missed anything?" Gunnar asked as he stepped onto the deck. "Ronald alright?"

"So far," Shane said, patting an empty seat. "Take a load off."

"Can't," Gunnar said. "Lucy is still not out of the woods. She lost a lot of blood. I'm going back to the infirmary right now. I just wanted to see if—OH, DAMN!"

Everyone jumped from their seats. Or the ones that felt like jumping did. They cheered and clapped their hands as Ronald lifted the Harris-Logan thing over his head then brought it down across his knee, snapping the things back in two.

There was a long, low howl and then silence.

Ronald walked the corpse over to the side of the ship and threw it overboard. The sounds of the sea dinos chomping down on the thing's body quickly followed.

"We win," Ballantine said, clapping politely. "Thank you, Ronald!"

Ronald waved to everyone as they thanked him as well.

"Okay, Grendel," Thorne said, hefting himself to his feet. "One last sweep then we let Cougher go scavenge for parts."

"You are sitting your ass down," Darren said to Thorne. "You are in no condition to do a deck by deck sweep with that wound in your side."

Thorne looked to Gunnar who shook his head.

"Not a chance, Vincent," Gunnar said.

"Fine," Thorne said. "But I want open coms the whole way. I ask what's going on and you answer me before I even ask the question."

"Control freak much?" Max whispered loudly.

"Come on, Grendel," Darren said. "One last mission then we help haul equipment over here."

There were some complaints, but not many since everyone was simply glad to still be living and able to haul equipment.

The deck cleared off quickly, leaving Thorne and Ballantine alone in the chairs.

"You know I have a lot of questions," Thorne said.

"And you know I probably won't answer many of them," Ballantine laughed. "Hell, I probably don't have answers to half of them, anyway."

"Nothing on that island made sense," Thorne said.

"You're telling me," Ballantine said and turned to look Thorne directly in the face. "I set this island up to recreate prehistoric biospheres, with some modern touches added, in order to study new creatures and how they react in different environments. The scientists I put in charge went well beyond that, lost their fucking minds, and turned it all to shit."

"I am getting a lot of conflicting stories," Thorne said. "Kinsey has one, you have one, what that Liu thing told me was another. Very few of the facts mesh and I have no idea what to believe."

"I'm right there with you," Ballantine said. "I don't know what to believe either. It's best we just forget this place and move on."

"And where are we moving on to?" Thorne asked. "How many of these secret islands do you have?"

"Too many," Ballantine said and stood up. "And I am willing to wager that more than a few of them are no longer secret. When it went to hell here, the island became visible to satellites once again. How many more have become visible? No way to know until we get there."

"Why?" Thorne asked.

"Why what?" Ballantine asked as he walked towards the main hatchway.

"Why do we have to get there?" Thorne asked. "Don't you think it's time to call it quits? Whatever you hired us for in the beginning has gone completely off the rails. Let it go, Ballantine."

"I wish I could, Commander," Ballantine said. His face looked tired, haggard. "God, I wish I could. But there are few things that happened on this island that makes me think the others aren't staying as isolated and anonymous as they should be."

"What does that mean?" Thorne asked.

"Not sure yet," Ballantine shrugged. "I'll let you know as soon as I do."

He walked through the hatchway, leaving Thorne to himself as the voices of Team Grendel began to fill the com in his ear.

***

The Beowulf III steamed at a steady ten knots south and east.

Lake glanced from the view out of the bridge windows and down at the control console every once in a while to make sure their heading was correct. He took a deep breath and let it out slowly, bored out of his mind.

"Anything yet?" Kinsey asked as she and Darren stepped onto the bridge from the outside hatch.

Kinsey was dressed in a bright red bikini and looking healthy and rested. Three weeks of no fighting, no running, just steaming along the South Pacific Ocean, was a good thing for the body.

Darren, dressed in blue swim trunks, looked tanned and equally as satisfied as Kinsey.

"Nope," Lake said. "Just water."

"Ballantine said we'd be reaching the next island any day now," Darren said.

"Yeah, I know," Lake replied.

"What's up your butt?" Darren asked.

"We ran out of beer," Lake said. "I had a stash, but I drank it."

"Oh, well," Kinsey said and patted him on the shoulder. "I'm sure you can find something to do instead of drink."

"You only say that because you're an ex-junkie and sober," Lake said. He looked at Darren. "Help me out here, D. You feel my pain, right?"

"The boys are finally all out of weed," Darren said. "There's a lot of pain going around."

"Welcome to sobriety, bitches!" Kinsey yelled and raised her hands in the air. "Woo hoo!"

"You suck, Thorne," Lake said.

"You know what, Marty? No, I don't," Kinsey said. "In fact, I'm pretty far from sucking."

She gave Lake a quick kiss on the cheek then left the bridge. Darren watched her go and placed a hand on Lake's shoulder.

"We'll get to civilization soon, Marty," Darren said. "Ballantine wants us to check out this one island first, though. He said there should be plenty of supplies, so maybe they'll have beer."

"You really believe that?" Lake laughed. "We'll be lucky if whatever is on this island doesn't drink us like beer. We barely got away from the last one with our lives."

"Says the guy that never stepped foot off this ship," Darren said then smiled before Lake could protest. "All good, Marty."

There was a crack and Lake jumped.

"Chill, it's just Max and Shane up in the crow's nest with Ingrid," Darren said. "She's getting a crash course in sniper school."

"Lucky her," Lake said. "She gets to do something different."

"You want me to take over being captain again?" Darren asked.

"You will have to pry this helm from my dead fingers, D," Lake said. "No way I'm letting you have my ship."

"Our ship," Darren said then left the bridge before Lake could argue.

Lake watched him go then said, "My ship."

***

Lucy sat in the mess, only a small bandage on her neck, as Kinsey came in to grab a drink.

"Just ran out of powdered lemonade," Lucy said, holding up a plastic cup. "Want the rest of mine?"

"I'm fine with water," Kinsey said. "How's the neck today?"

"I managed to make it through the week without tearing my stitches," Lucy said. She tapped the bandage. "Gunnar says that's a record for me."

"Listen, my dad has been talking," Kinsey said.

"I know," Lucy said. "He found me this morning after breakfast."

"Oh, cool," Kinsey said. "Uh…what did he say to you?"

"You don't know?" Lucy asked.

"I'd rather hear it from you," Kinsey said. "In case his plans changed."

"He's benching me," Lucy said. "I'm no longer on the Team. Not on the main Team anyway. I guess he's starting a ship security protocol since we always get boarded and have our asses handed to us before something saves the day."

"It's not a bad idea," Kinsey said, a little too brightly because Lucy gave her a sharp look. "I don't mean the benching you part. But the ship does need a dedicated security detail when we're off on ops. You'd be the veteran operator, so it would pretty much be your team."

"Yeah, your dad said as much," Lucy replied. "How long have you known?"

"We talked about it while you were still recovering in the infirmary," Kinsey said. "My dad wasn't going to even mention it to you unless the whole Team agreed."

Kinsey sat down and looked Lucy in the eyes.

"We've almost lost you twice, Luce," she said. "It's been dumb luck, but you know how things are. Sometimes luck is the only sign you're given."

"I know," Lucy said. "You guys are right. If I go on an op with the Team, half of you will be watching my back and waiting for me to take another bullet or get slashed or whatever. That puts the Team in danger."

"True," Kinsey said. They were quiet for a couple minutes. "I'll miss you out there."

"Miss me? Didn't your dad tell you?" Lucy said. "You're staying on the ship with me."

"What?" Kinsey cried.

"Got ya," Lucy laughed. "Man, that felt good."

"You bitch," Kinsey said and smiled. She stood up and stretched. "You staying here? I'm going to shower and get dressed then head to the observation deck for the sunset. Want to join?"

"You and Darren?" Lucy asked.

"Everyone," Kinsey said.

"Yeah, come grab me on your way up," Lucy said. "I'm going to chill in here for a bit."

"Cool," Kinsey replied. "See ya in a minute."

***

The shower room was already filled with steam when Kinsey stepped into it. She set her clothes on the bench and walked towards the sound of running water.

"Darby?" Kinsey asked as she saw the woman crouched on the floor of the shower, her head resting on her knees. "Darby, are you alright?" She hurried over to her and placed a hand on Darby's shoulder. "Darby?"

"I'm fine," Darby said and lifted her head. Her eyes looked hollow and sunken in.

"You don't look fine," Kinsey said. "And you're wrinkled like a fucking giant prune. Come on, let's get you dry."

She helped Darby to her feet, shut off the water, and walked her to a bench. She set Darby down and grabbed a towel for her, wrapping it around her shoulders.

"What's going on?" Kinsey asked.

"Nothing," Darby said.

"Bullshit," Kinsey responded. "Out with it or I go get Max."

"No!" Darby snapped then shook her head. "Don't get Max. He's already freaking out because of the nightmares."

"Nightmares?" Kinsey asked. "What nightmares?"

"I don't know," Darby said. "When I wake up, I can't remember them. I just know that something very bad happened in them. I'm always drenched in sweat and Max is trying to hold me down because I thrash so hard I almost cracked his skull open one night."

"Jesus," Kinsey said. "Have you talked to Gunnar about this?"

"Gunnar? No. Why would I talk to him?" Darby asked.

"He is a medical doctor," Kinsey said. "And he helped me through the rough patches when I was getting clean."

"But you've been friends with him since childhood," Darby said. "He can't help me. I'm losing my mind. That's not the same as chemical dependency."

"You are not losing your mind," Kinsey said.

"Yes, Kinsey, I am," Darby argued. "I keep having this feeling I'm not who I think I am. Then I'll get flashes of memory that aren't my memory. I know I didn't live them."

"That's probably your subconscious feeding you stuff from your nightmares," Kinsey said.

"Or my nightmares are being fed by my memory," Darby said quietly. "A memory I can't hang onto."

"Fuck that," Kinsey said. She punched Darby in the shoulder. Hard. "Get your ass dried and dressed, girl. I'm going to shower then we're all heading to the observation deck to watch the sunset. You are joining us."

"I really don't feel like going to watch a sunset," Darby said. "I'm going to go to my quarters and lie down."

"Bullshit," Kinsey said, a sense of déjà vu over her conversation with Lucy. "You're joining us. No arguments. Now get dressed and get your tiny ass up on deck."

"I'm not going to enjoy it. You can't make me," Darby said, but there was a small grin playing at her lips.

"Fair enough," Kinsey said as she stripped down then went and turned the water back on.

Kinsey stepped into the steaming hot stream and sighed. She looked over her shoulder and saw Darby toweling off. It was a start.

***

Everyone filtered past the briefing room on their way to the steps that led up to the observation deck. Ballantine watched them go, knowing the windows were tinted enough that even if they looked in they wouldn't see him sitting in the shadows. They also wouldn't see Dana Ballantine sitting right next to him.

"You know you can't win, right?" Dana said. "It's a zero sum game at the best."

"I don't believe that," Ballantine replied. "I have an amazing Team and a top notch crew."

"You have a band of misfits and malcontents running around with high-powered weapons blowing shit up for you," Dana laughed. "They are skilled, I'll give you that, but it is only a matter of time before a much better team arrives and stops the fun and games."

"That's why I have this," Ballantine said, gesturing around him at the ship. "Keep on the move. Never settle. Always be ready for what is coming."

"There is no way you can be ready," Dana said. "You know that too."

"Maybe," Ballantine said and shrugged. "Maybe not."

"God, you are as infuriating as ever," Dana said. "Sometimes I wish I had actually died so I wouldn't have to be in this position."

"What position is that?" Ballantine asked.

"At your mercy again," Dana said. "When our daughter—"

"Do not even start!" Ballantine snapped. "No! You do not get to talk about her!"

He stood up and loomed over her, his face hidden by shadows, but the anger very apparent as his body shook.

"We have been down this road before, Dana," Ballantine said. "It is a road that is closed. Permanently."

"You said my name," Dana responded after Ballantine had calmed down slightly. "That's the first time since I came on board."

"Since you came on board to kill me, you mean," Ballantine said.

"Only because you wanted to kill me," Dana said. "Kill me and everything I built."

"You had help building it," Ballantine said. "Those were the people I wanted dead. Not you. Never you."

Dana looked over at Ballantine as he sat down next to her once more.

"What?" Ballantine barked.

"You really didn't want me dead?" Dana asked.

"Not really," Ballantine said and shrugged. "Well, yes, I did, but only because I thought you were coming after me. So, if you are talking self-preservation then I did. If you're talking personal choice then I did not."

"That's the most honest thing you've said to me in a very long time," Dana said.

"If I'm telling the truth," Ballantine said and smirked.

They sat in silence for a few minutes before Ballantine reached out and took her hand.

"This doesn't mean we are on good terms," Ballantine said. "It just means I'm not going to kill you anytime soon. Unless you give me a reason."

"Do I still have to sleep in the brig?" Dana asked.

"It's a pretty comfortable brig," Ballantine said.

"Not as comfortable as a real cabin," Dana said, a little venom in her voice.

"Let's not push it," Ballantine said. "I just decided not to gut you and throw you overboard. Baby steps, dear."

"That's the only way you work," Dana said.

"Oh, I can take giant steps too," Ballantine said. "I have range."

The sliding glass door to the briefing room opened and Kinsey looked in.

"You are in here," she said then stopped. "Oh. She is too."

"Yes, she is," Ballantine said. "What can I help you with, Kinsey?"

"Apparently, not only am I the ship's counselor today, but I'm also cruise director," Kinsey replied. "The sun is about to set and I was sent to find you and see if you want to join the rest of the crew as we watch it go down."

"Watch the sun set?" Ballantine mused. "I think I could be talked into that. It sounds like a relaxing change of pace."

"Why now?" Dana asked. "Why this sunset?"

"Oh, well, because," Kinsey said.

"You can tell her, Kinsey," Ballantine said. "She isn't the enemy. Just my enemy."

"You fucking asshole," Dana said.

Ballantine gave her hand a squeeze. "I'm half joking. Guess which half was the joke?"

"Yeah, okay," Kinsey said and backed away from the briefing room. "You two need serious counseling and my work hours are over. Get out here and watch the sunset or don't, I couldn't give a fuck at this point."

Kinsey slid the door closed.

"She's an interesting young woman," Dana said. "Junkie?"

"You could tell?" Ballantine asked.

"There's a reason I made it as high up in the company as I did," Dana replied.

"Shall we?" Ballantine asked, standing up. He gripped her hand and waited.

"Yes," Dana replied as she stood. "But I have a feeling it's going to be cold out there."

"It's the tropics," Ballantine said. "It'll be perfect."

"That's not what I meant," Dana responded.

"I know," Ballantine said and led her to the sliding doors.

***

"This is nice," Ingrid said as she stood amidst the crew of the Beowulf III. "I don't think we've ever done anything like this. We need to watch more sunsets."

"This is one too many, if you ask me," Carlos grumbled.

No one asked him.

223

"Can I say a few words?" Kinsey asked as the sky before them glowed a deep orange with streaks of bright yellow and red. "I promise I'll be done before it's over."

"Go ahead, 'Sey," Darren said.

"I just want to say that other than my childhood growing up with my family and Darren and Gunnar around," Kinsey began, "this is probably the happiest I have ever been. It's been months since anyone has died. And we all survived our last op. Even Popeye is back. I'm sober and I have family around me. Not just my dad and cousins, or my ex-husband." She gave Darren a nod and he smiled warmly at her. "I consider all of you family. Every last one of you."

She shrugged and turned back to face the sunset.

"That's it," she said. "I just couldn't go much longer without saying I appreciate all of you."

"Nice speech, Sis," Max said.

"Yeah, good one," Shane agreed.

"Sis? I thought they were cousins?" Dana asked, leaning close to Ballantine as they stood at the back of the group.

"Nickname," Ballantine said. "Now hush and watch the pretty sky."

The sun lowered itself into the water. The whole world became a blaze of fire and glittering blue. It was breathtaking. No one moved until the last of the golden orb was lost below the horizon and the reds became purples.

"Beautiful," Ronald said. "Simply beautiful."

When the purples became deep blues, everyone moved to leave then something happened and they were glued to their spots.

Far off on the horizon, a ball of fire returned. It rose high into the air and mushroomed out, covering a huge distance across the sky.

Everyone shielded their eyes from the brightness and most ducked their heads, instinct telling them to get down. The mushroom cloud and fireball lifted higher and higher then dissipated finally.

All eyes turned to look at Ballantine.

"I didn't do that," Ballantine said.

"Was that the island we are headed for?" Thorne growled.

"Maybe," Ballantine replied. "Probably."

The entire crew turned back to the obvious nuclear explosion.

"We may want to get below decks before the shockwave reaches us," Ballantine said. "Ingrid? Carlos? Moshi? Thoughts on a possible EMP?"

"Not at that distance," Carlos said. "Not with our new precautions."

"Good," Ballantine said. "I think Cougher would slit my throat if we lose our engines again."

"I'd slit it as well," Lake said.

"Below, people," Thorne said. "Now. Batten down the hatches, literally. We ride this out below decks until we know things are safe. Then we figure shit out from there."

"How are your plans now?" Dana asked, leaning in to whisper in Ballantine's ear.

"Quiet, dear," Ballantine said. "Chaos is calling and I have to listen very carefully if we are going to make it out of this one."

The breeze picked up and everyone hurried to get things secured up on deck then they rushed below, sealing the hatches as they went.

Ballantine was the last to close a hatch and he spun the wheel as hard as he could, sighing when the solid thunk echoed in the passageway.

"Hello, Chaos, my old friend," he whispered before he pushed away from the hatch and made his way down to the mess where he knew everyone would be waiting for answers.

He didn't have any, but he had all the confidence in himself he'd figure some out before he got there.

The End

Jake Bible, Bram Stoker Award nominated-novelist, short story writer, independent screenwriter, podcaster, and inventor of the Drabble Novel, has entertained thousands with his horror and sci/fi tales. He reaches audiences of all ages with his uncanny ability to write a wide range of characters and genres.

Jake is the author of the bestselling Z-Burbia series set in Asheville, NC, the Apex Trilogy (DEAD MECH, The Americans, Metal and Ash) and the Mega series for Severed Press, as well as the YA zombie novel, Little Dead Man, the Bram Stoker Award nominated Teen horror novel, Intentional Haunting, the ScareScapes series, and the Reign of Four series for Permuted Press.

Find Jake at jakebible.com. Join him on Twitter @jakebible and find him on Facebook.

CHECK OUT OTHER GREAT DINOSAUR THRILLERS

THE VALLEY
by **Rick Jones**

In a dystopian future, a self-contained valley in Argentina serves as the 'far arena' for those convicted of a crime. Inside the Valley: carnivorous dinosaurs generated from preserved DNA. The goal: cross the Valley to get to the Gates of Freedom. The chance of survival: no one has ever completed the journey. Convicted of crimes with little or no merit, Ben Peyton and others must battle their way across fields filled with the world's deadliest apex predators in order to reach salvation. All the while the journey is caught on cameras and broadcast to the world as a reality show, the deaths and killings real, the macabre appetite of the audience needing to be satiated as Ben Peyton leads his team to escape not only from a legal system that's more interested in entertainment than in justice, but also from the predators of the Valley.

JURASSIC DEAD
by **Rick Chesler** & **David Sakmyster**

An Antarctic research team hoping to study microbial organisms in an underground lake discovers something far more amazing: perfectly preserved dinosaur corpses. After one thaws and wakes ravenously hungry, it becomes apparent that death, like life, will find a way.
Environmental activist Alex Ramirez, son of the expedition's paleontologist, came to Antarctica to defend the organisms from extinction, but soon learns that it is the human race that needs protecting.

CHECK OUT OTHER GREAT DINOSAUR THRILLERS

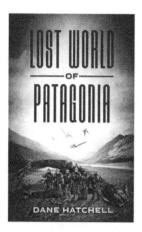

LOST WORLD OF PATAGONIA
by Dane Hatchell

An earthquake opens a path to a land hidden for millions of years. Under the guise of finding cryptid animals, Ace Corporation sends Alex Klasse, a Cryptozoologist and university professor, his associates, and a band of mercenaries to explore the Lost World of Patagonia. The crew boards a nuclear powered All-Terrain Tracked Carrier and takes a harrowing ride into the unknown.

The expedition soon discovers prehistoric creatures still exist. But the dangers won't prevent a sub-team from leaving the group in search of rare jewels. Tensions run high as personalities clash, and man proves to be just as deadly as the dinosaurs that roam the countryside.

Lost World of Patagonia is a prehistoric thriller filled with murder, mayhem, and savage dinosaur action.

SAVAGE ISLAND
by Alan Spencer

Somewhere in the Atlantic Ocean, an uncharted island has been used for the illegal dumping of chemicals and pollutants for years by Globo Corp's. Private investigator Pierce Range will learn plenty about the evil conglomerate when Susan Branch, an environmentalist from The Green Project, hires him to join the expedition to save her kidnapped father from Globo Corp's evil hands.

Things go to hell in a hurry once the team reaches the island. The bloodthirsty dinosaurs and voracious cannibals are only the beginning of the fight for survival. Pierce must unlock the mysteries surrounding the toxic operation and somehow remain in one piece to complete the rescue mission.

Ratchet up the body count, because this mission will leave the killing floor soaked in blood and chewed up corpses. When the insane battle ends, will there by anybody left alive to survive Savage Island?